Alfred the Great; Young Edward

(#3 in the King Alfred Sagas)

(# 9 in the overall series)

By Bruce Corbett

ISBN: 978-1-7380048-3-6

Dedication

This book is dedicated to
Jack and Miah, with love,
by a doting Granddad.

FOREWORD

This is the third book in the King Alfred series and the ninth in the adventures of Prince Ambrose. In this novel, an alliance of Viking leaders threatens the very existence of Wessex as the Danes invade in unheard of numbers.

The more I read about Alfred the Great, the more impressed I am with his foresight. His innovations in Wessex prevented the Danes from conquering the last Anglo-Saxon kingdom in Britain. In his lifetime, he went from hiding in a swamp to being hailed as *Bretwalda* - over-king - of most of England. His military reforms meant that never again were the Danes able to land and ravage more-or-less at will. His son, introduced here, inherited a kingdom with *burhs*, military strong points within a day's walk for most of the inhabitants, a separate summer and winter army, and permanent garrisons assigned to defend the women, children, and food supplies, leaving the rest of the king's sworn men, the *fyrdmen*, free to march where needed. His fleets sailed the coastal waters, and river forts stopped the Vikings from sailing up many of the rivers that had once been virtual highways for their sleek ships.

The titles of this and the two previous books have changed, since the main focus in these three novels is on Alfred the Great, though Ambrose, Polonius and Phillip will continue to play a major part in the war against the pagan Danes.

฿

Some years before this story begins, in 876 A.D., King Guthrum of the Danes invaded the Anglo-Saxon country of Wessex. Trapped at the town of Wareham by Alfred the Great and his West Saxon army, the Viking agreed to a truce, but, instead, slipped out and retreated to Exeter. After a Viking fleet was destroyed in a storm,

Guthrum was forced to sue for peace and retreated to East Anglia, a country that he and his ravaging Vikings had already conquered.

Just before Christmas 877, Alfred, whose army was disbanded for the winter, was caught by surprise by a second invasion of Guthrum's army. The Saxon king was forced into hiding in the forest of Selwood. Eventually he found his way to Athelney, an island surrounded by marshes. From there, he organized a secret gathering of his fighting men. Meantime, to the west, one of his *ealdormen*, Odda, destroyed a second Viking army newly arrived from Wales and led by Ubbi Ragnarsson.

A single major defeat could mean the end of Saxon Wessex. All of the Angle, Saxon and Jute kingdoms north of the Thames were reeling or had already fallen under the Viking onslaught. Alfred's army managed to gather in May, however, and they confronted the Vikings at Edington. Alfred was victorious and the Vikings fled to Chippenham. After a two week siege there, the Danish king, Guthrum agreed to be baptized and signed a peace treaty with Alfred. Wessex was saved. This story is told in **Alfred the Great; Viking Invasion**.

In 885, Wessex was threatened by a new enemy. Another Viking army, fresh from France, landed in Kent and besieged the town of Rochester. This is where **Alfred the Great; King's Revenge**, begins. Guthrum and his powerful army were bound by treaty to stay out of the fight, but his men were ever hungry for more land and adventure. The territory north of the Thames River belonged to Guthrum. If the Viking king joined his forces with the Danes from France, Wessex may have been finally overwhelmed. Alfred arrived with his army before the city fell, and the combined Saxon forces routed the Vikings, who fled precipitously, even leaving behind their entire horse herd.

In this story, **Alfred the Great; Young Edward**, a Viking alliance brings an unprecedented number of Viking warriors into Wessex. Again and again, Haesten, a pirate leader, invades Wessex. Again and again, he pillages, is eventually cornered and besieged, and then manages to break free and retreat to safe territory.

I found this portion of Alfred's story very difficult to write. All of my stories, though fiction, are as close to historically accurate as

I can make them. I actually enjoy doing the research as much as the creative writing.

I faithfully read the Anglo-Saxon Chronicles, and the story was both very sketchy and far from clear. I turned to three different expert interpretations of the Chronicles, only to find each had interpreted the same data quite differently! At last, I took the novelist's way out. Since there are serious differences in my sources, I just picked the parts I liked best, and where the Chronicles were silent, I invented plausible facts to make the story flow. Nevertheless, I stuck as closely to the story as told in the Anglo-Saxon Chronicles as I could. (See Appendix II) Ambrose, Polonius and Phillip, while old and dear friends of mine after eight stories together, are pure figments of my imagination.

Words in italics generally have special meaning and the details may be found in Appendix I. I hope you enjoy the story half as much as I did writing it.

The author,

Bruce Corbett

TABLE OF CONTENTS

CHARACTERS

Alfred: The younger brother of Ambrose, Ethelbert, and Ethelred. He was an intensely curious man who unexpectedly became king at the death of his brother, in 871 AD. A great general, he drove King Guthrum, leader of the Viking *Great Army*, out of Wessex, but was almost taken captive in a surprise winter attack. Hiding first in the forests, and then at an island base of Athelney, he started to strike back at the hated enemy. When his sworn men rallied to him in the spring, he was able to defeat King Guthrum. Surprisingly, he treated Guthrum generously and became his godfather.

In the second novel, Alfred was forced to lift the siege at Rochester, in Kent. After finding that fully half of the pirates were warriors sworn to King Guthrum, Alfred crossed the Thames and took London and part of Mercia. In this story, he faces his greatest threat yet; more than seven thousand enemy warriors and a network of hostile alliances, all intent on conquering the last Saxon kingdom in Britain

Ambrose the Dane-Slayer: (Fictitious) He was an Anglo-Saxon bastard prince of Wessex. Kidnapped by Viking slavers as a boy, he was taken to Denmark, and then fled to Norway and Sweden. Chased by the Danes, he joined Gunnar of the *Rus* Vikings, who sent him and his two companions, Phillip and Polonius, to trade on his behalf down the Russian rivers. Ambrose set up trading posts in Novgorod and then *Kiev*. Finally, he traveled to Constantinople as an emissary for the *Kiev* leaders. From there, he eventually returned to England to help his brothers fight against the

Viking raiders.

He and his friends became a legend when they first joined the Danish *Great Army*, and then stole a princess from a Viking stronghold in Ireland and spied on the Vikings from France. In this story, he helps his brother, and his nephew, fight against yet another major Viking invasion. Other names he used in various escapades were Hamar and Canuteson

Anarawd of Gwynedd: Welsh ruler of the one Welsh kingdom allied with the Danes of Northumbria. After Haesten and his defeated Vikings spent a winter as his guests, he asked to become an ally of Alfred!

Anwell: (Fictitious) He was the *ealdorman* of Cornwall who had previously made an alliance with the Danes in return for nominal independence.

Askold: He, with his cousin, Dir, are the *Rus* leaders who left Novgorod to settle at *Kiev*, a city they felt was ideally situated to control the Russian-Byzantine river trade. Under their leadership, the Dnieper River region came under *Varangian* control, and they participated in an attack on Constantinople itself. After the attack, in an attempt to end the hostilities, they appointed Ambrose and Polonius to negotiate with the Byzantine Emperor.

Bran: (Fictitious): a *fyrdman* who rode with the scouts in the attack on Benfleet.

Dag (the Dane) (Fictitious) The Viking commander of the treasure detail at Benfleet, he died bravely fighting Phillip.

Dir: See ASKOLD

Ealhswith: Wife of King Alfred.

Edred: was the *ealdorman* of Devonshire, replacing Odda.

Edwolf: was the *ealdorman* of Sussex, who was sent to Northumbria with Alfred's request for an oath of neutrality.

Edwy: a warrior and cook on the captured Danish ship sent to pick up Ambrose on the north bank of the Thames River.

Einarr: (Fictitious) A *jarl* chosen as a hostage by King Eohric. Einarr was hanged when his king broke his oath and sent men and ships against Alfred.

Eohric: King of East Anglia, he gave six hostages and a promise to Alfred to stay out of the war in 892. He later broke his promise.

Eric: (Haesten's son) (Fictitious) Haesten asked Alfred to baptize him. His Christian name was Marc.

Ethelflæd: daughter of Alfred the Great, she married Ethelred, *ealdorman* of Mercia.

Ethelhelm: *ealdorman* of Wiltshire, he was reluctant to lead his *fyrdmen* out of the shire.

Ethelnoth: *Ealdorman* of Somerset, he was loyal to Alfred.

Ethelred: The Mercian nobleman who conquered western Mercia and eventually married Alfred's daughter. In this story, he brought his *fyrdmen* to fight at Alfred's, and, later, Edward's side. When Mercia was invaded, he fought valiantly against the invading Vikings.

Ethelwold: Alfred's nephew and *ealdorman* of Dorset. His father was Ethelred, older brother of Alfred. Ethelred had been king of Wessex from AD. 866 to 871. Ethelwold was resentful that Alfred was chosen by the *Witan* as king over him, and plotted to become king. In this story he did little overtly against the king, because Alfred kept Ethelwold's son close by his side as hostage. At Alfred's death, he openly rebelled against Edward, and eventually fled north to join the Danes.

Folki: (Fictitious) A warrior of King Eohric of East Anglia, he was given to Alfred as a hostage and later hung.

Giric: (possibly along with Eochaid) was the king of the united kingdom of the Picts and the Scots. In this story, he was bribed to raid Northumbria.

Gretchen: (Fictitious) Was the daughter of Osmond, an *ealdorman* of Mercia, and distant cousin to the royal family of Wessex. Previous to this story, she first met Ambrose at the Wessex court, and then nursed him back to health when he was wounded during his earlier escape from the Danes. They were betrothed, but Gretchen was first kidnapped by Welsh, and then Viking brigands. Ambrose traveled to Ireland to free her. After many adventures, they were married.

Godric: (Fictitious) The young warrior (*Dreng*) who rode with Ambrose years earlier, he now escorts Ambrose, Phillip and Polonius from London to Exeter.

Godric: (Haesten's other son) (Fictitious) Haesten asked Alfred to baptize Godric. His Christian name was Pierre.

Guthfrith: The Danish king in Northumberland in 893, he pledged peace to Alfred but sent 100 ship crews to attack in Devon, under the pirate leader called Sigefrith.

Guthrum: A Dane who was king of East Anglia, Essex, and part of Mercia, he died in 890. Earlier, he attacked Wessex, was bought off, and then attacked from Mercia at Christmas of 878. After signing a treaty, he returned to East Anglia. In 885, he broke his treaty with Wessex by allowing his men to go south and join some Vikings from France besieging the West Saxon city of Rochester. Alfred went north to punish the attackers and seized Viking ships at the mouth of the Stour River. In response, Guthrum attacked with every ship he could muster, defeating Alfred. A second treaty was signed after Alfred seized London and defeated Guthrum in battle. King Eohric replaced Guthrum in 890.

Hagar: (Fictitious) The leader of the Viking raiding party who crossed the Lea River and captured Polonius.

Hakim: (Fictitious) The merchant from Alexandria who escaped from slavery with Ambrose, Phillip and Polonius, and who escorted the three of them across North Africa after the Byzantines came after the prince and his friends.

Halldorr: (Fictitious) A warrior of King Eohric of East Anglia, he was given to Alfred as a hostage and later hung.

Hamar: (Fictitious) Was the name Ambrose used previously when he pretended to be a Swedish trader in King Guthrum's camp some years before.

Kuralla: (Fictitious) She was a Slav chieftain's daughter whose village defied Bothi, a *Rus hersir* settled near Novgorod. Bothi ordered her father tortured and killed, and she was about to be given to his warriors when Ambrose purchased her to save her life. Polonius married her before they returned with Ambrose to England.

Leng the Bold: (Fictitious) The leader of the little band of Dorsetmen who stopped Ambrose on his journey to Alfred.

Odda: The elderly *ealdorman* of Devon, he had served four kings faithfully and killed Ubbi Ragnarsson when his army invaded Wessex. He died in 890 AD.

Oddr: (Fictitious) A warrior of King Eohric of East Anglia, he was given to Alfred as a hostage and later hung.

Osgar: (Fictitious) A scout who rode ahead to help clear the way for Edward's *Long Ride* to Benfleet.

Phillip: (Fictitious) A giant of a man, he was the free-born guardian of Ambrose when he was a youth, and companion later. Often called the Weapons-master, he had trained several generations of West Saxon noblemen in the military arts. Wherever Ambrose went, there was Phillip. His great goal in life was to protect his prince. When he spied on the *Great Army* in 868, he called himself Edgar.

Polonius: (Fictitious) He was born to noble Byzantine parents and given an excellent education. When his family had financial reverses, he and his sisters were sold into slavery. He was taken to Lombardy, France, and, eventually, Frisia. There, he chanced to meet Ambrose and Phillip. Together they embarked on a series of adventures that took him to Norway, Sweden, Novgorod, *Kiev*, and eventually Constantinople itself. An expert linguist and knife-thrower, he returned to England with Ambrose, and, as Nicholas, helped him spy on the Danish *Great Army*. Soon thereafter, he helped steal Gretchen back from the Irish Vikings. He taught Alfred to read, and in this story he acted as the king's military advisor and spy-master.

Ragnar Lodbrok: A powerful Danish chieftain who invaded England and France. Legend had it that he was killed in Northumbria by being thrown in a pit of snakes. His three sons were Halfdan, Ivar the Boneless, and Ubbi.

Sigefrith: A pirate sent from Northumbria with 100 ships. He landed in Devonshire and besieged Exeter.

Sigehelm: In a previous story he was the *ealdorman* of Kent, who sent his men into Rochester before the Vikings could attack. In this story he wrote to Alfred to tell him of the Viking twin invasions.

Sitric Ivarsson: The son of Ivar the Boneless. He previously met Ambrose at the Wessex court, where he was a spy with the identity of a *Frisian* peddler named Harold. Phillip rescued him from brigands, and they shared adventures in Ireland together. He did not join his uncle on his attack on Wessex. By 883, he was king of Dublin.

Snorri: (Fictitious) Cousin to King Eohric of East Anglia, he was given to Alfred as a hostage and later hung.

Torleik: (Fictitious) A warrior of King Eohric of East Anglia, he was given to Alfred as a hostage and later hung.

Treddian: (Fictitious) is the messenger who brought King Alfred the report that the Danes have fled their fort on the Lea River.

Ubbi: He was the younger brother of Halfdan and Ivar the Boneless. Ubbi was killed by Odda's *fyrdmen* when he brought his army into Wessex in 878 in support of Guthrum. At the time of this story, his Viking brother, Halfdan, ruled the land north of East Anglia.

Werian: (Fictitious) A young man who served with the Mercian scouts and who was first to clamber into the Danish fort on the Lea after the Vikings had fled.

CHAPTER 1

The Courier

The drivers' whips cracked and the massive oxen strained against their multiple yokes. One by one, the great wagons that made up the royal caravan crested the long rise. As the wagons appeared, dozens of armored Saxon riders swirled around. The riders quickly spread out into a protective ring that spilled out over the chalk downs.

The royal court of Alfred, King of Wessex, Sussex, Kent and Cornwall, was again on the move. The two dozen wagons and the hundreds of *drengs*, the young warriors who made up most of the king's Personal Guard, were gradually joined by an equal number of servants, noblemen, churchmen, and a vast assortment of children.

The immense caravan paused to give the oxen, horses and children a chance to catch their breaths.

Toward the rear of the caravan rode four figures. One, Ambrose the bastard prince, was short and slim. The second, a rail-thin and dark haired former Byzantine named Polonius, had many nicknames. Askold, *Rus* conqueror of *Kiev* and vast stretches of land along the Dnieper River, had once called him the most dangerous man he had ever met. He was alternatively known as the Scholar, the Spy-master, and the Wizard. Most important, the emaciated looking foreigner was friend to Ambrose and royal advisor to King Alfred the Great.

The third rider was so massive that he had been compared with a living oak tree. His name was Phillip, and he had been weapons-master to three generations of royal Wessex *athelings*.

The fourth rider was younger and handsome. His name was Edward, and he was the eldest son of King Alfred. Today he traveled with his father's caravan, but even at his young age he had already shown both exceptional maturity and intelligence. His father had recently given him responsibility for the entire expanse of land that made up the eastern portion of the empire of Wessex.

As the four riders topped the rise, Phillip called out and pointed back the way they had come.

"Someone is hard on our trail - riding hard."

Polonius spotted the man in the distance. "It is a bit early for my next courier, but I was expecting one from Winchester somewhat later this evening."

Even as they watched, the rider appeared appreciably nearer. Ambrose shook his head. "Well, Scholar, that man is close to foundering his horse. He had better be carrying important news!"

"We will see soon enough, Prince Ambrose. He will be here in a matter of minutes if he keeps up that brutal pace."

Ambrose stared back down the hill. "I am never happy when I see a courier killing his horse to bring us news. It is generally a hint that something is very wrong."

The royal courier let his mount slow from its headlong gallop to make the long climb up to the chalk downs, but he still urged it on at a merciless pace. The rider recognized each of the group waiting for him, but he rode directly to Polonius, long known as King Alfred's spy-master.

"Lord Polonius, I have an urgent message from Sigehelm, E*aldorman* of Kent!"

Polonius dismounted and took the leather pouch from the rider's hands. He removed the single rolled sheet of parchment and broke the wax seal. After scanning the sheet quickly, he looked up.

"It is grave news, indeed. Prince Edward, would you please alert your father?"

"Polonius, he is finally sleeping after that last dose of elixir you gave him. He is not at all well."

"Prince, he needs to hear this now. Wessex is about to go to war. Wake him if you must."

"Very well! Before I disturb him, however, I will order the chamberlain to call a halt and to set up camp right here. Second, I will have the royal campaign tent erected immediately. You know that he will want to consult his precious maps.

The food supply caravan was supposed to reach us in another

mile or two, so supplies should not be a problem. I guess there is no reason we cannot simply stay right here for the night. Phillip, would you please be so kind as to find all the available members of the *Witan* and alert them to a possible council meeting?"

Within minutes, the efficient servants had started to set up a comfortable camp. Alfred's campaign tent rose almost magically, and Edward escorted his father directly to it. The king appeared wan and *held his stomach*, but he looked alert when he caught the eyes of Ambrose, Edward and Polonius.

"It is rarely good news when a king is roused from his sickbed. What is the problem, my friends?"

Polonius held out the parchment toward the king. "Sire, I was expecting a dispatch from the continent, forwarded through Winchester, but this is direct and urgent, from *Ealdorman* Sigehelm of Kent."

Alfred took it in his hands, but didn't look down at it. "Spymaster, I have recently noticed that my arms are getting too short to allow me to see the letters clearly, and my stomach is not doing well. Just tell me what it says."

"Sire, you know that Eudes, Count of Paris, managed to defeat the Danes last year?"

"I remember, Scholar. Haesten and his Danes were soundly trounced. You told me all about it."

"And then Arnulf managed to inflict an even more crushing defeat on Haesten and his Vikings at the River Dyle."

"The story is etched forever in my mind. Scholar, just tell me what happened."

"Of course, Sire." Polonius took a deep breath and looked at the sheet again before speaking. "Two hundred and fifty Viking ships left Bastogne last week, and they subsequently landed in Kent."

Alfred groaned. "God's breath! I feel this is a bad dream. Edward! A chair for your father, before I fall down!

Was it only six years ago that I heard those same words?"

Ambrose spoke. "Then there was an initial fifteen ships at Rochester, but we defeated them, brother."

"Aye, that we did, though it cost us dearly in both treasure and lives, and fifteen is very different than two hundred and fifty!'

The king sank gratefully into the chair his son had brought him. 'Two hundred and fifty! Well, we have been preparing for a major attack for many years. We knew it would come one day, and truthfully, we have never been in a better position to defeat the pagan Danes than we are right now."

Polonius continued. "*Ealdorman* Sigehelm's scouts estimated the force at a little more than five thousand warriors - with their own horses brought from *Francia*."

"That alone is serious cause for worry. Usually it takes them several weeks to steal enough horses to become mobile. This cuts into the time we have to react . . . Polonius, what else does our good *ealdorman* tell us?"

"Only that the Vikings beached at the mouth of the Lympne River."

Alfred idly pulled at his beard. "Well, that could be worse. It is boggy land thereabouts and I don't remember any strong point there that they can occupy. They will at least be tied down for a considerable time while they build a defensive position."

"Except they went up-river to the Forest of the Weald."

"Better. Then we can block the lower reaches and trap their fleet."

"Except Appledore, our soon-to-be completed fort for the region, was almost empty, and the Danes occupied it."

"By the cloak of St. Peter! So the pagan devils have both a strongly fortified strong point and are mobile . . . we have prepared for years for this eventuality, but Merciful God! Five thousand warriors? That is probably the largest invasion force in my lifetime . . . perhaps a little dose of your elixir would be in order, Polonius. Just a little to ease the pain. I can not afford to have my wits dulled right now."

King Alfred scanned the map that lay on the trestle table before him. "There are clearly pieces of a puzzle that I am missing. Ambrose, would you just land and attack a country with a strong fleet, dozens of fortified *burhs*, each with its own permanent garrison, and not one, but two *fyrds* - each numbering well over three thousand sworn warriors?"

"If I could raise a force of five thousand battle-hardened and eager warriors, brother - probably. You have a summer and winter army, but after the debacle at Chippenham, when you were left with few sworn men to fight with, I might conclude that you are unlikely to call up both together, and the garrisons, while they provide security for your subjects, eat up many thousand more *fyrdmen*. So, you would not, in actual fact, outnumber me on the battlefield."

"But my mounted and armored *fyrdmen* can be supplemented by five or even ten thousand other followers."

"The *fyrdmen* are the equal of the Viking warriors, brother, but the churls are not all well-trained or equipped. They and the slaves might hold their own behind a city wall, but generally break before a determined Viking shield-wall. It is only your trained *fyrdmen* that I would fear, and that I outnumber. I would also be very aware that most of your sworn men have not faced serious action in six years.'

"And if I did call up both of my armies at the same time?"

"I would sit behind my walls until your *fyrdmens'* service time is up and they went home, leaving you with little more than your Personal Guard to face me."

"And if I ordered in the Saxon fleet?"

"Against two hundred and fifty ships? It is true that a few of your vessels are larger and higher than the Viking ships. On a one to one basis, the Saxon ships have shown themselves to be capable of holding their own, but we have dozens, brother, not hundreds, and you have already recruited most of the *Frisian* seamen that are available. Our fleet can play little part in this struggle - unless you want to lose it - as happened when we went against King Guthrum some years ago."

"Is it possible that this is a simple raid?"

Ambrose shook his head. "This wouldn't be the first time the Danes have tried to overthrow your kingdom, Alfred. To move five thousand warriors, and all their horses, is a massive undertaking. It has to be more than a simple raid."

"Ah, now we get to the meat of it! Polonius, pen and paper, please. Let us make a list of what we are likely to face."

Ambrose spoke first. "If I was the Danish commander, Brother, I would make big promises to any disaffected noblemen in the West Saxon Empire. I would offer to make any traitorous *ealdormen* into kings - until it is time, of course, to *practice archery* or perform the *Blood-eagle* on them."

Alfred nodded. "Noted. I have a short list of possible suspects in my mind. Both Ethelwold of Dorset and Anwell in Cornwall did their best to betray us when the Vikings invaded last time . . . Polonius, the sons of our two suspect shire commanders are needed immediately in Winchester. I have decided to allow them the honor of fighting in my Personal Guard. I will need their presence for the duration of the war. Please make sure . . . quietly . . . that their fathers understand that disobedience to this command will be construed as treason and punished with the utmost severity."

Polonius smiled. "Would you like me to arrange for their kidnapping, Sire, like last time?"

"No, I am, perhaps naively, hoping that their fathers learned their lesson from their last experience. Let us try a more subtle approach this time, but be sure the fathers understand all of the implications."

Polonius bowed his head. "I will send one of your most articulate senior *duguos* with both the public summons and the private message, Sire."

Alfred looked around the table. "What is next on our list?"

Polonius spoke. "Personally, I would have sent agents to Northumbria, East Anglia, Ireland, and Denmark itself, calling on any restless Danes to go a-viking."

"And how do we counteract that?"

Ambrose looked at the map. "Last time, we offered Guthrum legitimacy, if he respected our treaty and supported us."

Alfred frowned. "For all the good it did!"

"Brother, he did not openly lead his army against us. He merely did not prevent his warriors from coming south individually and joining their cousins."

"That is sophistry! Fifteen out of the thirty ships at Rochester were East Anglian . . . but Guthrum did pay for his perfidy . . . and the real truth is, which I will never admit to outside of this tent, I needed an excuse to seize both old London and Saxon *Lundenwic.'* The king sighed. 'So what do we do this time?"

Ambrose replied. "Brother, thanks to you seizing London and

supporting your son-in-law Ethelred in Mercia, we are in a much stronger position north of the Thames. After Ethelred made repeated incursions into Wales, two of the major Welsh kingdoms begged to become your allies and acknowledge you as *Bretwalda*, and the East Anglian Vikings are well aware that you could have destroyed them if you had wanted, after you defeated Guthrum. The priests continue to make inroads amongst the Danes there, and in a generation or two, the Danelaw should be solidly Christian. Why do we not demand hostages from East Anglia and Northumbria both?"

Alfred looked around the table. "Please note that, Polonius. We shall do it. And what else can we expect?"

Polonius spoke. "I would arrange as many feints as I could, splintering your forces and, hopefully, leaving the main force relatively unopposed."

"Then if this is more than a raid, we should expect more landings. All lookouts are to be on the alert for new landings. Polonius, is it noted?"

"It is all noted, Sire."

"Well, my friends, what have we missed?"

Edward turned to Alfred. "Father, I think that is a very thorough list."

Alfred smiled through his pain. "This is possibly the biggest crisis I have ever faced, but at least we have prepared for this day. If we survive this onslaught, my son, then you just might inherit a secure throne. My dream is to see all *Angleland* united as one country. Perhaps in your life you will make it happen, but first I fear we must deal with more than five thousand seasoned warriors, plus whatever other devilment Haesten, Eohric, and Guthfrith have dreamed up for us. Polonius, are you still in contact with the Picts of Northumbria?"

"Sire, they will never love Saxons, but, as an old saying in my country goes, the enemy of your enemy can be your ally. We still have some influential friends amongst them, and their leaders are never averse to our gold and weapons."

"Let us wait to hear the answer from Northumbria before we foment more rebellions in the north, but it is an option that I won't forget. The Northumbrian Danes may hesitate to send their young men south when the Scots and Picts keep swarming over their northern borders. Polonius, how about your spies?"

"I will have a half-hundred riding north before the week is over, Sire."

The king held his belly. "Be not stingy, my friend. I would rather deplete my kingdom of gold than lives . . . one more small dose of your elixir, and then I must sit down with the *Witan* . . . oh, and Polonius?"

"Yes, Sire?"

"I will excuse you from the meeting of the *Witan*. Asser can act as secretary. We will no doubt meet until the dawn and painstakingly hammer out many important and intricate details, but the truth is, I want the couriers on their way by dawn. Will you see to the writing of the messages for me?"

"I will collect all the literate priests and clerks I can find, Sire, except Asser, and put them to work. What, specifically, do you want the summons to say?"

"The summer *fyrd* from Hampshire east is to answer the summons in full force and immediately. I expect the *ealdormen* to have their *fyrd* on the move within *seven-night* or less. They are to ride for Winchester or wait along the Dover Road for my Personal Guard to reach their position.

I expect strong mounted contingents from the western shires, but I do not want to denude those shires of the possibility of forming a mobile force for their own defense. I expect every subject in the eastern shires to head for the fortified *burhs*, without delay. I want every man, woman and child out of reach of the heathen devils, along with their pigs and cows and even their chickens - let the Vikings learn to eat grass . . . Garrison troops are to man their walls forthwith - throughout the kingdom. All coastal watchers are to man their posts, both by day and night. The sailors should hold themselves ready, but they are not to man their ships until called upon . . . You know what to say, Polonius. You are the man responsible for much of our preparation."

Polonius bowed to his king. "It will be as you say, Sire."

Even as Polonius spoke, a mud-splattered courier pushed his way into the command tent. Seeing his king staring at him, he dropped to his knees and held out his courier pouch.

"Excuse me, my King, but I carry an urgent message from *Ealdorman* Sigehelm!"

Alfred nodded toward Polonius, who took the pouch, removed the parchment, broke the wax seal, and read the message.

"Well?" the king said, impatiently.

"It is another message from *Ealdorman* Sigehelm of Kent, Majesty. *Jarl* Haesten himself, with an estimated eighty ships, has landed at Milton Royal, on the bank of the Swale River."

"By all that is holy! I think God must be testing me.' He took a deep breath.

'No, that is just my frustration speaking. I will pray tonight for true humility and for divine guidance. Ambrose, you said that there would be more surprises. Here is the first . . . only eighty ships. If they are operating in concert, and we can assume for the moment that they are, why the discrepancy in numbers?"

"Brother, East Anglia is close to Haesten's camp. I would assume he expects considerable reinforcements from north of the Thames."

Alfred nodded. "That makes sense. This could also be, however, their first mistake."

Ambrose looked surprised. "How so, brother?"

"Seven thousand warriors would be more than we can handle without calling up every *fyrdman* in the empire. Two separate camps, however, splits their forces, whereas we will have one single force. If we are careful, then we can set up camp between the two armies, strike in either direction, and do our best to keep the two Viking forces apart."

Edward spoke. "Father, this could add up to two thousand more veteran warriors to the struggle. Our main force will be heavily outnumbered. Surely we should consider calling up the winter *fyrd* as well as the summer army."

"Son, if we call up both *fyrds* for immediate duty, we will be left with nothing when they start to go home in six months. After

Guthrum caught us at Chippenham with no army that winter, I swore I would never again be without an army at my back. You were young then, but it was a bitter winter, and only the swamps around Athelney kept us from dying at Guthrum's hands. What we will do is build one of Polonius' Roman marching forts for protection, and then we will strike separately at the heathens."

"Father, if both Viking armies catch up to us at the same time, our *fyrdmen* are likely to be overwhelmed."

"You are right, Edward, if we are caught in the open. There is a risk, but Kent is our land and there are a lot of marshes and trees to slow the Danes. With the help of Sigehelm's foresters, we will systematically kill their couriers and scouts so they cannot communicate effectively. We should be able to ambush any Viking forces smaller than ours, and we will use Kentish scouts and the game trails to fade away before any larger ones."

The couriers rode with the dawn. Over a hundred riders spread out from the little encampment at the edge of the chalk downs. North, east, south and west, the riders rode hard to call the fighting men of Wessex to war. Seven thousand enemies had already landed on their shores, and it would take every *fyrdman* in the empire to prevent the final destruction of the last independent Anglo-Saxon kingdom on the island of Britain.

Ambrose sat across from his brother, and spoke. "Alfred, let me be the one to go to Eohric's court. It shows how seriously you take the threat of his army, and he will not play games with me. We will talk Dane to Dane."

Alfred sighed. "I was afraid you would ask that."

Ambrose smiled. "I will be safe enough, brother. I will take Phillip and a white shield. The Danes treat emissaries with great respect. It is part of their culture to do so."

The king nodded. "I hope you will forgive me if I keep Polonius with me. I have great need of his skills."

"Of course, brother. The best place he can be is at the center of his web, feeling for various vibrations through his many contacts. It is what he does best."

CHAPTER 2

**"Upon this (arrival of Viking armies) King
Alfred gathered his army, and advanced, so
that he encamped between the two armies at the
highest point he could find defended by wood
and by water, that he might reach either, if they
would seek any field."
......The Anglo-Saxon Chronicles**

Thousands strong, but stretched out for miles, the armored and mounted *fyrdmen* trickled into the site. Behind, thousands more, *churls* and slaves, traders and prostitutes, trudged along, followed by hundreds of wives, lovers, and even children.

Alfred stared from the high spot his scouts had chosen. There was water nearby, and Polonius' engineers had already hammered in pegs that denoted the size of the walls and the location of the various shire encampments. He spoke to the emaciated-looking Byzantine who sat his horse near the king's side.

"Well, Wizard, we are half way between Milton Royal and Appledore. We are now going to play a dangerous game."

"And what is that, Sire?"

"First I need a secure fort to rise here. I need you to use every devious trick you know to set up a fort that can hold out against several times our numbers."

"Sire, if you count the unmounted *churls* and slaves, you already outnumber the Danes, and more *fyrdmen* will be trickling in for days to come."

Alfred sighed. "After we have established a strong defensive position here, I do not want to sit on my hands. I want to send most of the men out to strike hard against any wandering Viking bands, and I want the entire forest to be filled with the bodies of Viking scouts hanging by their necks."

"And so there will be times when we have relatively few men to man the walls."

"Exactly so, Wizard, but I am also keenly aware that after our first rank or two of veteran *fyrdmen*, our battle lines will consist largely of our poorly trained *churls* and former slaves. In order to help make up for the lack of heavily armed and veteran *fyrdmen*, I intend to strike at any foraging parties with overwhelmingly massive forces."

"That is a recipe for success, Sire. If the veteran *fyrdmen* can break the Danish lines, the rest can kill as efficiently as your best warriors."

"But, Polonius, we are between a hammer and an anvil. If one Viking force can hold our attention, and the other can manage to secretly approach our rear, we will be massacred. We will use your maxim of local superiority and rapid mobility, but the truth is, their two separate forces, if united, would probably be able to chew their way through our veterans, and if that happened, we could be in very serious trouble."

"Thus the need for a strong fort, Sire. Even an untrained man on the wall is more than the equal of the best warrior on open ground."

Alfred was in pain, but he smiled. "Exactly so, Wizard. That is the very thing I am counting on."

"And my new title is a hint that I am in charge of having this miraculous fort built, preferably before the sun sets tonight."

"Astute as ever, my friend. I don't want to make you nervous, but there are five thousand Viking warriors over that way . . . and perhaps two thousand, armed and very hostile, in that direction. If they find us here, without those stout walls, we would be in serious trouble."

"Your logic is impeccable, Sire. Perhaps I should get to work."

The king *held his stomach*, but his voice, when he spoke, sounded normal. "Just tell me what you need, my friend, and you shall have it."

"I need every man and woman who is here, Sire. You are right. The fort must be a priority. The walls and ditches should be completed before anyone so much as unpacks."

Alfred turned. "Edward - spread the word to all the *ealdormen*. Until further notice, all men and women will work solely on our defenses - until Polonius here declares that he is completely satisfied."

"Father, it is going to be dark in a few hours, and everyone is exhausted from the march here."

"Then we will work by firelight, son-of-mine. The walls must be complete before the God-cursed pagans find our location. It could literally be a matter of life and death for all of us!"

Edward just nodded, turned his horse, and headed after the various shire *fyrds* and their commanders.

"I will pass on the word, father . . . and then I will go find a shovel."

Within minutes, tired men were driven to strip off their armor and outer clothing, and take up shovels, mattocks and pickaxes. A deep ditch was laboriously dug, and the dirt and rocks were mounded on the inside, while others took axes and started to cut poles for the palisades. Four centuries after the last Romans abandoned the island of Britannica, a Roman marching fort began to appear on a modest height in the middle of Kent.

When the first rays of light illuminated the tents and shelters of the West Saxon *fyrd*, formidable walls surrounded the sleeping warriors. The work had taken long into the night, and Alfred allowed most of the men to sleep late. Everyone was exhausted from the long march and the back-breaking labor, but they were safe behind stout ramparts. Kentish scouts had been excused from the labor, and, as they had all night, they constantly patrolled the nearby forest trails. Somewhere in the Forest of the Weald were thousands of brutal raiders, intent on pillaging and raping, and, if they could, conquering the last free Anglo-Saxon kingdom on the island. Only Alfred of Wessex, his son-in-law, Ethelred of Mercia, and their sworn men, stood between the Danes and their final victory.

CHAPTER 3

**"The Northumbrians and East-Angles had
given oaths to King Alfred, and the East-Angles
six hostages; nevertheless, contrary to the truce,
as oft as the other plunderers went out with all
their army, then went they also, either with
them, or in a separate division."
......The Anglo-Saxon Chronicles**

Ambrose and Phillip crossed the Thames from Southwark to London, and then, after exiting through Aldgate, they rode east and north, along with an escort of twenty riders. After resting one night on the trail, they crossed the frontier into East Anglia. They rode without incident for another day, speaking to occasional farm laborers in either Saxon or Danish.

On the second day, a force of mounted Danes spotted them and rode after them. The commander, a giant of a man with crooked teeth, a crooked nose and a battle axe clenched in one hand, ordered them to halt.

"You smell like mangy Saxon dogs! What are you doing north of the Thames?"

Ambrose spoke in perfect Danish. "My name is Ambrose, Prince of Wessex, and I am emissary from King Alfred to King Eohric. Now that you have found us, you can arrange for an escort to your king."

"Any Saxon dog in this country, whether he speaks a human tongue or not, wears an iron collar and obeys his betters! You need training, Saxon!"

Ambrose replied. "Well, my loudmouthed friend, I have yet to meet a Dane who is my better. Many have tried to teach me manners, but they all died a violent death."

"Do you have a death wish, stranger, that you, a pipsqueak of a man, would dare to speak to a *hersir* so?"

"Others call me Canuteson the Dane-Slayer, loudmouth, but all you need to know is that I am an emissary, carrying a white shield. It is thus your sacred duty to get me safely to your king!"

"It is my sacred duty to put you into the ground, Saxon dog! Get off your fine horse, and I will hew you like a Quaking Aspen."

The second-in-command spoke up. "*Hersir*, he is right! I know of this man. It is he who they sing about, and look, his companion is a giant. It is really them! We must get them to the king as soon as possible."

The commander looked at Ambrose with smoldering anger. "One day we will meet, Canuteson, when you are not an emissary. On that day you will learn to fear a Dane."

"And you will see *Asgard*, if you are capable of dying bravely. I will look forward to the opportunity to rid the world of another a Dane who does not know his duty to his king!"

"You go too far, Saxon!"

Ambrose sighed. "You are right, Dane. I am forbidden to take a life, even one such as yours, as long as I am an emissary. Take me to King Eohric!"

⚑

The newly enlarged column rode deeper and deeper into the heartland of East Anglia. At last, when Ambrose could smell salt in the air, they approached a sturdy fortified *tun*. Horns blew at their approach, and hundreds of well-armed Vikings swarmed to the walls. By the intensity of the reaction to their arrival, Ambrose was sure that had finally found the East Anglian king.

The prince was led through the open gate, and his escort stopped in front of a large and beautifully constructed Mead Hall, more than fifty paces long. The massive door flew open, and King Eohric himself came hurrying out.

"What is all this fuss about? Are we being attacked? Well, if it isn't the brother of my very favorite Saxon king."

Ambrose smiled as he slipped from his saddle. "It is the brother of the only Saxon king left on the island, King Eohric, thanks to you and some of your friends from the north."

Eohric chuckled. "You flatter me, Prince . . ."

Hakon, the commander of the king's royal bodyguard, came through the doorway and immediately growled at the prince. "On your knees to a Viking king, you Christian dog!"

Ambrose turned and stared at the big Dane. "In another time, and another place, *Victory-Maker* would be pleased to teach you manners, Viking. I am the adopted son of a Danish warrior, so you may call me Canuteson the Dane-Slayer. I bow to no man but my king."

"You dare to call yourself that in front of me?"

"Why not? It is what people have taken to calling me."

Eohric raised his hand. "Peace, Hakon! You are speaking to a royal prince of Wessex, who is my welcome guest and will be treated as such! This man refused to bow to the emperor of Byzantium, and I would call him friend. You insult my guest and may remove yourself from my presence."

The big Dane glowered at Ambrose, but finally stalked away.

"Now, Prince Ambrose, as I was about to say, before I was interrupted, you know that we Danes are, while brave and ferocious, yet a people poor in land. It is sad necessity that thousands of our young men must go a-viking each year. You, yourself have lived in my homeland, and know that there are just too many people for the land to support."

"My visit to your homeland was not voluntary, King. I wore chains and worked those insufficient fields you talk about."

"And I see that it was the making of you! Here you are, a prince and a legendary warrior whose ballads are sung even by your enemies. Few men alive have made the journeys you have made, prince, nor had such adventures."

"It is true that I have had an eventful life, but that is not why I have come to see you, King."

"Prince, I am told that you were welcome in Guthrum's court, and you are always welcome in mine."

"I thank you, King Eohric. You honor me."

"Come inside my Mead Hall, Prince. Let's you and I talk alone.

The mead cools in the river even as we speak, and two friends and allies must do their best to honor the nectar of the gods."

"I thank you, King. It has been a long and hot trail, and I would welcome good mead."

Eohric smiled. "Come, then, Prince. Several *ambats* have already gone to fetch a supply from the river depths. Not only is the mead good, but the girls expose all their assets when their dresses are soaked. You may choose any one that catches your fancy for a bed companion."

So saying, the king led his guest past his bodyguards and into the dim interior of his Mead Hall. They walked past the pit fire that illuminated the interior, and Eohric took him to a trestle table where two chairs were set up.

"Sit, Prince. You need not worry about your men. Phillip and the rest of your escort will be fed and provided with food and the same good mead as we are about to taste."

After the mead was poured by several pretty serving wenches still soaked from retrieving the mead from the cooling river, Eohric waved them away and grew more serious. "Ambrose, you have ridden a long way when I know your kingdom is in crisis. You obviously want something from me. Speak, Prince, so I know how I can help you."

"You are very astute, King Eohric, and what you say is true. As you know, King *Athelstan* . . . Guthrum . . . signed a treaty of friendship with my brother."

"I know it well, Prince, and although I do not consider myself bound by its covenants, I have yet tried to be faithful to them. Priests wander my domains at will, and convert any who express a desire to follow your strange three-gods-in-one. Difficult as it is to stop, I forbid my young men from raiding into your brother's shire of Mercia. I even told your brother once that he is welcome to hang any he can catch, without having to pay *wergeld*."

"And Alfred appreciates your forbearance. He welcomes you as an ally and neighbor - as long as the covenants are upheld. And he holds back Ethelred's wolves, who are hungry to re-acquire much of their homeland."

Eohric smiled. "Yes, I watched Ethelred's assault on the Welsh with great interest and some amusement. After he quite thoroughly ravaged their lands, two of the Welsh kings asked to submit to Alfred so your brother would rein in his son-in-law's human wolves. It was brilliantly done. One hand attacks, while the other protects. Now you tell me that the wolves are restless again."

Ambrose sipped from his horn of mead. "As long as you respect the covenants between our two kingdoms, Alfred will control the wolves of Mercia. Even after Guthrum marched against London, and then was defeated in battle, Alfred held back the *fyrdmen* from launching an all-out attack on your heartland. There were not enough East Anglian warriors left to stop us, but we returned to Wessex. Guthrum was allowed to live."

"You are right, Ambrose, though Alfred did end up with his treaty, London, and the rest of Mercia. I also sometimes wonder if Rollo and his Danes in *Francia* had anything to do with that decision."

"With Guthrum and most of his warriors dead, Rollo would have had little reason to cross over from *Francia* . . .' Ambrose smiled suddenly, 'and we had already paid him well to stay away."

"Ambrose, you well know an invasion against fortified positions may have cost your brother more casualties than he wished to pay. I repeat, however, I have been a good neighbor. What can I do for Wessex?"

"The bald truth?"

The king smiled. "I would have nothing less between two Danes, Canuteson."

"One. Do not allow Wessex's enemies to stay on your soil."

"Ambrose, many of my tribesmen have cousins and friends in the armies of Haesten. It is hard for me to tell them that the cousins cannot come, in friendship, to my land."

"King Guthrum once said almost the same thing to me, and I told him that we understood, but would come after any Viking who landed in Wessex, and then crossed into East Anglia or Essex. It helped to cause the war between us . . . which East Anglia lost.

Two. You must not allow your warriors to invade Wessex or reinforce the Viking armies in Kent. Alfred will take that as an abrogation of our treaty and we would be at war.

Three. I need your assurances on both these matters. Today."

King Eohric pulled idly at his beard. "Prince, you ask a great deal."

"I promised to be blunt, King. I am sure that your scouts have already reported that the wolves of Mercia have paused on their way south, and have already gathered along your frontier. They can be burning down this Mead Hall within the week. You cannot call up enough warriors in time to stop Ethelred if Alfred but gives the word."

"Ambrose, I have no wish for war, and would be a good neighbor. I will command that no sworn man of mine may cross your borders. I will swear it on my armband and by *Odin*, if you wish."

"Eohric, as you say, I have lived as a Viking and been adopted as a Dane. I know that your oaths to a Christian king are meaningless."

Eohric sighed. "Prince, I will deliver to your custody six of my most beloved members of this royal court. They will go back with you, and their heads will be my guarantee of my good faith. I cannot do better than that."

"King Eohric, I will accept your offer, with thanks. I would still like an oath from you, sworn to me personally."

"Prince, why would you ask such a thing?"

"Because I am the adopted son of a Dane, I think an oath from you to Canuteson has much more meaning than one to a Christian king."

Eohric hesitated, then nodded his head slowly. "To Canuteson the Dane-Slayer? You ask much, Prince."

"It is what I need to assure me that we are not going to war."

Eohric sighed. "If it is a matter of peace between us, then you have it."

"Then with your permission, King, I will return to Wessex immediately. I would like to get back in time to prevent an invasion of your happy land."

"And the Mercian wolves?"

"There are many Danes to kill in Kent."

"I think we understand each other. May peace be with you,

Prince."

"May we stay at peace, King Eohric . . . For the sake of both our people."

"Return to your men, Prince. I have made available a house and food. You can rest and plan for your return trip. When I have had a chance to talk with the hostages and prepared them, I will send for you."

ᚠ

King Eohric had Ambrose escorted back to his Mead Hall. There, the prince saw six men standing in rich garments. The king saw him enter, and turned to face Ambrose. He spoke.

"I promised you six important members of my court to act as surety, and here they are. Meet Snorri, an esteemed cousin of mine. Meet Einarr, an important *jarl* from what you probably still call Essex. The others are four of my greatest warriors, Oddr, Torleik, and Folki. Hakon you have already met. In return for their agreeing to accompany you, I expect that you and Alfred will treat them with the utmost courtesy."

Ambrose nodded. "As long as you respect the conditions we discussed, King, they will be treated as the noblest of royal guests."

Ambrose, his escort, and their hostages rode out together and headed south and west. The Vikings followed peacefully enough. Ambrose rode along the trail until they hit the old Roman road leading to London. Instead of turning west, however, the prince led his band almost due south. Einarr the *jarl* spurred his horse and caught up with Ambrose. He spoke in his guttural voice.

"Prince, I think you are confused. London lies in that direction, along the road we just crossed."

"True, *Jarl*, but it is a long ride to London, and Alfred is due south of us."

"Prince, I do worry about you. The Thames has joined the ocean some Roman miles west of here. There is no way we can cross to the southern shore."

"Ships, good Einarr. We Saxons also own ships."

"Ships!' the *jarl* snorted derisively. 'Haesten has eighty

long-ships not far away. The Thames is a highway for us. Any Saxon ship we find we take. You have no chance finding a ship and making it across."

"Thank you for the information, Einarr. As long as I am commanding and you are a hostage, we go south."

The further south they went, the more upset the hostages became. Ambrose finally rode next to Phillip. "Old friend, our friends are becoming agitated. I think it might be wise if you were to check our back-trail."

The big man smiled as he turned his horse around. "Consider it done, Prince!"

The weapons-master returned more than an hour later. When Ambrose looked at him, he just shook his head negatively. Ambrose dropped back, and Phillip joined him. Ambrose spoke quietly to the giant *thane*.

"Well, Weapons-master?"

"There seems to be nobody on our trail, and with thirty-odd riders, it would hardly be difficult to follow."

"Phillip, if the Danes mean us some mischief, they do not have to follow closely. They expect us to head for London, and fast couriers could be sent ahead to arrange whatever they want."

"And our guests?"

"They are growing more and more unhappy. It seems that we are doing something that they do not much like."

"That is telling, Prince. Why would they care how we travel back to Wessex? Even if Haesten did find us and refuse to accept our emissary status, he would hardly harm the Viking hostages."

"Why, indeed, Phillip . . . unless they are already arranging an ambush for us somewhere, perhaps, near London."

"Wouldn't it have been simpler for King Eohric to just tell us we are going to war?"

"Agreed, old friend . . . unless . . . perhaps if some of Haesten's Vikings were to ambush us, or at least his banners flew during an unexpected attack. Eohric keeps his pledge, but the incompetent Saxons are unable to protect their hostages. Alfred is in his debt, Ethelred has been called off, Eohric has his men back, and you and I would probably be dead."

"Which would mean that Eohric already has plans to attack Wessex in some way and doesn't want to sacrifice the hostages.' Phillip grinned wolfishly. 'But we mess up his plan if we take a different route back!"

"Exactly, old friend. We are nearing the sea. I think there is a risk of running into Haesten's army. Perhaps our *fyrdmen* should string their bows as a precaution."

Phillip smiled again. "Aye, Prince. I will see to it. It is our job, after all, to protect our guests."

As dusk neared, the group passed the large rock that served as a guidepost to mariners coasting along the northern shore. Ambrose ordered that their camp be built on the shore of the Thames, about a mile to the east of the landmark. The horses were tied, and everyone made ready for sleep, but Ambrose instructed Phillip to take a couple of *fyrdmen* and build twin bonfires right at the high water mark.

As the cold breeze swept in from the sea, and the sky to the east began to lighten, Phillip shook Ambrose awake. He spoke quietly.

"They are here, Prince."

"Excellent. Shake our *fyrdmen* awake first. I want them up, with bows strung and arrows nocked."

"Are you expecting trouble?"

Ambrose shivered in the early morning cold. "I am just trying to prevent any, old friend. How soon until the ship is close enough to board?"

"It will come into the shallows just as soon as it is light enough to see the rocks clearly."

Ambrose stood and stretched. The first thing he did was strap on **Victory-Maker**.

Within minutes, the Saxon escort was armed and armored. Only then did Ambrose move to waken their guests. As the Danes got up in the dim morning light, the first thing they spotted was a small *long-ship* just feet off the beach. The second thing they spotted, when they looked inland, was twenty Saxon *fyrdmen* holding bows with arrows nocked. Only Phillip was missing.

Einarr the *Jarl* was belligerent. "What is this ship and why have your men drawn arrows again?"

"We expected a Saxon ship this morning, *Jarl*, but want to be ready in case one of Haesten's ship captains saw our campfires and decided to investigate. It is our sworn duty, after all, to protect you with our very lives."

"But we can't go aboard a ship here! Our horses . . ."

"It is regrettable that we must leave the faithful beasts here, *Jarl*. They have served us well, but Alfred himself will replace them with the finest animals we can find in Wessex . . . now if you don't mind, we need you and our other guests aboard ship. As you say, this is a dangerous coast, and we must not linger."

At that point, Hakon stepped forward and drew his sword. "I am not going to board a ship! I am going to climb on my horse and ride to London and no one is going to stop me."

Einerr spoke in rapid Danish. "You will follow your king's instructions, Hakon! Haesten's ships will capture this scow!"

Hakon was shaking with anger. "I am riding. You! Daneslayer! Perhaps you would like to stop me!"

Ambrose drew **Victory-Maker**. The magnificent blade gleamed red in the early morning light.

"Hakon, by disobeying my instruction, you have broken the bond between guest and protector. You have both insulted me and dishonored your king. It would, indeed, be my pleasure to teach you some manners."

Hakon sneered. "You, little man, with your toy sword? Einarr, give the little man a real weapon. You clearly don't need it."

As he jeered Ambrose, he approached him. Suddenly, like a venomous snake, he attacked without warning. His long blade swept low, and if Ambrose had not been watching the man's eyes, he might not have jumped quickly enough to evade the long sweep. Ambrose landed and rolled. Suddenly he was ten feet from Hakon, and his sword was ready for the next attack.

He smiled. "Is that the cut you use on old men and women, Viking? I thought you were going to teach me a lesson."

"I was going to let you live, little man. Now I am not so sure."

Again he sidled forward as he spoke. This time he exploded into a series of powerful slashes.

Ambrose parried each one easily, and soon he was facing a

panting and tired warrior. He spoke.

"You seem to be out of practice, Hakon. You have been indulging in too much food and not enough exercise. Perhaps Eohric chose you because he couldn't find any old women to send along."

With a roar of rage, Hakon charged Ambrose, but instead of closing, he ran right past the prince and leapt on to the back of one of the horses peacefully grazing on the lush grass. He kicked the startled animal into motion, but before the horse could go more than a dozen paces, a yard-long shaft buried itself in the animal's chest. Mortally wounded, the poor beast screamed and then fell to the ground.

Hakon rolled free as the animal fell, but when he went to get to his feet he discovered his sword was out of reach and a second arrow was aimed in his direction. Phillip stepped out from behind a cluster of trees, the arrow touching his ear.

"On your feet, Viking scum! Today you made me kill a faithful and beautiful animal. I would far rather have put the arrow through you. Now obey my prince and get on the God-cursed boat!"

Hakon stepped over to where his sword lay. Phillip spoke.

"Pick it up and you die! You have dishonored your king and lost the privilege of wearing a warrior's sword."

Hakon looked at his sword and then carefully stepped over it. The Viking, followed by Phillip, Einarr and Ambrose, all headed for the waiting ship.

Einarr tried again. "Prince, you are sailing a Danish highway. You will never reach the southern shore alive! Let us ride around, through London."

Ambrose spoke. "I think you misunderstand the role of a hostage, *Jarl*. We decide where you go and how we get there. You obey. It is that simple."

As they argued, the rest of the escort and hostages made it aboard. Finally, with great reluctance, Einarr clambered aboard.

"Mark my words, Prince, a Saxon ship will never make it across!"

The oarsmen pulled the ship clear of the shallows, and then the captain, in perfect Danish, ordered the square sail hoisted.

Einarr stared, dumbfounded, as Eohric's emblem suddenly

appeared in the early morning light. He turned to Ambrose, who smiled back at him.

"This is a Danish ship, Einarr, and all our crewmen speak Danish. As you say, the Thames is a Viking highway, at least as far as Southwark, and what is one more Danish vessel plying its waters? Why would we not make it safely to the southern shore?"

"But that is Eohric's emblem on your sail!"

"Of course it is. *Jarl* Einarr, the previous owners were pirates who spent too long ashore on a raiding expedition. Those who did not die in the fight were all hung. My brother is very serious about his boast of six feet of ground and a good rope for every Viking who invades his land."

Ambrose stepped over to the crewman who acted as cook for the crew. "Greetings, Edwy."

"Greetings, Prince Ambrose."

"Edwy, you should be carrying some pigeons for me."

"Yes, Prince, the king was most particular about that. Polonius the Wizard delivered them personally, with clear instructions not to eat them. Prince, I don't know why you would want to. We have some particularly fine chickens for supper."

"Where are the pigeons?"

"They are in the cage near the mainmast."

"This is very important, my friend. I want you to ring the neck of the two black ones. They are for the supper pot tonight."

"And the two white ones?"

"You are to say a short prayer of thanks to God, and then release them both."

The Saxon looked strangely at Ambrose. At last he just shrugged.

"Aye, Master. As you say."

As Ambrose idly watched the two white pigeons spiral higher and higher, he felt a presence at his side. Snorri stood beside him. The bearded warrior spoke in Danish.

"I hope that they were not our dinner tonight, Prince. Is it customary amongst Saxons to release some of your food animals?"

Ambrose smiled. "It is a custom I learned in Africa. Look at the beauty of the birds as they ascend toward heaven. Can you think of a better way to send a prayer for peace to Almighty God?"

"I don't know, Prince. I worship the true gods, the Viking gods, but above all, I call upon *Odin* to help me in my times of need. Your three gods in one is a puzzle to me."

⚑

The little party landed at Rochester and requisitioned enough horses to re-mount the little force and their guests. Within hours after a peaceful trip across the Thames, Ambrose was leading his little force toward Alfred and his army.

⚑

Ambrose signaled his little column to slow, and then galloped ahead. At the head of the large mounted force just ahead of them on the old Roman highway rode a king on a splendid white stallion. When Ambrose approached, several guardsmen maneuvered their horses between him and Alfred, but when they recognized the dusty rider, they just grinned and cleared out of the way.

Ambrose thus caught up with his brother. He called out. "Greetings, king of the West Saxons! Have we won the war yet?"

"Ambrose, you rascal. Praise God! You do not know how I worried about you! Did you have any trouble?"

"King Eohric promised all that we discussed, and even sent six hostages."

"Excellent, so you had no trouble."

"Nothing we couldn't handle. Our guests seemed very disturbed when we took the sea route back here, so I am very suspicious. If I had to hazard a guess about what they were planning, I would suspect that we might have been ambushed by Vikings waving Haesten's banners if we had returned via London."

"But what would be the point, brother?"

"Actually, it would have been quite clever. Eohric would have his hostages back safe and sound, we would be blaming Haesten for the deed. Having lost your hostages to 'raiders', you would have failed your side of the agreement and would be greatly in his debt, I would be out of his hair, and, far from least, you would have called off Ethelred and his warriors, giving Eohric time to call up his own warriors and throw together some kind of coherent defense. The truth is, with Ethelred's *fyrdmen* unexpectedly shifted eastward to the frontier, we had Eohric by the balls, and he knew it."

"And did we call off Ethelred and his *fyrd*?"

"I am still not sure what game Eohric is playing, but he did give his oath, and he did give us hostages. I therefore felt I had no choice but to send the white pigeons."

"Do you have any proof of any plot?"

"Not a shred, brother - Eohric was happy to swear an oath to you, but was strangely reluctant to give me a personal oath. The other item was the behavior of the hostages. It should not have mattered a bit to them which route we took to return to Wessex, yet they were very upset when they realized that we were not planning to take the Roman road back to London.

One particularly unpleasant specimen, Hakon, drew his blade and tried to run away by going through me."

Alfred grinned. "And how did that go?"

"I didn't touch a hair on his head, but Phillip had to shoot a horse out from under him."

"How did you handle the rest of them?"

Ambrose smiled. "Well, the boat could have been Danish - correction - it was once Danish, so our faithful escort strung their bows and nocked arrows - just in case. We, of course, never threatened any of the other guests with violence. They got the message, however, and eventually clambered aboard.

Einarr, in particular, then bragged that we would be taken on the water by Haesten's sailors . . . until he saw Haesten's emblem when we raised the sail. Then he was furious."

Alfred stroked his beard absent-mindedly. "The case is hardly irrefutable, but your logic is impeccable, brother. I fear that we will have to watch our 'friend and ally' very carefully."

Ambrose smiled. "I don't think for a moment that you

considered doing anything else, Alfred."

Alfred grinned. "You are quite right, big brother!"

"And what about you, little brother?"

"We have our fort just east of here, but there are two large Viking armies nearby. We patrol daily, and have hung many Viking scouts and couriers."

"Have the Danes met you with serious forces, Alfred?"

"So far they have only sent out relatively small patrols. I think we have managed to keep them blind and deaf, so they are bumbling through the forest."

"So what are we doing today?"

Alfred smiled. "Since you finally found me, I think I should take you to our new home. There is a Byzantine there who is eager to talk with you!"

CHAPTER 4

"Then went they (Alfred's fyrdmen) forth in quest of the wealds, in troops and companies, wheresoever the country was defenseless."
......The Anglo-Saxon Chronicles

Alfred stood before Edward and Polonius. Behind them, but slowly falling into formation, were two thousand of his finest veteran *fyrdmen*, each well armored and mounted.

"My son, if the *Witan* is ever to choose you as king, then you must learn to lead men in battle. Never forget that cousin Ethelwold is ten years older than you, and has an excellent claim to the throne. The *Witan* has the right to choose from among the *athelings* the man whom they think will best rule.

It would be, however, a sad day if that traitor sits on the throne. Thus you need some experience leading fighting men, and an unblemished record."

"Father, do you really feel I am ready to lead seasoned warriors?"

"I fear that you may have to be, perhaps sooner than you would wish. I am not well, Edward, and I want you to get some experience. I am sending with you three living legends, however, and I expect you to take their advice. It is largely because of these three that Wessex did not fall to the pagans long ago, and I pray to God that they are able to serve you as faithfully as they have me.

You know, I marched to war with my brother the king while still a beardless youth. We lost as many battles as we won, but in the end we either bribed the Vikings or we vanquished them.

I will pray for your success, my son. Remember, if you wish to beat Ethelwold to the throne, you can afford no serious defeats. If you outnumber the Danes, kill them ruthlessly. If the numbers are close, I expect you to retreat to the safety of the fort. Polonius here has taught me an important lesson."

"And what is that, father?"

"He taught me that the purpose of war is to win. I am an old man now, and if I have learned one thing - it is that there is no glory in battle. Do not spend Saxon lives foolishly.

I do not want - what did you call him, Polonius?"

"Call who, King?"

"That Greek king who defeated the Romans but destroyed his own army in the process."

"King Pyrrhus?"

"That's the one. Edward, I do not want a '*Pyrrhic victory*', where we defeat the enemy but leave the cream of our warriors dead on the battlefield."

Edward bowed to his father. "Fear not, father. We will overwhelm small foraging parties, and hide from ones that come even close to matching our numbers. With Sigehelm's Kentish foresters scouting for us, we should be able to deliver some surprise punches with relatively small risk."

Ambrose smiled. "Excellent. That is what I want to hear. May God protect you and look after you, my son!"

⚑

The day warmed, but the Saxons did not stir. The warriors had lain half the night behind the trees and bushes that lined the single road through the forest. They lay in ambush, while, slowly approaching, were several hundred Viking warriors.

It had been hard for the Saxons. They had heard the noise of battle in the distance when the Viking raiding party had swept over a still-occupied village in the gathering dusk the night before. They had heard the screams of the women being raped, and the sounds of the men being tortured for their paltry treasures or killed because they tried to protect their loved ones. The coppery smell of blood had wafted their way, and, finally, the smells of cooking meat, when the villagers' livestock was roasted on spits over bonfires. Through it all, the Saxon tight discipline prevailed.

The men were eager to avenge the villagers, but the formidable palisades, while they had not much slowed the Danes who had taken the *vill* by surprise, would erase any advantage the Saxons might have had. They needed the Vikings in the open and vulnerable. The men ate cold provisions, cut brush far from the road to act as screens, and then lay down to wait. In the morning the Danes would leave the protection of the palisades, advance along the forest road, and revenge would be sweet.

In the ruddy light of dawn, the Vikings finished chaining their captives into coffles, ate from the vast trove of meat, and slowly made their way westward along the old Roman road.

Edward watched as squads of scouts galloped past their position. The scouts were riding hard to get far ahead of the advancing force and search out any Saxon threats, but they did not bother to scour the brush on either side of the road so close to the little *vill*.

Edward was beside himself with excitement. He whispered to Phillip. "When should I give the order, Weapons-master?"

The giant whispered back. "Soon, Prince. We want the first ranks to reach Ambrose's position before you signal the attack."

"But Weapons-master, their vanguard might escape if we wait that long!"

"Better a few escape than the main body. Our task is to hit them so we kill as many as possible with the least risk to our own warriors . . . I would say that now would be a good time, Prince."

Edward rose to his feet and shouted "For Wessex! Attack!"

Throwing off blankets covered with vegetation or heaving aside cut branches, a thousand warriors staggered to their feet and, yelling the Saxon battle cry, charged forward.

Bowmen did their best to empty their quivers, and the rest of the *fyrdmen* launched their Roman-style *pilums* as soon as they got close enough. The Danes, for the most part mounted, tried to slip off their horses and form their famed *skjaldborg*, but they were vulnerable as they dismounted, and the arrows sought out unprotected backs. The

Saxons hurled their spears at the riders, or killed the horses. The Danes were all experienced from long years of combat on the Continent, and many managed to safely dismount. Once on the ground, they lifted their shields to provide protection against the rain of missiles. The Saxon spears, however, with their narrow heads, bit deeply into the Viking shields. When the Danes tried to remove them, the long iron shanks bent, rendering the spears useless and weighing down the shields. When the frustrated Vikings cast aside their shields, the arrows quickly sought them out.

Within a few hundred heartbeats, the barrage of missiles ceased abruptly and the Saxon *fyrdmen* closed with the hated enemy. The Vikings were brave men. Ambrose had heard of old men who begged their sons to take them one last time to join the shield-wall so they could die fighting rather than gasp out their last breaths in bed. The reward for the bravest was a seat in *Asgard* in the halls of the gods. Taught to laugh at pain, they stood bravely against the overwhelming numbers of Saxon attackers.

The Vikings tried repeatedly to form their *skjaldborg*, but the Saxons rushed at them from both sides and the Danes had trouble forming a cohesive defensive line. Within minutes, most of the Danes lay dead or wounded on the old Roman road. Edward, under the watchful eyes of both Polonius and Phillip, swung his sword lustily against several Vikings in turn, but his enemies were overwhelmed by the avalanche of vengeful *fyrdmen*. One bearded Viking giant, seeing the gold *torque* Edward wore, charged right at the *atheling*, but a dagger pierced his left eyeball, and the man fell screaming back into the mass of struggling warriors. Within moments, the big Dane was trampled on and dead.

The Saxon warriors methodically slit the throats of any enemy wounded and looted the bodies of the newly dead. Shielded by Phillip, Edward vomited until nothing more could come up.

Ambrose quietly took charge and had the warriors collect the surviving horses and freed the captives, mostly young women and older children. He sent for their own horses, and, within minutes, the bastard prince had the re-mounted column heading back for the Roman marching fort that was their temporary home and shelter. Though they were a thousand strong, there were even larger enemy forces loose in the forest, and Ambrose knew the Vikings would be hot for revenge once they learned what had happened to their foraging party.

The prosperous-looking merchants whipped their horses savagely as they fled along the forest road. Their heavily-burdened pack animals slowed their progress and the riders seemed to panic.

Hard on their trail came more than a hundred Danes, grinning and calling out to the fleeing Saxons to wait for them. Suddenly the rearmost Saxon slowed his horse. A half-dozen armored riders exited the forest and formed a defensive line across the road. The Danes jeered the few defenders, drew their weapons and advanced eagerly. Suddenly the forest on both sides vomited Saxon warriors. Lines of archers appeared amongst the trees, and they filled the air with clouds of arrows. The Danes, with no time to dismount and form their *skjaldborg*, wheeled and charged toward the archers. The Viking warriors quickly found the *caltrops* scattered thickly along the edge of the road, and another line of *fyrdmen* rose to their feet and firmly planted twenty foot lances against the ground. Horses and men alike were impaled on the deadly points, and within moments the desperate charge was broken. Dozens of men and horses had been cut down, and the Saxon *fyrdmen* advanced cautiously toward the few survivors.

Just a few minutes after the battle started, it was over. The ground was red from the blood of horses and Danish warriors.

Phillip ordered the *fyrdmen* to mount up. They were near Appledore, and thousands of enemy warriors were much too close. The Saxons rode for the safety of Alfred's fort.

Three of the graceful *long-ships* bumped the river bank and disgorged their crews. The Danes playfully leapt over the railing and quickly formed up on the river bank. With a minimum of noise, the several hundred veteran warriors started jogging toward the nearby

Kentish village.

The Danes had found little food in the Forest of the Weald. Following Alfred's instructions, the villagers had transported their food stock and livestock to the nearest fortified *burh*, and the Saxons had even burned supplies they could not take with them. The Vikings were getting hungry, and thus they had planned a ship-born assault on one of the few villages that their scouts reported had not been abandoned, because it was not connected to the rest of Kent by a road.

Haesten, commander of the secondary force of 80 ships, and established at Milton Royal, led the raiders himself. His belly was empty, and he was damned if he and his men would eat any more of their precious horses. The scouts had told him that the village was positively groaning with livestock and refugees. Good food and Saxons to enslave were lures that the *jarl* could not pass up.

His warriors approached the town with caution and Haesten inspected the palisade disdainfully. It might keep out wolves, but it was much too frail to more than slow the Vikings a little.

He swept his hand forward. Three hundred warriors erupted from the surrounding forest. Roaming cattle and pigs mooed and grunted in panic at the sudden appearance of a mass of strangers. The Vikings ignored the animals and raced toward the village. The attackers had to reach the open gates before the defenders could react and close them. Three hundred men hacked their way through the palisades, climbed over them, or simply flooded through the main gate.

Chickens flew and dogs barked, but no villagers confronted the invaders. The Danes, in a fighting frenzy, found no one standing against them. They milled about in confusion. Food was cooking over fire pits, but there was no enemy to be seen.

Haesten stared in surprise, and then took command. He called out to his officers. "The villagers must have got word that we were coming. That means there could be armed men in the forest and reinforcements may have been sent for. Have your men get to work. I want the grain and livestock gathered and transported to the ships as soon as possible. I expect that this haul will feed our crews for at least a week or two."

As the men began to search out the town's food stocks, Saxon war horns started to bugle.

Haesten ran to the main gate and arrived just in time to see a seemingly endless line of Saxon warriors step out of the surrounding woods. The warrior *thanes* of Wessex closed ranks as they exited the woods and then advanced in shield-wall formation. The unbroken line of armored *fyrdmen* was followed by a rabble of archers, slingers and spearmen. The Vikings lined the palisades and beat their shields with their axes or swords, but all the noise in the world could not hide the fact that the Danes were both surrounded and outnumbered by a five to one margin. As Haesten had already noted, the palisade itself was adequate to keep out wild animals, but there was no ditch and the rotted wooden palisade would no more slow the Saxons than it had the Vikings.

A quick survey by the *jarl* determined that all four sides of the little village were completely surrounded by Saxon warriors. There was no opening through which the Vikings could escape, unless they somehow managed to carve out an opening with their own blood and steel.

Jarl Haesten held up his shield draped with a white cloth as he stepped through the gate. He called out in guttural Danish. "Who speaks for you?"

The shield wall opened and an older man with a crown on his head stepped forward, flanked by a giant, an emaciated looking dark-skinned man, and a short blond warrior.

The dark-skinned man spoke in perfect Danish.

"My master is Alfred, King of Wessex. Who are you?"

"I am *Jarl* Haesten, leader of eighty ships and two thousand fierce warriors. And who are you?"

"I am Polonius, advisor to King Alfred."

Haesten smiled. "Ah, the Byzantine. Your knife-belt gives you away. You are known to my people as 'spy-master' and 'scholar'. Some of the more foolish ones even call you 'wizard'. I know of you. Then that must be Ambrose, or should I say Canuteson and Phillip at your side."

Polonius smiled and made a little nod. "You are correct, *Jarl*."

"At last I meet the men who traveled all the way to *Miklagard*, sailed Viking ships to steal back princesses, and spied on the Danish *Great Army* by serving in it. I have often heard the ballads about you three."

"My master, Prince Ambrose, also served for a time in Guthrum's army, *Jarl*, and my people have taken to calling him 'Dane-Slayer' . . . Have you come to surrender your men?"

"Your King Alfred is not well known for his mercy to Viking adventurers, Byzantine. I am told that each Viking is treated to six feet of good Wessex soil and a piece of rope. Why, with my own eyes, I have seen dozens of good scouts and warriors hanging in the trees surrounding my fort. This does not encourage either me or my warriors to submit ourselves to Christian charity."

"Then why are you here? You know it would be our pleasure to send you and all your men to *Asgard* this very day. It seems to be the only object lesson that thick-headed Danes seem to understand."

Haesten hesitated. "If the tales about you are true, then you have fought at the side of Viking warriors, Byzantine, even if they were only *Rus* Vikings. You know that we will not die easily, and many Saxon widows will also be grieving before this day ends . . . Tell your king that I have a proposal for him."

Alfred spoke in poor Danish. "I am listening, *Jarl*."

"I concede that you will probably be victorious today, King, but it will be very, very expensive. I am willing to give my oath that, if you allow us to return to our vessels, I will take my eighty ships and leave your lands forever. I will be gone, along with my two thousand warriors, and it will not cost you a single Saxon life."

Alfred spoke through Polonius. "*Jarl*, you do not know the number of times that I have heard those words. Ambrose, my brother, has lived with both the Danes and the *Rus* Vikings, and he tells me that an oath from you to a non-believer such as myself is worthless – unless it can be backed with my naked sword."

"I will swear by my sacred armbands, King, and you may choose several hostages from amongst my commanders. Their lives will be yours to do whatever you want with, if I do not speak the truth to you."

"*Jarl* Haesten, I have hanged brothers of Viking kings. I have hanged royal cousins and I have hanged great *jarls*. Still I am lied to."

"As well, King, I will agree that two of my sons will be baptized in your Christian religion. The mother of my two children, who was once a princess of *Francia*, wishes it, so I make you the offer. What is it to be, King of Wessex, grieving widows or peace between us and two more Christian souls saved?"

"I must choose the hostages from amongst your court and your children will also be hostage. It must be understood that they will all pay with their lives for any treachery on your part."

"My sons will stay with you until I sail, and they will serve as hostages until then. When I am ready to leave, you will return them to me, but the men will stay a further six months with you. Are we agreed?"

Alfred spoke. "We are agreed, *Jarl* Haesten."

"And my men must have some silver and gold to pay for their troubles. They have come a long way and collected very little. We have even had to eat some of our precious horse herd."

"Your men may have the choice of hemp or steel from me, *Jarl*, but not a single silver or gold coin. I will honor your children, and your hostages, with generous gifts at the end of their visits, but not one coin for *Danegeld*. A victor does not pay tribute, and I am not the loser today. On this we must be very clear."

Hasten suddenly grinned. "I had to ask. You might have been foolish enough to agree.

Then, King, I swear on my sacred armband that I will return directly to my camp, and, within a single cycle of the moon, take my eighty shiploads of warriors away from Wessex."

"*Seven-night* - and stay away forever."

"Two *seven-nights* - and stay away forever." The *jarl* suddenly smiled again. "There is much to pack."

"We are agreed, *Jarl* Haesten, but I expect you to be my guest for the baptism."

"With your personal promise of a safe-conduct, I would be pleased to agree, king of the Saxons. You are known as a harsh foe, but a man of your word."

ڡ

Edward rode beside his father as they headed back to their base. "Father, why do you let the pirate live when we had the chance to strike off the head of the snake?"

"Edward, it is a good question, and if you are to eventually rule, then you will have to learn strategic thinking. Ambrose once told me a story told to him by his friend Hakim, merchant of Alexandria."

"The merchant who saved his life in Alexandria and then escorted him all the way across North Africa? I have heard Uncle Ambrose talk of him, father."

"You have heard of the terrible Moors of Spain?"

"Of course, father. They poured in from the desert of North Africa, and in the space of a few years, conquered all of the southern Christian kingdoms on the Iberian Peninsula. Uncle Ambrose was even enslaved by a colony of theirs on Crete."

"What I did not know, Edward, until Ambrose enlightened me, is that the Moors are not Arab."

"Really? Then where did they come from?"

"They were the children and grandchildren of the Berbers, who were Christian or pagan, and who fought bitterly against the arrival of Islam in their lands."

"Father, I do not understand."

"The Arabs, when they swept along the coast of Africa, conquered the tribes who lived there, including the Berbers. The Berbers fiercely resisted conversion and the Arabs did not force the Christians among them to become Muslim, but their leaders' children were taken to Bagdad to be educated. In only a generation or two, the children accepted the teachings of Mohammed, and it was their children who were sent by the Caliph to conquer Christian lands across the Mediterranean."

"Then if I am following you correctly, it was the grandchildren of Christians who conquered Christian kingdoms for their Muslim rulers? Father, I suspect you are trying to tell me something here."

Alfred smiled fondly at his son. "Edward, in my treaty with

King Guthrum of East Anglia, he agreed to stop persecuting God's priests in his land. Already, in less than a single generation, many pagan Danes have seen the light of God's truth. Within another generation or two, I expect to have Viking Christians acting as a buffer against their own cousins.

Don't you see? It is not so much the two souls we save, although Bishop Asser tells me that God is well pleased with that, but I look at the promise of saving hundreds more down the road. In time, one of these two boys will likely replace his father as *jarl*. He will be a Christian, and perhaps influence his pagan followers to convert. Is it better we kill a man who might have inadvertently let in the light of God to his people, or allow the sacred light to spread to his benighted followers?"

"Father, are you convinced that the *jarl* will keep his word?"

"He probably won't, and if and when he breaks his word, we will hang all of his hostages, except the boys. God has another purpose for them. Meanwhile, we have a chance to turn to God's light the next generation of pagan Vikings. The children of Christian and pagan Berbers became an all conquering force for Islam. Why should we not do the same with the Danes . . . now would you find Bishop Asser for me and tell him to arrange for a baptism as soon as we reach Milton Royal? Oh, and tell Polonius to send for two thousand more of our best mounted *fyrdmen*. I want them to follow in our wake - at a discrete distance – and I will want some very generous gifts ready to present to the boys and *Jarl* Haesten."

"Father, are you really going to reward a Viking for invading Kent? You always told me that we should hang every Viking we can get our hands on."

"The truth? I am going to reward a Viking for letting us baptize his children, and I intend to give him enough 'gifts' that he just may really stay away from Wessex. Edward, you know that if the two Viking armies manage to join, our *fyrdmen* are seriously outnumbered?"

"If we include all the adult men under our banners, then that is not strictly true, but I will concede that, trained warrior to trained warrior, we would, indeed, be outnumbered with only the summer *fyrd* at our back."

"But if Haesten takes his fleet away, even for a few months, then we hold a clear numerical advantage."

"I see that, father."

"Then the moment *Ealdorman* Sigehelm's scouts tell us that Haesten has really gone and our backs are safe, we are going to turn our full attention on to Appledore, besiege it, and reduce it to rubble. One enemy at a time we can handle."

"And Northumbria and East Anglia?"

"I do not think for one moment that their kings will remain innocent spectators in all this. Eohric's behavior with Ambrose was very suspicious. I just pray they stay out of the fight for a few more months, at least until we finish off Appledore. We will move quickly and decisively - before they can get an attack organized. After that, I would not mind a crack at them. I think God would be pleased if we could return the northern conquered kingdoms to Christian rule. In fact, my son, I hope that in your lifetime you rule a united land that stretches at least as far north as the Humber River. I pray you will rule a land where Danes and Saxons live as equals, and all are God-fearing Christians. It is my fondest dream."

CHAPTER 5

Baptism

Bishop Asser called his acolyte to him. Today he was going to preside over a baptism of two young boys whose father was a ferocious pirate and a mother who had been savagely torn from the bosom of her royal family and made a Viking slave. As godparents, he had no less than the king of Wessex and his son-in-law, Ethelred of Mercia.

He had discussed the baptism at length with King Alfred. He knew that the heathen pirate was lost to God, but he was excited that the boys, baptized by him, would one day be leaders amongst the Danes. The king was right, it was an exceptional opportunity to try and convert the brutal pagans to the way of Almighty God. This was one baptism he wanted to get right!

"Clywd! We have three of the most powerful people in all Britain going to ride into this *tun* at any moment and you still do not have me ready! Tell me again why I did not send you home to my sister years ago!"

Clywd smiled and spoke calmly. "Partly because my mother, your sainted sister, would probably box your ears, but more importantly, I am the best acolyte you have ever had. Please relax, Bishop. I have it on good authority that they will not start the ceremony without you."

Suddenly, Asser broke out in laughter. "I suppose you are right, you rascal. It is not a good thing, however, to have a king and a pirate mad at you."

Clywd turned with the bishop's alb in his hands. "If you would raise your arms, Bishop, I will slip this over your head."

"And now the red chasuble, Clywd."

"I still remember the day, lord Bishop, when I was young and foolish, and tried to give you the green one for that Danish king's baptism. You were not happy with me."

"Bring the Dalmatic and Stole, Clywd. Let us save the reminiscences for another day. The king could arrive at any moment! Now where is my miter and staff? Rascal, have you hidden them on me again?"

Clywd reached over to the staff leaning against the wall. "Would this one be satisfactory, lord Bishop?"

"I knew it! Why must you hide everything on me?"

Clywd smiled. "So I can have the pleasure of finding it for you, lord Bishop."

ೀ

Bishop Asser made it outside in time to see the participants arrive. The procession, led by King Alfred himself and *Ealdorman* Ethelred, stretched almost out of sight. Asser groaned. The only church available held less than a hundred, and it looked like a lot more than that were approaching. He quickly formed up his column of priests. They would lead the high and mighty through the *tun* and into the tiny church.

The king approached, and Bishop Asser led his column into the center of the road that led to the church. King and *ealdorman* swung in behind the chanting priests, and the entire column slowly crossed the old Roman bridge and approached the church.

The passage was marked with a cloud of incense, and the priests chanted sonorously as they marched. The small church was of wood and had few windows, but the interior was lit by flaring torches stuck into fixtures mounted on the wall.

Bishop Asser led his king and the pirate chieftain through the door. Haesten the Dane held a little hand from each of his sons, and led them into the dim interior. Asser led the little group to a position just before the font of holy water. The King, *ealdorman*, Haesten and his two boys formed a semi-circle around the bishop and the font, while as many noblemen, ambassadors and Viking warriors as could fit filled the rest of the church. Asser stepped behind the two boys and tied the chrism, a white piece of linen cloth, around their foreheads. Both of the newly baptized boys were expected to wear the symbol of their new faith for eight days.

The king and *ealdorman*, in their role as godfathers, stood beside the children, while Bishop Asser dipped a scallop shell into the holy water and sprinkled a few drops on each boy in turn. As he moved from one boy to the next, Bishop Asser chanted the mysterious Latin words that gave the boys hope of eternal salvation. "I baptize thee in the name of the Father, and of the Son, and the Holy Ghost. Amen.'

Once the task was completed, Bishop Asser returned and stood in front of the king and the *ealdorman*. 'And now, King Alfred and *Ealdorman* Ethelred, do you have Christian names for these new lambs of God?"

"Aye, Bishop, but first let us introduce our guests to the mysteries of the church.' Turning to the boys, he spoke to them in the Frankish tongue. 'Each of you dip your hand into the holy water, and make a sign of the cross, like this . . . Excellent. Now please follow me and *Ealdorman* Ethelred."

The king and nobleman led the two boys down the length of the nave to the alter, where the two of them repeated the sign of the cross. The two boys followed, watched, and carefully imitated them.

Alfred spoke. "Godric and Eric, today your soul has been saved. Kneel with us before the power and glory of God. Shed your heathen names and then rise, as Marc and Pierre."

The two boys followed Alfred's lead, and then rose. Alfred and Ethelred each embraced a boy in a great bear hug, and Alfred broke the silence again. "Welcome to God's Holy Church, Marc and Pierre!"

Alfred smiled as he faced the pirate leader and his most powerful commanders. "Haesten, I hope you will let me provide food and drink to celebrate the salvation of your two boys' souls."

Haesten rubbed his belly and replied in Danish. "I never say 'no' to good food, King!"

Alfred then turned to Bishop Asser. "My lord Bishop, I hope that you can come and offer God's blessing to our joyous feast this evening."

"It would be my pleasure, Sire."

Alfred sat in his intricately carved seat-of-honor, and beside him sat Haesten and his two boys. Next were Ambrose, Polonius, Phillip, and Ethelred. Slaves and *churls* rushed to set up the trestle tables and benches in the king's hall, while women prepared food and poured the ale and mead for the waiting guests. Over two hundred guests were milling around just outside the hall, or were arriving.

At Polonius' curt nod, the signal horn brayed, and the many guests hurried to receive a warm cloth and wash their hands. Once their ablations were completed, they lined up to file past the door-wardens, who had them escorted to their pre-designated seats.

The trestle tables stretched the length of the hall. On either side of the first table were the ealdormen of the empire, mixed in with bishops of the church, ambassadors of foreign lands, and, lower down the table, the more prominent *drengs* and *duguos* who made up Alfred's real power.

At the next table sat Haesten's chief officers and the warriors who made up the pirate chief's escort. Bishop Asser invoked the blessing, and Alfred then signaled for the feast to begin. From the far end, close to the outdoor summer kitchens, began a procession of heavily laden servers. The servers started with large roasted portions of venison and boars, roasted with their heads still intact. Heaping platters of beef and lamb followed.

A second wave of servers brought out entire flocks of roasted chickens and hundreds of smaller birds that had been roasted on skewers.

Some two dozen servants circulated with huge pitchers of mead, ale and wine, which they poured endlessly into the waiting drinking horns. Baskets full of fresh loaves of bread, cheese, and vegetables were heaped between the platters of meat, until the tables groaned with their burden of food.

While the Saxons and Danes got down to serious eating, Alfred's favorite *scop* tuned his harp and sang the epic ballads.

After the food was cleared away, Alfred rose to his feet, and the crowd quickly hushed. The king addressed the assembled guests.

"My friends, members of the court, and honored guests! Today

Ealdorman Ethelred and I have had the honor of becoming godfathers to two strapping young lads, the sons of Haesten the Dane. It is a great honor for me. I hope that, this night, as we welcome Marc and Pierre into our midst as Christians in the sight of God, will be a memorable one!

In honor of this momentous occasion, I would like to present Haesten and his two sons with some tokens of our good will."

With that said, Alfred clapped his hands rapidly three times. The curtains at the far end parted again, but this time it was not platters of steaming food that arrived. Three comely maidens marched in slowly, each carrying a small wooden casket. Solemnly, the maidens advanced until they were next to the Danish *jarl* and his two sons. Each bent low, and they presented the caskets to the *jarl* and his two sons.

Haesten received his first. He thanked the pretty girl who presented it to him, and then eagerly opened the box. He withdrew a jewel encrusted sax made of the finest Damascus steel. It was of exquisite workmanship and the men closest to the Danish chieftain gasped as he held the beautiful blade up to the light.

Haesten, overcome by the beauty of the gift, stood and embraced Alfred. He spoke in his deep voice, and Polonius translated his words so the Saxons and Angles could understand.

"I am overcome with the generosity of King Alfred's gift, and I thank him with all my heart. Now boys, it is your turn!

Excited, the two boys threw open their caskets, and withdrew two identical golden crosses studded with jewels. Their father nodded to them. Pierre was too shy to speak, but Marc piped up in his reedy voice. "Thank you, great King . . . no, I must call you godfather now. You have been most kind this day, and my mother will be very pleased that our souls have been saved. It was a great worry to her."

Polonius translated the Frankish words, and then all in the hall burst into cheers. The boys soon fell asleep beside their father, but the ale and mead flowed until the sun rose.

CHAPTER 6

Plans for Appledore

Ambrose examined Alfred as he entered his brother's command tent. He noted that the king had more color and no longer *held his stomach*. He looked much better.

When Alfred looked up from the map, Ambrose spoke. "Brother, have we heard from Northumbria yet?"

"Edwolf has not yet reported in, but he sent fast couriers ahead the moment he reached London. His report arrived just last night."

"And are we at war with Northumbria?" asked Ambrose.

Alfred smiled. "No. They offered no hostages, but have sworn eternal love and affection."

"Do we believe them?"

"Even less than Eohric."

"So what are we doing about it?"

Alfred replied. "There are over three hundred Viking ship crews in Kent. That must be our first priority."

"Brother, on another matter . . . did I not hear that we captured another Danish *long-ship* last week near Dover?"

Alfred smiled. "That will teach the crewmen to sleep on the shore and have their sentries fall asleep. Our local *fyrdmen* took great pleasure in making sure that the entire crew had the opportunity to sleep until Judgment Day."

"And I understand that it was one of Haesten's ships?"

"It is too late to ask the crew, but it was his emblem on the sail."

"Brother, I would like to have that *long-ship* . . ."

Alfred interrupted. "Big brother, if you are going to tell me you want to use it to sneak into the Viking camp . . . forget it! You have managed that little trick, against all odds, far too many times. Even the Danes sing the ballads about you and how you tricked numerous

Viking kings and *jarls*. You have humiliated a lot of very powerful people. The Danes are a proud people and not forgiving of such insults. You told me that yourself!'

Alfred suddenly grinned. 'You are planning something, brother - I can see it written across your face."

Ambrose smiled in response. "Peace, brother. I merely want to do what worked so well in North Africa."

"And that is?"

"In North Africa we bought a little fishing boat, sailed right up to the moored Byzantine fleet in the dark, while a hundred archers distracted the sailors in the fort with fire arrows, and threw containers full of Polonius' favorite flammable concoctions at the ships. We actually destroyed one *dromon* and put two out of commission for a month or more."

Alfred sighed. "What exactly are you proposing, brother-of-mine?"

"Alfred, what do you want the most out of this campaign?"

"To kill all the Vikings with no loss to our own *fyrdmen*. That would send an effective message to all the raiders and *jarls* out there that *Angleland* is not a healthy place for them to come to."

Ambrose grinned. "A worthy goal, but probably unobtainable even with me and the Wizard both at your side. What is your second choice?"

Alfred looked puzzled. "What are you trying to get at, Ambrose?"

"If the choice was between a bitter struggle where you drive the Vikings into their boats after large losses on both sides, or just the Vikings fleeing in their ships, which would you choose?"

"In my heart I would prefer a victory where we leave thousands of the pirates dead, but considering the cost in lives it would take to bring it about, I guess I would reluctantly accept their departure. I think you were right, the Danes are not through with us, and I do not want our army bled white through battle. I am still waiting for the other boot to fall."

"Then I think we have a plan worthy of Polonius' old friend, *Sun Tzu*, brother. Without Haesten's army skulking somewhere behind you, our forces will pour into the Appledore region, finally decisively outnumbering the Danes. The vast manpower means you can quickly throw up siege works, and within a day or two, Polonius' catapults go to work."

Edward interrupted. "But Uncle Ambrose, you yourself told me that the Vikings, when hungry or seriously threatened, just take to their ships, sail somewhere else, and start over."

"Exactly, young Prince. Their ships are their ultimate escape plan. Imagine the river beside Appledore. Two hundred and fifty ships. So many they cannot all be beached. Palisades will run down to the water, protecting the flanks, but with so many ships, many will be tied to ships that are beached, and more ships will be tied to them. It is vital to the well-being of the Danes that the ships are well-protected against any land attacks from our forces."

Edward spoke again in excitement. "Are you saying that if you could threaten their fleet, they would immediately flee?"

"Five thousand warriors is a great force, but without ships they are stranded. If besieged, they would soon be starving. Their only hope would be to break through our defensive lines with a massive attack, and then walk many miles through Saxon territory, largely composed of forest and bogs, subject to harassment all the way, cross the Thames, where our ships rule, and then, depending on where they crossed, have to fight ashore and then through Ethelred's Mercians."

Alfred spoke ruefully. "Not an impossible task, brother. Viking armies have broken out on us before, in spite of all our precautions. Wareham comes to mind."

"True, brother, but when they did it last, they were desperate because we had chased away part of Guthrum's relief fleet, and I think it was pretty clear that Ethelwold had a lot to do with their escape from Wareham. Given enough pressure, they have always taken to their ships."

Alfred nodded. "So if we can seriously threaten their fleet, they would likely decide to withdraw."

Ambrose replied. "They wouldn't have to, but the alternative is to risk all in a war of attrition, and the Viking commanders sacrifice their warriors' lives cautiously. Even five thousand warriors can be killed, one by one, though it could cost us ten thousand men to do it.

In the end, they cannot afford such a war of attrition, and we can, distasteful as it might be."

Alfred spoke. "Then what are you proposing, brother-of-mine?"

"We take an old captured Viking *long-ship*, attach one of our smaller oared boats behind, perhaps making it look like a captured prize, fill the *long-ship* with Danish-speakers, archers and flammable material, sail upriver to Appledore, use grappling hooks to attach ourselves to the vast fleet, ignite the materials, jump into the small boat, and row like the devil is after us!"

Edward was excited. "And that would be enough to drive them off?"

"I think so, if we build up to it. We would first openly parade our superior numbers before them. We can have each man tend more than one camp fire at night to give the impression of even more men than we have. They would see the ditches and palisades, and realize that they are hemmed in. Soon the catapults would work their magic. Then the fire ship. With luck, it would destroy at least several Viking long-ships. Yes, I think the fear of losing their only means of escape would entice them to leave."

Alfred stared at his brother. "But you will not land and play the part of a Dane?"

Ambrose smiled. "Not if it causes you anxiety, brother."

Alfred looked around the table. "Then are we agreed?"

Phillip, Polonius, Edward and Ambrose each nodded. "Then we just need confirmation that Haesten has actually left."

Alfred called for Polonius. "Scholar! Where are you, man?"

Polonius entered the command tent. "Here, Sire!"

"Polonius, I heard couriers arrive. Do we finally have that confirmation that *Jarl* Haesten has departed from Milton Royal?"

"Aye, Sire. It came just now. Sigehelm's watchers on the lower Thames report some eighty *long-ships* exiting from behind the Isle of Sheppey, and then sailing north."

"May the Lord be praised! I no longer feel the weight of thousands of Danes behind me whichever way I turn. Now we can start to take decisive action."

"What are your instructions, Sire?"

"Appledore. Phase one of Ambrose's plan. Concentrate every warrior we have there. I expect every *burh* this side of Winchester to strip half of its garrison, and to bring more men with them from amongst the refugees. I want all the available *fyrdmen* we can find, I want huntsmen, foresters and archers, and I want large numbers of laborers to march on Appledore, immediately!"

Polonius spoke. "Our forces will be arriving piecemeal, and they will be very vulnerable, Sire."

Alfred sighed. "You are right, Scholar. That is why our main *fyrd* will arrive first, and will then proceed to build yet another one of your damn fortified camps."

Polonius smiled. "A wise plan, Sire."

"And, Wizard, how are your plans coming along?"

"The wagon train with my chemicals is on its way, Sire, as are a half dozen of my catapults - in pieces. I have several hundred carpenters cutting and trimming lumber to build more, and Ethelred sent his lieutenant to *Lundenwic* to scrounge all the rope he can find."

"Excellent. And Ambrose's ship?"

"It has made it safely as far as Dover, Sire, and it is tied up alongside the *Black Arrow*. The Danish speaking sailors are already there, and they but await their sailing date from you, Sire."

"And they think they can make it past the Danish ships along the south coast?"

Polonius shrugged. "Why not? It worked for Prince Ambrose when he crossed the Thames a *seven-night* ago. They sail on a Danish vessel, wear Danish clothing, speak Danish, and tow a captured Saxon rowing boat . . . an altogether too frequent sight along our coasts. Most of the flammable liquids they will use to set fire to the fleet are in barrels, so at the moment they just look like cargo. We will not use a corvus, as the Danes would probably now recognize it as a Saxon thing, and I went with bolt-throwers rather than catapults, since they have a lower profile and are not easily seen from another ship deck."

"But they will do the job?"

"I have had large clay containers designed that will fasten to the tips of the bolts. They proved quite satisfactory in the trials."

"May God be praised! Polonius, before I order the attack on the fleet, we must discourage the Vikings sufficiently that they will panic when we attempt to fire their fleet. If they do not flee, then we really will have to settle into a siege."

"That should be our last resort, Sire."

"I well remember the wise words of your old friend, *Sun Tzu*, on the frustrations of siege warfare."

Polonius replied. "Though he was not my friend, since he died hundreds of years before I was born, yet *Sun Tzu* was right. Siege warfare really is the lowest form of warfare."

"I have to agree with your statement. In fact, that is why I wanted to see you today."

"What can I do, King?"

"I need our forces to decisively outnumber the Danes."

"That has already been arranged, Sire. It will just take a little time to gather them all."

Alfred stroked his beard. "We will build earthworks that will make it hard for them to escape. Once they are trapped, I want you to rain fire and brimstone upon them."

"Only God may rain fire and brimstone, my King."

"I know, my friend, but I will settle for quantities of your various chemicals, as well as very large rocks. Many large rocks."

"I think, Sire, that what you are trying to tell me is that you would like the catapults to soften them up so that when Ambrose sails the fire ship into their midst, they will break and flee."

Alfred grinned. "You have a remarkable ability to cut through the chaff when you put your mind to it, Wizard."

"In fact, I think my new title indicates that you expect me to present you with a new miracle, Sire."

"Prescient as ever, Polonius. If they do not flee, then I want to kill them, without losing a lot of Saxon lives. Can you find a way to do it?"

"With the catapults I have on the way, along with the oils and chemicals, and the blacksmiths and carpenters working away under the direction of Phillip - I can at least promise you I can make life inside Appledore very unpleasant."

Edward interrupted. "Father, why do we not build a fort near the mouth of the river? We could sink their ships if they try to flee."

Alfred looked fondly at his son, and replied. "The idea has merit, but if the Danes are trapped, we will force them to fight to the last man. They die hard. Much as it would please me to send all their souls to perdition, their complete destruction would likely cost us the flower of our army, and there is a very real risk that we could lose the battle. I must balance the satisfaction I would get against the loss of my best warriors. Polonius' spies have now confirmed that this is not an isolated raid. Danes are being recruited in Ireland, in Northumbria, and in East Anglia. I have therefore decided to intentionally allow their escape if we can make them take to their boats, and thus keep my army intact for whatever comes next . . . but, son-of-mine, you have given me an idea . . . Polonius!"

"Yes, King?"

"Our *fyrd* will march to a pre-chosen site, throw up a Roman marching fort, and wait for the half-garrisons and others to answer our summons."

"Understood, Sire."

"We will then march on Appledore in a vast array, and proceed to besiege the fort."

"Unless the Danes wish to abandon their walls and meet us in the open."

"That is a real possibility, Scholar. That is a concern to me. If they choose to meet us, then we will have to put our trust in God, in the right arms of our best *fyrdmen*, and in our superior numbers."

"I will do what I can to equip the men for battle, Sire. I have ordered the blacksmiths, as soon as they have completed the catapult parts, to make hundreds more *caltrops*, and as many *pilums* as they can."

Alfred nodded. "Then for the moment, we will assume that the Danes will stay behind their walls."

Polonius answered. "Then our task is to convince them of the futility of their cause."

"Agreed, Scholar. Hence the large labor force, the catapults, and the flaming chemicals."

Edward smiled. "And Ambrose's fire ship!"

Alfred smiled in turn. "What if we tried Edward's idea and we started to set up a river fort?"

Polonius frowned. "You said it yourself, Sire. A strong garrison with enough catapults to effectively close the river means that they will fight to the last man, out of sheer desperation."

"Agreed, Scholar, but what if we were seen to start construction on the river fort?"

"Then the Vikings would be forced to choose between meeting us in all-out battle, starving, or fleeing in their ships before the fort is completed," said Polonius.

Alfred smiled. "Exactly. Then let us start on building Edward's river fort, but visibly and slowly."

"I think we need not fear, Sire, that the Danes will know about the fort. They regularly have ships arriving and departing."

Alfred stood up and held his belly. "Then I think we are ready. Polonius, would you be so kind as to draft up orders for the commanders? I want the *fyrd* to move toward Appledore come the dawn. I think that I shall now retire . . . Polonius, a drop or two of your elixir before I go would be much appreciated."

CHAPTER 7

**". . . the main army had come thither, that sat
before in the mouth of the Limne at
Appledore."
......The Anglo-Saxon Chronicles**

With the dawn came the Saxons. By the hundreds, then the
thousands, they marched out of the forest and arrayed themselves in
a shield-wall that stretched all the way around the fort to the river.
Behind the well-armored *fyrdmen* came more, the men who did not
own a horse or armor, but were still prepared to fight for their king.
They were part-time warriors and laborers. Some wore no armor at
all, or only leather with metal plates and bones sewn on at strategic
points. More carried axes and spears than swords, but many also
carried bows and quivers full of arrows. They couldn't, by
themselves, hold against a Viking *skjaldborg*, but, protected by
well-armed *fyrdmen*, they could kill effectively, and at a distance.
Most important, there were thousands of them. Behind them came
hundreds more mounted fyrdmen. While Polonius had only trained
a few hundred in the mounted tactics of the steppe, yet the rest at
least served as a mobile reserve in case the Danes came out to fight.

When the Vikings refused to come out and meet the Saxons in
the open, the center of the shield-wall split. Several thousand
infantrymen and slaves ran forward, each carrying a shovel or
pickaxe, or supporting a section of a rudimentary defensive wall
composed of sharpened logs tied securely to crossbars. As one group
of workers built a rough palisade with their pre-assembled logs, the
other started energetically digging a ditch and piling the removed
earth behind.

Alfred watched with great trepidation. If the Vikings wanted to
fight, today would be the day. Once the ditches were dug and the

walls built with the earth, the Saxons would have a massive advantage. Already, Polonius had half of the men of the mobile squadron dismounted and working on yet another Roman marching fort.

The Danes jeered and laughed, but none exited from Appledore. Their walls gave them a ten to one advantage, and they seemed to have no intention of giving it up. Alfred smiled through his pain. He, too, would have a secure fort before the sun set. After he had his secure base of operations, his ditch would grow slowly but inexorably, until it touched the river at two points and the Danes were effectively cut off from the land.

Ambrose signaled the men at the steering oar to turn into the river. The winds were not cooperating, so the captain ordered the crew to lower the sail and man the oars. The crewmen were Danish-speaking veteran sailors from Alfred's fleet, and the order was carried out with swift efficiency. As the river mouth narrowed, two *long-ships* came down-river. They swerved to run alongside the approaching vessel. The captain of the first, a huge, barrel shaped man laden with a gold *torque* and ornate armbands, pointed at the Saxon boat bobbing behind the *long-ship*. "I see you had good hunting!"

Ambrose smiled and spoke in Danish. "The Saxons clearly wanted us to have it. They hardly put up a fight."

"Where are you from, stranger?"

"We were in Northumbria, and heard that ship crews were being recruited hereabouts."

"Well, you heard right, stranger. Head on up the river for an hour or two, and you will come to our fort. The Saxons call the place 'Appledore'."

"Thank you. I hope you can return as easily as you leave!"

"What do you mean, stranger?"

"Not far back, I saw a Saxon construction crew by the narrows near the river mouth. It looked like they starting to build a fort right beside the river."

"A captain reported that two days past. I don't understand why they bother. Alfred has already encircled the Appledore fort with his *Odin*-cursed ditches and walls."

"My friend, the Saxons have now closed the Thames River to our wooden steeds at Cricklade, Wallingford, Sashes, and Southwark. The river forts there have ballistae large enough to sink any ships that try to force a passage. I have heard of this Polonius, an Eastern Roman scholar who teaches King Alfred the military techniques of the mighty Byzantine Empire. I fear we will see the mouth of this river closed before long."

The big captain looked concerned. "Be sure to report on the progress to the commanders when you land. I will be back in two days, and I will report on how much more they have done then."

"May the gods be with you!"

"And you, stranger!"

Ambrose smiled as they headed up-river. He had been right. There were no Viking patrol boats on the river. What Saxon would be foolish enough to attack some two hundred and fifty shiploads of Danes?

As they turned a broad bend in the river, the fort could be seen, along with an immense fleet tied together and to the shore. Stout palisades protected the ships, although not far away there was a bee hive of activity as the Saxons industriously reinforced their already impressive ditches and walls around the fort of Appledore.

Ambrose turned to his captain. "Byram, please row us upriver past the fleet, so the current will bring the ship back down-river. Have the bolt-throwers uncovered and the bolts prepared. You will have time to launch a dozen flaming bolts, and then I want this ship set aflame and aimed at the center of the fleet."

"Prince, do you think we can really get away with it?"

"Why not? No one has challenged us so far, the Danes are soon going to be very busy fighting multiple fires, and we are towing the fastest courier ship in the Saxon fleet."

As soon as the current moved the ship near the moored Viking fleet, the bolt throwers went to work. The twisted rope gave the large spears tremendous power, and the clay amphora attached to their tips shattered on decks deep in the fleet. The rest of the crew dipped their arrows into fire buckets and proceeded to launch shaft after flaming shaft. The fires produced by the arrows were small, and many went out spontaneously, but some hit flammable material and then new flames climbed skywards.

Finally, as the last crewman leapt to the safety of the courier ship, the vast cargo of flammable materials went up with a whoosh. Along the shore Danes shook their fists at the fleeing vessel, or leapt into the nearest *long-ship* in an attempt to get to and save their personal vessels. The fire-ship became a flaming inferno, and Ambrose watched in awe as the ship, still moved by the current, plowed into the up-river edge of the Viking fleet. He turned to Byram. "We row, my friend. If the Danes get a fully-crewed ship untangled from that mess, they will be on our tail, and I suspect that they will not be in a charitable mood."

"Prince, what do we do if they catch up? We have no chance against a *long-ship*."

"Relax, Captain. If it looks like a ship is likely to catch us, we head for the shore. The land here is Kent, and all the riders you see are friendly *fyrdmen*. I would just hate to lose this ship. It is the fastest courier vessel in the entire Saxon fleet."

Within hours after the fire ship caused extensive damage to the moored ships, Polonius' giant catapults, long delayed by rain, mud and bad roads, finally went to work. In the inky darkness, huge flaming balls of flammable material arced high into the sky and then plummeted into the fort of Appledore. Once the range was determined, the stones followed. Hour after hour, a steady rain of stones outweighing a heavy man and flaming balls fell indiscriminately within the fort. Sometimes tents burst into flames, sometimes a single man, or an entire tent full, were smashed to bloody pulp. Most missed any targets and landed harmlessly, but in the stygian darkness, the terrorizing effect of the rocks were multiplied many fold. Men fled their shelters, only to find there was no place of refuge to huddle in.

The Saxons watched in awe as, ship by ship, the entire Viking fleet slipped into the water, rowed down-river through the Forest of the Weald, and, once they hit the open waters, hauled up their sails to take advantage of the offshore breezes, and coasted eastward.

The little fort at the river mouth that was designed to scare the Vikings into leaving was manned, although far from complete. It even had single catapult for show. Its crew ratcheted the arm down and loaded a ship-killer rock. The boulder arced high, splashing the crew of a passing *long-ship*. Encouraged, the Saxon crew went to work, but more than two hundred ships passed by with none sunk.

CHAPTER 8

A Ship from the North

A messenger rode up to Alfred's command tent. He saw Polonius and spoke breathlessly. "Lord Polonius, there is a Viking ship just off the coast."

"Just one?"

"Yes, Lord."

"And why is it unusual?"

"They rowed close to our watching position and waved a white shield."

"What did they want?"

"They want you, Lord. They said they needed to meet with you."

"Did they fly any identifying banners or flags?"

"Yes, Lord. They flew a long green pennant."

Polonius nodded. "Excellent. I will get a horse and you can escort me back to the ship."

Ambrose, who had been listening quietly, spoke up. "What is it, Scholar?"

"It am hoping that it is news from the north. I pay several *jarls* there to send me important news."

"Then let Phillip and me round up some horses and an escort, and we will join you."

"Gladly, Master."

Prince Edward spoke. "May I come, too, Polonius?"

"Of course, Prince. How many poor scholars get to have two princes as an escort?"

When Polonius unfurled a green banner and waved it enthusiastically, the crew of the *long-ship* launched a rowboat, and a man heavily adorned with a gold *torque* climbed dexterously into the smaller boat.

The small boat paused just out of effective bow range, and the man spoke in Danish.

"Are you Polonius?"

"Yes, I am."

"How do I know that?"

"Alfred is *Bretwalda*."

"Now, those are the very words that I wanted to hear. And is an old Dane welcome ashore?"

"Friends of the Saxons are always welcome. I will protect your life with my own."

"In that case, I will land. I have important news for you."

"Please. I am grateful that you came so far to bring it."

"It was dangerous, but I will let you hear it and decide on the size of the reward."

"Wessex rewards its friends generously, *Jarl*."

The *jarl* leapt ashore and strode to where Polonius stood. "Would you like to see my half-coin, Spy-master?"

Polonius smiled. "I do not think that is necessary, *Jarl*. The fact that you are here at all is enough proof for me . . . Now what is the news that is so urgent?"

"Spy-master, Guthfrith of Northumbria has sent out word to his *jarls*. He wants a fleet of a full hundred ships to form up and then coast south and west as far as Devon. He has appointed Sigefrith the Pirate as commander. There, Sigefrith is to land, seize a secure location and cause as much damage as possible."

"A hundred ships! That is news, indeed."

"And there is more, Spy-master. There are rumors that Eohric of East Anglia will send a further forty, also to land somewhere in the west."

"The news you have brought is very important, and I am grateful that you risked so much to bring me word."

"I knew that you would be aware of the great risk I have taken and reward me accordingly."

"Do you know the landing sites?"

"That is only known in the highest councils, Spy-master. I was not privy to that information."

Polonius spoke. "If you would give me a few minutes, I will have a generous measure of gold brought to you."

The big man grinned, showing that he was missing several of his teeth. "It is always a pleasure to serve Wessex. If you don't mind, however, I will wait offshore on my wooden steed. You Saxons with your nooses make my Danes very nervous."

Polonius smiled. "Then we will leave the gold on this very rock and then withdraw."

"That would alleviate much anxiety on the part of my men."

⚑

As they rode back, Prince Edward spoke to Polonius. "Is it really possible that Northumbria and East Anglia would send a hundred and forty ships between them?"

"Why does it surprise you, Prince?"

Edward looked indignant. "We have a solemn oath from Guthfrith and we hold hostages from Eohric's own family. Eohric risks the hostages' lives, and both risk a war with Wessex."

"There is no risk, Prince. Your father will hang the hostages, just as soon as he sees evidence that East Anglia is involved."

"Then Eohric is killing his own people."

"Prince, a Viking will promise anything to a foreigner, but never mean it."

"You mean the barbarians have no honor!"

"They have a very strong sense of honor, but only amongst themselves. A promise to us is meaningless, unless they deem us worthy of respect in their eyes. That is why Prince Ambrose attempted to extract a personal oath from Eohric. An oath to another Dane does have meaning."

"You once told me Captain Hammar of the *Rus* risked his ship and his life in order to allow you to escape the clutches of the co-emperor of Byzantium."

"The man was High Chamberlain at the time, but the story is

true. Your uncle and Phillip earned *Rus* respect with the prowess of their swords. Until they had met, and defeated several Vikings and many enemies, however, they were derided as foreigners."

"And you, Scholar?"

"I would like to say that I earned respect with the quality of my mind. We helped Askold and Dir win against great odds, against both the Pechenegs and Byzantines because of strategies I dredged out of the past."

"And was it enough to get you accepted?"

Polonius grinned. "I also used my skill with the throwing knives to defeat all who challenged me. I suspect that it was the latter that was more important than the former . . . let us not forget, however, who Dir and Askold sent as emissaries to Constantinople after they had wrecked havoc around the Byzantine capital the summer before."

Edward smiled. "Surely it was because of your brilliant mind and language skills?"

"I would like to think so, but if the Byzantine Emperor had decided to torture us as an example to the too daring barbarians to the north, no *Rus* warrior would have died - just a few outlanders."

"Then you are saying that Eohric and Guthfrith do not respect my father."

"Sitric Ivarsson was a true friend to your uncle. He protected all three of us in Dublin from his uncle, a very angry commander of the *Great Army*, who we had made to look like a fool. Sitric even lent us the *long-ships* which we used to rescue your aunt Gretchen. King Guthrum respected your father, and so he allowed the priests north and refused to lead his East Anglian Danes against your father until after we took London."

"He sent his warriors south across the Thames, when he swore he would not!"

"He did not refuse them permission to join their cousins south of the river, but he did not personally bring any warriors against us until we invaded his territory north of the river and took the Saxon settlement of *Lundenwic* and the old city of London."

"I don't understand how Eohric could so callously throw away the lives of the hostages! As you say, he knows what father will do."

Polonius hesitated. "Don't forget that at the time we had Ethelred's entire *fyrd* poised on his border, and Eohric had no adequate force to counter it. Six hostages bought him enough time to call up his warriors, Prince. I guess they also think the conquest of Wessex is worth the lives of a few of their own leaders. Perhaps he sent a cousin who he would be glad to be rid of. Most likely, he intended that they would never reach King Alfred. That, at least, is Prince Ambrose's theory, and I suspect that he is right.

Prince Edward, we have never before faced such a concerted attack, against so many enemy warriors. Even with all our preparation, I fear for Wessex."

"Polonius, we have already driven off two armies!"

"But defeated neither. They have changed their location, but they have not gone home!"

CHAPTER 9

"Then collected together those that dwell in Northumbria and East-Anglia about a hundred ships, and went south about; and with some forty more went north about, and besieged a fort in Devonshire by the north sea; and those who went south about beset Exeter."
......The Anglo-Saxon Chronicles

Alfred held his belly when he heard the news. "Two fleets, totaling a hundred and forty ship crews! I have to tell you, I am beginning to despair!"

The king composed himself. "We have not lost yet. With God's grace, I will take the *fyrd* west, call up more men from the western shires, and defeat these heathens, too. What is the word on Haesten and the other Frankish Danes?"

Polonius replied. "The Danes from Appledore have joined Haesten at Benfleet, Sire."

"May God damn their souls to eternal hell! Then I fear that we are not done with them yet.'

King Alfred sighed. 'Edward, I am going to have to leave you with Ambrose and Polonius. I intend to go west to deal with this new threat. Thank the Merciful Lord that we have at least had advance warning. I will leave you part of the *fyrd*, and you and Ethelred will have to call up more men when we finally find out what Haesten is up to at Benfleet."

Ambrose spoke. "We knew Guthfrith and Eohric were coming, brother."

"I know, big brother. It was just a question of when and with how many. I hope God will forgive what I am about to order.

Polonius!"

"Sire?"

"We must strike back, and ruthlessly. Polonius, loose the Welsh allies. They love to raid. Tell them their *Bretwalda* will support them in need, and Mercia will not only let them pass unimpeded through its territory, but supply them with food as best they can. We will even offer weapons and other incentives."

"The messengers will ride at dawn, Sire."

"Anarawd of Gwynedd has been altogether too friendly with Guthfrith. Perhaps Ethelred could launch a punitive raid in support of our Welsh allies.

Next, we should offer the Picts and Scots gold to cross their frontiers. I want Northumbria to be so busy fighting invaders that they cannot afford to send ships south. We might even consider raiding their coast with our own fleet."

Polonius spoke. "The Picts and Scots will be happy to take both our weapons and our gold, Sire. They need little incentive to attack Northumbria. It is one of their favorite pastimes."

"Will you see to it, my friend?"

"Consider it done, Sire."

"What about the fleet? Do we risk it?"

Polonius shook his head. "If you send it as far as Northumbria, Sire, it is unlikely that we will ever see it again. There are just too many very large Viking fleets sailing along the coast."

Alfred sighed. "Then it will remain tied up unless we can use it along the Thames."

Polonius nodded. "I think that would be wise, Sire."

CHAPTER 10

"But the army rode before them, fought with them at Farnham, routed their forces, and there arrested the booty."
......The Anglo-Saxon Chronicles

Edward turned to his little group of advisors. "Polonius' scouts have brought good news! The Viking army is in Sussex and probably going to move north on the Winchester road."

Ethelred frowned. "And how is more than six thousand pillaging barbarians heading for my shire good news, brother-in-law?"

"I would like to say 'because they are leaving mine', but in the circumstances, I feel that would not be appropriate. It is good news because for once we also have some six thousand men under arms, including your Mercians, because we know the land where we will be fighting intimately, and because they are coming to us."

Ethelred still looked dubious. "That means they will be more footsore than our own *fyrdmen*, but I see few other advantages."

Edward smiled. "It means, brother-in-law, that we can block their only available road and choose the location for battle. It means that our favorite magician here will have time to pull a few tricks out of his hat."

"And I suppose it means that we can crush the heathens before they cross into Mercia!"

Edward grinned. "Aye, it means that, too. So do I have your support? I will need all the *fyrdmen* you can bring to the battleground if we are to surpass them in numbers."

"I am a loyal vassal of Wessex, Prince, and, besides, you would tell your sister on me if I did not co-operate. If I may borrow

Polonius later, and as many scribes as he can locate, then the couriers will ride with the summons come the dawn."

"Good, then it is settled. All that remains is to decide where we will meet the heathen host, and the details of how we shall defeat them."

☞

Edward stared down from the height. "This seems perfect, Polonius. As you requested, we have a spot where our shield-wall in the valley below will be buttressed at both ends - by this knoll on one end, and the lake on the other. We will be astride the only road, so there is no easy way around us."

"Young Prince, that makes it even. They can't outflank us. The question is - how are we going to beat them?"

"I assumed that you will set out *caltrops*, and I know you have had hundreds of throwing *pilums* made up."

"The Danes are by now well-aware that we use *caltrops* and *pilums*, and, in turn, they will reciprocate by using throwing axes to try and destroy or weigh down our shields. The trick is hardly new to them."

Edward looked distinctly nervous. "Scholar, do you have any other suggestions?"

"I would suggest we dig man-traps, Prince. It will not stop the Danes, but it will help break up their *skjaldborg*. I would suggest we fortify the knoll and place a few hundred archers there. If they manage to push our shield-wall back, we have their backs for targets, and if they attack, it will be costly."

"And?"

"And the Surrey scouts tell me that there is a hidden valley two kilometers to the south. I would suggest we place five hundred riders there. Once the Vikings form their *Skjaldborg*, the riders can arrive unexpectedly behind them. Five hundred lances thundering in from the rear should be enough to shake them up."

Edward smiled. "I like it! And?"

"You want more?"

"I want victory, Polonius. My father told me we can afford

nothing less."

"I probably have the time to make a couple of catapults and place them behind our men."

"Polonius, you told me that they are not accurate enough to hit a moving shield-wall."

"They are not accurate enough to hit a shield-wall consistently, especially one that is moving, but we know that they will eventually try their *svinfylka*, their boar's snout formation, to try and break through our shield-wall. If we determine where the boar's snout is likely to form up, then we can pre-aim the catapults. Low shots that bounce will wreck havoc with a deep formations of warriors. For that, however, I will need a team of stone masons."

"Stone masons?"

"Only round rocks roll. It is stone masons, or I make up balls from iron."

Edward shrugged. "Then, if the smiths have enough iron after the *caltrops* and *pilums* are done, let's use iron. Iron balls should solve the problem of consistent aim, since the balls can easily be made to a uniform weight.'

Edward smiled again. 'And?"

"We can put a few bolt-throwers on the knoll, but after that I fear that the rest is up to God."

The young prince looked around at Phillip, Ambrose and Ethelred. "Are we all in agreement?"

After receiving a nod from each, Edward sighed. "Then, God help us, we are finally going to face Haesten's entire Viking army."

CHAPTER 11

A Battle, and the Vikings Flee

The first hint of the Viking army's arrival was the horns. The Saxon war horns brayed, and the rhythmic thunder of thousands of Viking swords on thousands of shields was the response. From his perch on the knoll, Ambrose watched the Viking warriors dismount and form a sinuous column that thickened and coalesced into the *skjaldborg*, the famous Viking shield-wall. The Vikings were clearly prepared to accept the challenge.

The Saxons stood still in their formation, waiting for the next response from the Danes. It came soon enough. The Viking horns blared and the entire *skjaldborg* began to advance at a slow walk. Ambrose was impressed with the professionalism of the Viking warriors, but he was not surprised. He had fought beside the *Rus* Vikings somewhere in that great land mass that was north of Constantinople and even the Black Sea. He knew that every warrior who had followed Haesten from *Francia* was a veteran. They had fought against the Franks for years there, and a slow warrior in battle was a dead warrior.

The Vikings did not even pause to parley. Secure in their numbers, they were eager to destroy the last standing army between them and the Thames, and most of the *fyrdmen* they had faced so far had ran and hid behind *burh* walls. The first rank moved forward. Each warrior held two throwing axes.

As soon as the Saxons were in range, the weapons would hurtle toward them. If the axes did not kill or maim, they might split shields or at least weigh them down. A gap in a shield-wall on either side could be fatal. Only a continuous and unyielding wall of locked shields could hold back the thousands who pressed forward.

As the first rank neared, there were sudden screams, and dozens of warriors disappeared into the cunningly hidden pits that Polonius had ordered dug. Sharpened stakes awaited the unfortunate, and few warriors managed to climb out again.

The Vikings were both brave and expert at war, however, and the rest just closed the gaps while warriors of the second rank moved up. Next were the *caltrops*. Dozens of Vikings screamed as the sharp metal spikes penetrated their feet. Once the warriors were aware of the dangerous objects hiding in the tall grass, they advanced at a much slower pace, using a sidling movement. The front rank continued to advance, although the *skjaldborg* was leaking casualties.

Phillip waved the yellow flag, and suddenly the air filled with hundreds of arrows with sharp bodkin points, each capable of penetrating thick metal armor at close quarters. The Vikings raised their shields higher and continued to stoically advance, and Phillip waved the blue flag. The *pilums*, modeled on the ones used by Roman legionaries centuries before, began their arcing journeys. The shields of the first rank of Vikings soon looked like a hound's nose that had run up against a porcupine.

Their shields rendered all but useless by the hail of missiles, the Vikings hesitated. With a single blare of a signal horn, however, the first two ranks smoothly switched position. Within a five count, the *skjaldborg* was advancing again, this time with fresh men and unencumbered shields in the front rank.

The two lines met, and the brutal battle began. Swords and spears snaked out under or over the shields. Big men locked their shields with neighbors and shoved. Hundreds of men, stretched across the road and meadow from the lake to the knoll, shoved, sweated, and stabbed. Hundreds more waited their turn in the shield-wall. A wall of dead bodies built up, and the ground was stained red.

Edward watched nervously from his position atop the knoll. He turned to his uncle. "I thought that battle against the heathen would be beautiful to behold. This is more like a charnel house. I think I am going to be sick!"

"Edward, those men are dying for Wessex, and for you. I know your belly is turning to jelly and you are feeling terror. Phillip told me many years ago, when I was younger than you, that to feel fear in battle is normal. It is what you do in spite of your fear that counts."

"But you, a veteran of a hundred battles can stand and watch so casually. I feel like screaming and running."

"As do I, Edward."

"You?"

"Me. Repetition does not make it any easier. I feel as sick as I did in my first battle."

"But, Ambrose, you appear to be calm and in complete control."

"Those warriors are dying because we give the order. It is the least I can do for the brave *fyrdmen*, and make no mistake, the *fyrdmen* watch us closely and take their cues from us. If we appear nervous or frightened, it will infect the whole army within minutes."

As he spoke, Ambrose saw a *hersir* wave part of the Viking mobile reserve off their horses and urge them toward the hill where he stood. "Speaking of what we can do for our men, it is time we consider preparing for defense! Look toward the mounted men, Edward."

"They are dismounting and forming up, Uncle!"

"They are coming our way, Edward. We have only seconds to prepare!"

"Uncle, why would they attack up such a steep hill? It is suicidal."

"The Vikings are not stupid. If they take the hill and kill us, then the army is leaderless and our *fyrdmen* will likely break and run. Why kill the *fyrdmen* one by one when they can just cut off the head?"

"So what do we do?"

"Do? We fight! You might want to direct the archers to the new threat, and alert the young men of your Personal Guard. We are going to need their swords, and soon!"

Edward did not look at all well, but his voice, when he spoke, was strong and steady. "Archers! Empty your quivers at the Danes who are trying to climb the hill! Men of my Personal Guard, into line with *pilums*!

Phillip! Put the spear throwers into action!"

As the Vikings reached the base of the hill and struggled through the thickets of sharpened stakes and *caltrops*, the arrows started to fall, followed by a rain of *pilums* that could penetrate the strongest armor. The Vikings just accepted the casualties, however, and climbed over their own dead and wounded.

Phillip had the spear throwers uncovered, and soon the massive iron bolts were hurtling down the hill. The power of the twisted ropes was so great that the bolts went right through their primary targets and impaled a second or even third Viking.

The Vikings kept coming, however, and Edward turned to Ambrose. "We are not killing them fast enough to stop them! What do we do now?"

Ambrose drew **Victory-Maker**, the mysterious sword his Danish master had taken from the sands of North Africa and given to him when he was but a young slave and unable to wield a heavy Viking blade. "We fight, Edward. If we fall, the entire army dies."

Edward watched as Polonius and Phillip closed on his uncle. Legendary fighters, the three had fought as a unit for many, many years. Ambrose smiled at his nephew. "Come, Edward, you are about to experience your first concerted attack. I doubt it is an experience you will much enjoy. Come, we shall protect you . . . and bring your Personal Guard."

The four leaders joined the line of warriors and archers manning the crest of the hill. Edward's sworn men, young *drengs*, warriors who had yet to prove themselves in battle but had attached themselves to the young *atheling*, followed him to the defensive line.

Almost simultaneously, the struggling Viking warriors finally crested the hill and attacked lustily. With swords and battle axes, they attempted to kill the hilltop defenders. Ambrose's sword flicked out again and again, leaving dead and dying men in its wake. Phillip's huge blade carved an arc of death and, when it appeared that a Viking would slip past the guard of either man, a dagger flashed from Polonius' hand. Edward drew his own blade and attacked a burly Viking who was trying to slip behind Polonius. He felt the blade penetrate the man's unprotected neck, and he shuddered. He froze as the enemy turned to look at him, and then slid to the ground. Almost before the enemy was prone, however, a tall, thin Viking with a massive axe closed on the young prince. As he had been taught, the prince raised his shield and prepared a counter stroke. The axe blow, when it came, almost drove him to the ground, but while the warrior's axe was still stuck in his shield, the young prince swung his sword in a low horizontal cut. The Viking screamed when Edward's blade bit deep into his leg. Edward withdrew his blade and then struck at the hand that was holding the axe. Axe and hand fell to the ground, and Edward struck for the man's neck. As the warrior, now fatally wounded, collapsed on the ground, Edward attacked an obese Viking who had managed to get behind Ambrose.

Time passed in a blur of action and blood. At last the Danes ran out of fresh bodies to throw at the hill, and the wave of enemy warriors receded from the top, leaving behind dozens of dead or wounded. The Saxon survivors on the crest struggled to catch their breath and treat any personal wounds. Then they began the sad task of removing their own dead and helping the seriously wounded. Any enemy warriors they found who were still alive had their throats slit.

Ambrose and Edward resumed their position overlooking the battlefield. While they had faced a determined attack, the rest of the army was still fighting for its life, All along the lines, brave men fell, and others, waiting their turn, filled the gaps with their bodies. The sounds of steel against steel was deafening, although sometimes blocked by the sheer volume of screams of pain and anger that emanated from the mouths of thousands of struggling warriors.

Edward watched the struggle. There were hundreds dead, but neither side had managed to make any major gains from their original positions. He turned to the bastard prince and uncle who stood by his side.

"Ambrose, for all the dying, it appears that there is a stalemate. What will happen now?"

"Both sides will attempt to punch through the other's shield-wall. If one side succeeds, then they pump the men of the next few ranks through the gap. Generally, the second and third rank can deal with a break-through, but if not, then the battle is close to being won . . . or lost."

"And if neither side can break through?"

"The Vikings have two tricks. Sometimes they pull back, and send their berserkers out."

"Berserkers? You mean the crazy men?"

"The men dedicate their lives to their gods, strip off their clothes, and attack our ranks naked."

"Then they should be easy to stop."

"You would think so, but our men are superstitious, and they back away from the mad men. I have seen an entire shield-wall break in superstitious fear. I have also seen a berserker with a spear and a dozen arrows in him, continue to advance and fight. They show super-human strength and bravery. They eventually bleed out and die, but if our men have broken, then it is too late."

"You said they had two tricks."

"Yes, the other, the boar's snout, is the battle formation we planned for."

"How does that defeat us?"

"It has in the past. A thick wedge of veterans just charge right through our lines. They literally use their weight to push our men out of the way, and once they have penetrated the last rank, they split our force into two. The Byzantine soldiers I saw in the east would just form into two separate formations, but our men are less well-trained. Once the force is split into two, then generally the men break and run."

"But to run would mean being butchered."

"You and I know that . . . And probably the *fyrdmen* know it too. There are enemy warriors both behind and ahead of you, panic sets in, and you break. Even the Vikings, brave as they are, can be made to break and run."

"How would we stop the boar's snout?"

"You told Polonius to go ahead and make iron balls. That is our little surprise for the Danes - as long as they form their boar's snout in the right place. You saw the catapults shoot ranging shots with the iron balls."

Edward interrupted. "Look, Ambrose! The Viking fourth rank is forming into column!"

"First a column, then a wedge. Now, Edward, we know which

trick they intend to play on us . . . Polonius!"

"I see it, Master. The boar's snout is forming even as we watch."

Edward spoke nervously. "Scholar, are they forming in the right spot for our catapults?"

Polonius looked a little smug. "Exactly where I predicted."

"And the men are ready?"

"As soon as I wave the black flag."

Edward spoke. "In the name of God, Polonius, what are we waiting for?"

"Prince Edward, we are going to get one chance at this. If we tip them off too early, they will merely form up elsewhere, and we will not have the range."

"I am sorry, Polonius. I am just very nervous."

"As am I, Prince, but my discipline must outweigh my panic."

"You, too, Polonius? But you are considered to be one of the greatest military strategists living."

"I have not been able to eat for two days, and I clean out my bowels hourly. Prince, any man who has seen a battle and is not nervous, is an utter and complete fool . . . Phillip . . . the black flag - now!

Almost instantly, round iron balls arced over the various Saxon ranks, to fall right in the boar's snout formation. Just missing the heads of the Saxons, the heavy metal balls tore into the packed ranks of the Viking formation. Each ball crushed a dozen or more Danes. Phillip waved the black flag a second time, and the Saxons on the knoll manned the bolt throwers again. The great metal darts also tore into the same formation, and several Vikings were transfixed by them.

The mass confusion of the men of the boar's snout breaking and running in all directions disturbed the other ranks. At Phillip's signal, all of the Saxon signal horns brayed a continuous note.

Edward crossed himself, and even Ambrose showed nervousness. The prince knew that the next five minutes might decide the fate of all Wessex.

While the Danes were confused and reeling, they had not yet suffered grievous losses, and, consummate professionals that they were, they could yet recover and win the day. Most of Polonius' tricks had been used up, and they only had one maneuver left up their sleeves.

The continuous blaring was matched from the woods behind the Danes, and Ambrose heaved a sigh of relief. Five hundred riders, all equipped with Polonius' beloved lances, broke from the brush and whipped their horses into a charge. The thundering hooves alerted the Vikings, and they turned just in time to see tons of horse flesh and hundreds of lances leveled right at them.

Ambrose knew that a well-prepared Viking shield-wall was capable of containing even a charge of massed and determined horsemen. He had seen it with his own eyes on the Asian steppes. In fact, he knew that it was the reason that the *Rus* Vikings, unwelcome traders in a strange land, had been invited to settle at Novgorod, their first foothold along the great river system that stretched all the way from the frozen north to Constantinople. The Slav infantry could never hold against the nomad cavalry, and they were in awe of men who could stop a cavalry charge cold. With Polonius' help, the *Rus* had held against even massed Pecheneg cavalry.

Polonius broke out of his brief reverie. The Viking warriors here were still reeling from the arching metal balls falling amongst them, and they were trapped between hundreds of sharp lances and a Saxon shield-wall that showed no sign of breaking. Instead, the Danes broke. Throwing away anything that would impede their progress, they ran for the forest and for their lives. Ambrose did note that, expert warriors that they were, none threw away their personal weapons.

Edward watched from his position on the knoll. "Sweet merciful God! They broke! We have won! Polonius, what do we do next?"

"If they manage to form up again, Prince, then the victory will not be so great. You may rest assured that they will try. What we do next is very important."

"Then in the love of God, please help a poor ignorant prince know what to do!"

One. Send my lancers after the Danes. We must harry them without mercy. The lancers will never be the equal of the Khazar and Pecheneg horsemen I saw on the Russian steppes, but they are quite capable of stabbing running Danes in the back. We want to inflict the largest possible casualties we can before the Vikings recover. Panic is infectious, and we want to encourage it for as long as we can. A panicked army cannot fight."

"Ambrose, would you please give the orders?"

Ambrose smiled. "Happily, nephew."

"Two. Send Ethelred, with a strong force of his best and most trustworthy men, to take the wagon train. We could use the supplies the Danes have stolen, and there will be a great deal of loot that can be added to your father's treasury - as long as you get to it before it is looted by your own army."

"Agreed. Ethelred?"

"I ride, Edward."

"Three. You have a lot of dead and dying men down there. It is vital that you get the wounded to our healers as quickly as possible. I would also suggest we visit the injured as soon as we have an area set up for care."

"Polonius, I am not sure I can bear seeing what I have done to some of those men."

"Prince, you must. They fought for you, and they will cherish a visit from their commander and future king. You owe them nothing less."

Edward sighed. "You are right. I will do it! Polonius, would you please see to the care of our wounded men?"

"I shall arrange it immediately, Prince."

CHAPTER 12

"And they (defeated Vikings) flew over Thames without any ford, then up by the Colne on an island."
......The Anglo-Saxon Chronicles

The riders spurred after the running Vikings. Even the bravest Dane had little chance by himself against armored horsemen, and Polonius' lancers, poor as they were, yet drove their lances into hundreds of Viking backs. The Danes instinctively headed for the densest forest they could find. There, in twos and threes, they gathered, and then fled northward. Thousands of Vikings made it to the Thames riverbank. The Saxon riders patrolled the banks as best they could and Edward sent mounted *fyrdmen* to the fords along the river, but under cover of darkness the pagan northerners swam, or slipped across on logs or in stolen boats.

Edward's main force moved slowly northward. They flushed out as many fugitives as they could, but the Vikings, now without their loot or captives to worry about, moved surprisingly fast.

Edward ordered that a marching fort be set up on the north bank of the Thames, and then waited for his scouts to make contact with the enemy. On the second day, as the tired men rested, a scout galloped into the fortification and threw himself off his lathered mount in front of his prince.

"*Atheling*! One group of our scouts finally caught up with the Vikings. It is like you said. They had a secret rendezvous point, and several thousand have congregated some twenty miles north of here!

"Where are they located?"

"We were able to follow their trail from the north side of the Thames. They followed the Colne River upriver as far as Thorney Island, and there they stopped."

"Then they are on the island?"

"Yes, *Atheling*."

"You say there are several thousand on the island?"

"We killed hundreds of stragglers, *Atheling*, but there are still thousands who made it safely to the island. They are fortifying it and seem determined to make a stand there."

"Go get something to eat, and then report back to me here. I may have more questions for you later."

Edward called his inner circle of advisors together. He looked around the table at Polonius, Phillip, Ambrose and Ethelred, in whose land they were now in.

"My friends, the scout who just rode in has reported that Haesten and his cutthroats have finally gone to ground."

Ambrose smiled. "Excellent. Then let's go finish him off before he gets reinforcements."

Edward looked puzzled. "Reinforcements? He is trapped here in Mercia."

Polonius spoke up. "Prince, Northumbria and East Anglia have raised a lot more than a hundred and forty ship crews, some of our old friends in Ireland are taking back the land conquered by the Danes and the *Norse*, the Scots and Picts are making it hot in the far north, and the Franks are fortifying many of their rivers. There are a lot of landless Danes and Norsemen who are looking for another opportunity to steal loot and perhaps even take land. I do not think for one second that killing Haesten will end this conflict. The coordinated attacks we have seen so far indicate a vast Viking alliance."

"Then you think new armies will march to relieve Haesten?"

"I do not know, Prince, but I think that eventually we will see many more warriors from the Viking kingdoms arrive."

"What are you telling me, Polonius?"

"That we should move north as soon as our baggage train catches up. The sooner we crush Haesten, the less likely it is that he will get support."

"Polonius, I do not know what I would do without you. You are right, of course. Let's send the mounted *fyrdmen* northward now. If we can bottle up the Danes on the island, then they will not be able to forage. We took their supply train, so they are probably already hungry."

Ethelred spoke. "When the sun rises, my couriers will go forth. Any food supplies in Mercia that cannot be safely carried to a defensive position will be destroyed. Let's starve the heathens into submission. And speaking of supplies, I will ride to London in the morning. There I will arrange for part of the garrison to join you and I will send some food supplies by boat along the Thames and up the Colne River."

⚑

Edward and his advisors gathered on the little point of land. Just visible, upriver, was Thorney Island. Ambrose could see, in the distance, hundreds of warriors, like industrious ants, busy building a palisade and throwing up shelters. He knew then for certain that they had at last caught up with the fast-moving Viking raiders. For some reason, the Vikings had decided to stop running and make a stand.

Ambrose spoke. "Polonius, can you rain Alfred's 'fire and brimstone' down on them?"

"I will have to ride all the way around the island to answer your question properly, but from what I can see from here, I would have to say I can drop stones on the edge of the island, but if you are asking can I hit anywhere on the island, then the answer is no."

"And can we make a full-out attack?"

"Even if we scrounged every boat for a hundred miles around, we would take terrible losses as we approached the shore of that island."

Edward turned to the two men. "Then what does my uncle and my chief advisor recommend?"

"All we can do is besiege them and let them starve."

Edward nodded. "Then so be it."

Ethelred had just returned from London with fresh *fyrdmen* and much needed supplies. He stared for a few moments and then spoke. "Come the dawn I will send for thousands of Mercian *churls* and slave laborers. We will ring the island with palisades, Prince."

Edward looked at the island again. "It is a massive undertaking, *Ealdorman*."

"Prince Edward, my people built Offa's Dyke, a hundred and sixty-nine Roman miles long, to keep the Welsh out of our lands. Now **that** was a massive undertaking."

Within days, the conscripted workmen began to show up, and, under the protection of the massed *fyrdmen*, earth walls surmounted with wooden palisades grew on all the shores around the island.

CHAPTER 13

"Then the king's forces beset them without as long as they had food; but they had their time set, and their meat noted."
......The Anglo-Saxon Chronicles

The *hersir* held the white shield high. He walked boldly out to the end of the dock and called across in Danish to the watching Saxons.

"My master, Haesten, High Commander of this army and blessed of *Odin*, wishes to talk with your commander."

Polonius turned to Edward. "His master, Haesten, wishes to parley with you. Are you interested?"

Edward nodded. "It can't hurt to hear what the man has to say. Tell him I will speak to Haesten."

Polonius called out. "*Atheling* Edward, son of the great King Alfred, deigns to speak with the pirate Haesten of the Danes."

Haesten himself walked out to the end of the wharf, though Ambrose noted that two warriors helped him stay on his feet. He was not dressed in armor, and his middle was wrapped around in linen.

The Viking *jarl* called out. "May I approach in a rowboat? Yelling is not seemly for a future king of *Angleland*."

"The future king of Wessex gives you permission to approach."

"I actually meant me, not your young pup."

"We have accepted your flag-of-truce. Do not waste the *atheling's* time any further."

"I see that Alfred's young pup now commands. It is an important promotion, young pup. In my land, such an honor must be earned."

Polonius replied in his perfect Danish. "The young pup also commanded at Farnham, *Jarl*. Perhaps you already forget who ran like frightened women. If you have something intelligent to say, then speak. My prince is a busy man and you are continuing to waste his time."

"Peace, Byzantine. I am here to save Saxon lives. That should be worth something to you."

"Each man on the island with you is entitled to six feet of good Saxon ground and a rope. That is the king's promise to all Vikings who invade our territory."

Haesten smiled. "I am sometimes a slow learner, but eventually even I see the error of my ways. My men and I would like to leave this desolate land and return to Benfleet."

"I am sure you would. You are out of range of most of our catapults, but you are starving and have no hope of launching a successful attack against my prince's *fyrdmen*. The water that keeps us from attacking you also keeps you captive. I am sure that you are about to tell me your fleet is even now on is way to your rescue. In answer, I have but one word in reply. Southwark. That one fort, by itself, is capable of blocking your entire fleet from coming to your rescue. I think that perhaps you have bitten off more than you can chew, and now expect the soft Christians to forgive all and get out of your way so you can just go home. There are burned churches, thousands of dead Saxons, and an endless string of raped women and girls in your wake, *Jarl*. Even the most devote Christian would have trouble forgiving what you have done."

Haesten spoke. "A Christian monk once told me that a true Christian must both love and forgive his enemies. It is your duty."

Polonius responded. "In the same holy book, it also says 'an eye for an eye'. We will do our best to forgive you when you and all your men are all safely dead."

Ambrose could see the *jarl* trying to control himself. At last he calmed down.

The *jarl* spoke. "My council has sent me here to make a proposal."

"My prince is listening, *Jarl*."

"If you withdraw your forces, we will swear to withdraw to Essex and leave Wessex alone forever. This is our offer. You cannot hurt us with your toys, Byzantine. We are five thousand brave men on the island, and you will never defeat us."

"*Jarl*, again you seem to have forgotten that we already defeated you in open battle. Thousands of Viking corpses litter the roads and fields all the way from Farnham to your cozy little island. Five thousand men, if you have somehow discovered thousands of replacement warriors on your way here, eat a lot of food, and you have none. You are welcome to starve and die on the island, if that is your wish."

"Those are my terms, Byzantine. Tell your royal pup what I have said. I will expect your answer tomorrow."

☙

Edward looked around the table in his campaign tent. "Well, my friends, what do we tell Haesten tomorrow?"

Phillip spoke up. "Prince, I say we let them starve on the island and kill any who try to escape. We have a ring of steel around him that Haesten cannot break."

Polonius looked up and spoke. "Prince Edward, I have two major concerns."

"And what is that, my faithful advisor?"

"Your *fyrdmen* have already served their six months, and our own food supplies are very low. If we take more from the locals, then they will not survive the winter. The men are eager to return home and see if their families are all right, and to gather in as much of their crops as they can. It is their right to do so."

Edward looked alarmed. "Can we not ask them to stay on until the winter *fyrd* is here and we are at full strength?"

Ambrose looked to the ealdorman of Mercia. "Ethelred, what do you think?"

"I think I could persuade my Mercians to stay for a few days, but after that, they will just start slipping away in the night, and, truth be told, I would have a hard time hanging a brave warrior who has served his time faithfully and already stayed beyond his required term. I think we all expected to have King Alfred join us before now, with the winter *fyrd* at his back."

Ambrose spoke again. "He has promised to come, as soon as he has successfully dealt with Sigefrith and the two Viking armies in Devon. Unfortunately, that is taking longer than he expected. How long will it take us to raise five thousand warriors of the winter *fyrd*?"

Ethelred spoke. "Truthfully? Several weeks."

The bastard prince looked at Ethelred. "Then you are telling me that soon we will be heavily outnumbered by the Vikings on the island."

Ethelred flushed. "My London garrison troops were newly called up, and will stay for their half year. Thousands of other *fyrdmen* have responded to the call and are on their way, Prince. They come from some six shires, however, and some must march for a week or two just to get here."

Ambrose pursed his lips before speaking. "Then our choice is between watching the Danes break free and ravage their way through the breadth of Mercia, or coming to an agreement and attempting to direct them into Danish held Mercia."

Edward spoke. "Or we quietly let the summer *fyrdmen* slip away and replace them with the winter *fyrdmen* as they arrive. With luck, the Danes might never suspect that our numbers are down."

Ambrose shook his head. "Edward, make no mistake. The Vikings are starving, and they will attempt to break free before they are too weak to fight effectively. It is in the nature and the religion of the Vikings that they would rather die on our swords than die of starvation. Only in that way can they be chosen by the *Valkyries* to go to *Asgard*. If we are too few to hold them, well, that is just a bonus to them."

"Uncle, are you sure they will attempt an attack on us?"

"You can count on it, Edward. They will come, and sooner rather than later."

"Then what terms can we offer them?"

"One. They will march directly to Danish-held Mercia.

Two. They will not loot or enslave on the way. In return, we will have to promise to provide some food.

Three. Haesten swears by his gods that he will not return to Wessex.

Four. They give us a dozen leaders to act as hostages."

Five. They turn over all prisoners and loot before we even let them come ashore."

Edward looked worried. "Do you think it will really work, Uncle?"

Ambrose replied. "They will leave as promised. The question is - will they come back again? If and when they do, we will at least have a fresh army to meet them with."

Edward sighed and looked all around the table at the rest. "Is everyone agreed? Then let's try it."

Ambrose turned to Phillip. "Old friend, can we have additional camp fires this night?"

Phillip smiled. "I think I hear the new *fyrdmen* arriving even as we speak. I will make sure hundreds of new *fyrdmen* are heard this evening, Prince, though I am not sure that the conjuring will last long past dawn."

⚑

Haesten had his boat rowed toward the shore early the next morning. The white shield was held prominently. The *jarl* called out as he neared the river bank.

"Where is the young pup today? Haesten would speak with him, and he, too, is a busy man."

Polonius stepped to the river bank. "If only you could fight as well as you yell, then you would not be in this predicament. What is it you want, *Jarl?*"

"I laid out terms yesterday, and I want to know if you are going to accept, or if we have to come over there and teach you to respect my brave Vikings."

"Edward, Prince of Wessex, Sussex, Kent and Cornwall, has prepared an answer, but I regret I cannot pass it on to you as long as you continue to forget who lost the last battle, and who is starving. When you remember your manners, then pray return so we can talk a little more constructively."

Polonius then turned away. Before he got ten feet, however, Haesten called out.

"Byzantine . . . perhaps I was a little hasty. I am prepared to hear what the young pup has to say."

"Very well, *Jarl*. Prince Edward proposes the following. We will retreat two Roman miles down river, and you and your men will walk, or crawl due east, until you hit Danish Mercia."

Haesten interrupted. "We will also ride, Byzantine. You may be surprised to know that we have not eaten the entire horse herd yet."

"I will get to that. On that journey you will neither rape, forage, loot nor enslave. You will also free all Saxon captives you currently hold and return all the stolen loot you have . . . before you so much as set foot on dry land."

"Stop right there, Byzantine. If we do not forage, we will starve. I will admit that we are a little hungry, and we need provisions."

"And Prince Edward will arrange for you to receive adequate cattle and pigs for slaughter. We will use a little of the treasure you have already gifted us with to buy them. We will choose an even dozen hostages from amongst your officers. If you break any details of our agreement, they will hang in the trees - just like your last hostages."

"Your king is a hard man, Byzantine. He hung some good men!"

"Put the blame where it is due, Viking! You were the one who hung them - by breaking your word. In all my years of fighting for the *Rus* Vikings, I never met a man with so little honor - who would betray his companions as you did."

"Byzantine, I have killed many men for less! You have impugned my honor."

"Then challenge me, man-with-no-honor. Pick the island and declare *holmgang*. I will meet you anytime - anywhere. You are twice my size and I will fight only with the knives I wear. You may bring whatever weapons you want."

"I have heard the ballads about you, Wizard. It is said that your knives have powerful magic and you never miss."

"If you do not like my words, then name the time and place, Haesten. That way you could redeem your honor by dying bravely . . . You are not interested in defending your honor? Then to continue. You will swear by *Odin* and *Thor* both that you will not return to Wessex for as long as you live, and you will turn over your golden armbands to Edward since, having broken your last oath sworn on them, you are no longer worthy of wearing them. Oh, and not least, you will turn over whatever horses you have left. Prince Edward believes that you having to walk the breadth of the land might teach you a little humility."

"Beware, Byzantine. You go too far!"

"If you are not happy with the conditions, Haesten, then go back to your stinking little island and starve. Personally, I would prefer you choose that option. My prince wants your answer by tomorrow at dawn, *Jarl*."

"Your pup may have my answer now, Byzantine, as may you. If I was not so badly injured, I would be pleased to teach you a lesson in manners, one that would include removing your impertinent tongue. Sadly, having just got out of my sickbed, I cannot do that at this time. As for your pup, you may tell him that I will agree, on the condition we keep the horses."

"Then we have no agreement, Viking. You walk, or you die on the island."

"You leave me little honor, Byzantine."

"My preference is to leave you with no life, Viking. As for your honor, I fear that you lost it long ago, but my knives patiently await your challenge if you wish to disagree with me."

"You will get the horses, Byzantine."

"And the captives, and whatever little treasure you have left, *Jarl*. War is an expensive business, and you have done much damage."

Ambrose watched the Viking commander speak through clenched teeth.

"Tell your pup that you will have it all."

⌐

Edward stared at Polonius. "Scholar, would you have really met Haesten in a *holmgang*? He is one of the most feared fighters in the entire Viking army."

"Prince, to even say it sent the butterflies rushing around my stomach, but, to answer your question, I would never make such a challenge without meaning it. Above all else, the Vikings respect strength and bravery. Thus, by insulting him without him challenging me in return, I diminished the respect in which his own warriors hold him, and showed that we are not soft. Christian mercy and compassion, to a Viking, are just weaknesses to be exploited. It is my hope that, in response to Haesten's belittling, some of his strongest men will decide to challenge him for leadership."

"But what if he called you out, Scholar?"

"The truth? If God is merciful to me on that day, I would have won. I have never lost a duel with the knives yet."

"I admit, Scholar, I have often heard stories about you and your magic knives, but, until our battle against the Danes at Farnham, I had never seen you in action. Now that I think back, I was having trouble with a big warrior and even bigger axe, when suddenly a dagger sprouted in one of his eyes. I never did thank you for that. You may well have saved my life."

"You have much to do before God calls you to his side, Prince. It is going to fall to you to complete your father's work. Wessex must reclaim the land where the heathens rule. For the task ahead, you must remain well and healthy. If I could help you stay that way, then I have done my duty."

"It is my hope, Polonius, that my father is able to complete the task in his lifetime."

"Mine too, Prince. It is my fondest wish that your father has many more years to complete his great task. Yet you and I both know that he is not a well man, and God is going to call him to his side sooner rather than later. That is why he was so desperate for you to earn a reputation. Some days I think I should just challenge your cousin Ethelwold to a duel so I can rid the world of such evil."

CHAPTER 14

Edward Finds out Haesten Is Raiding in Mercia Again

Ambrose was walking along the battlements of the London fort with his wife, Gretchen, when she stopped and pointed northward.

"What is that, husband?"

"What do you see, my love?"

"Look, just on the horizon. Is that not a signal fire?"

Ambrose stared into the darkness before he spoke. "I see it now! May God damn them all to hell! It can only mean that the Danes are loose again! I will put the garrison on alert and send out some scouts. My love, you are going to have to excuse me again."

"Do what you have to do, my Saxon lover. This kingdom depends on you."

༄

The courier entered the fort via the open Cripplegate at a gallop. "Make way! Message for my *ealdorman!*"

In short order, the exhausted rider was brought into Ethelred's presence. Ambrose, Edward, Phillip and Polonius all rushed to join the *ealdorman* of Mercia and governor of London.

The courier could barely speak. "My lords . . . The Danes have marched north . . . from Benfleet and are pillaging . . . in Northern Mercia. The *thanes* have asked for all the help you can give . . . They are up against an army of thousands!"

Ambrose turned to Ethelred. "Can you send word for the *burhs* to lock up? It is vital that the villagers move their livestock to secure areas."

Ethelred looked unhappy. "Prince Ambrose, my wife has been

harassing me to emulate her father and establish *burhs* every twenty miles, but we have just started the process, and it is going to be years before Mercia is as well organized as Wessex. Still, it is our best hope, and the orders will go out by tomorrow."

Ambrose turned to Polonius. "What do you think, Scholar?"

Polonius looked up from reading the actual message the courier had brought. "It sounds like Haesten has almost stripped Benfleet of warriors. The army is huge, and well mounted. Worse, they are operating near the border with Danish Mercia, so if we match their numbers and press them too hard, then they will just cross the border. Then we will have a dilemma."

Edward spoke up. "What is the dilemma, Scholar?"

Polonius answered. "If we cross into Eohric's territory, we are expanding the war. Can we afford to do that at this time?"

Edward thought for a bit. "Eohric has already sent warriors into Devon. Hasn't he already expanded the war?"

Ambrose responded. "We know both Northumbrian and East Anglian Vikings have been sent south, and Eohric has called up enough warriors to protect his borders, but Polonius' spies have not yet reported a mass call-up. If Eohric makes a general call-up of all his warriors, and then joins with Haesten, we would be heavily outnumbered, at least until King Alfred arrives with the rest of the West Saxon army."

CHAPTER 15

"Haesten had formerly constructed that work at Barnfleet, and was then gone out on plunder, the main army being at home. Then came the king's troops, and routed the enemy, broke down the work, took all that was therein money, women, and children and brought all to London."
......The Anglo-Saxon Chronicles

Edward looked up from a map and spoke when Ambrose entered the planning room at the London Fort. "Uncle, Polonius mentioned the *Long Ride*, or, as he called it, the *Long Gallop*, in passing last evening. Could you please tell me a little about what exactly it is?"

"Well, it was a trick we learned when we were living in *Kiev*. It almost cost us our lives."

"How so, Uncle?"

"The Pechenegs liked to raid the towns along the Dnieper River."

"The Pechenegs?"

"They are fierce nomads that wander the steppes of Asia."

"Forgive my ignorance, Uncle. What, exactly are the steppes?"

"Think of steppes as grasslands that would take weeks or even months of hard riding to cross. The nomads who roam them have little liking or respect for farmers. In fact, they burn cities and enslave who they catch, or at least extort gold and goods from any they can.

I guess they decided that *Kiev* was recovered enough from their last visit that it was worth another visit. The entire Pecheneg nation was being driven gradually west by other nomad tribes, the *Khazars* and Ghuz, and I suppose they also needed food supplies and gold. Whatever the reason, they used the *Long Ride* on *Kiev*."

"Exactly how did they do that, Uncle?"

"First they sent tribesmen disguised as traders up the trails from the steppes toward *Kiev*. There is a *Varangian* fort less than a night's ride south of *Kiev*, called Vitchev Hill. It is not much of a fort, but it is on a height, and it is manned by one or two dozen warriors. Its main purpose is as an observation center. At all times, a signal pyre is kept ready, as well as some fast horses and a boat. Its main purpose is to signal *Kiev* in case of danger coming from the south."

"Uncle, you called the fort '*Varangian*', but you have always said that Dir and Askold were of the *Rus* tribe."

"Edward, the *Rus* made up the majority of the first landing party that took *Kiev*, but many other Vikings, of many different tribes had flooded to the area and joined the *Rus* settlers. *Varangian* is a word that came to describe the various Vikings and the Slavs, together."

"Then you knew the Pechenegs were coming?"

"The first hint we had in *Kiev* was when a crew of exhausted *Rus* warriors arrived by ship. They had seen the destruction at Vitchev Hill, and had rowed through the night to reach us before the enemy. It was a close thing. The crewmen were reporting what they had seen when the Pechenegs broke out of the forest and charged for the main gate of the town. It was a close race, but the *Varangians* were able to close the gate seconds before the first of the Pecheneg riders got there."

"But why did the men at Vitchev Hill not warn you of the impending attack?"

"Dir and Askold, the joint rulers of *Kiev*, asked the same question."

"And what was the answer?"

"We will never know for sure. All of the men at the fort were later found dead. The most likely scenario was that the Pechenegs sent scouts disguised as traders to block the trails north of the fort. The courier boat was stove in, and the fort's horses were gone, so the assumption was that a band of traders set up camp beside the fort. It was not uncommon. Many caravans would want to stop by such a fort, in the hope it would offer some protection against other hostile tribesmen. In any case, it is likely that the trap was sprung shortly before the main body of the Long Riders arrived.

However it was done, the fort was somehow taken and destroyed, and no *Varangian* watchers made it from the fort to *Kiev* by boat or horse."

"Uncle, you said that the Pechenegs had sent riders north of Vitchev Hill."

"Yes. That is part of the *Long Ride*. Scouts gradually infiltrate any trails leading to the target. At a given moment, they throw off their disguises and wait in ambush for any enemy scouts or couriers.

The whole essence of the *Long Ride* is that the riders must outstrip any who might warn the town. All trails are blocked, and each Long Rider has at least two mounts. It is grueling. The participants ride non-stop. If anyone slows for any reason, they are simply left behind. When the horses become exhausted, the Long Riders scramble onto fresher riderless horses and keep going.

If the scouts supporting the *Long Ride* manage to catch all the watchers and couriers, then the force arrives at its target with no warning. They ride for the gates, and, if they achieve success, then they charge through and keep the gate open. After that, the rest of the attacking horde eventually catches up, and the city inevitably falls."

Edward listened raptly. "Uncle, is that the trick you and father used to capture Carnarvon when you rescued Aunt Gretchen?"

"We used a variation of the same trick. We sent several dozen 'traders' to the town, and then bought a massive hay wagon. Polonius rigged the wagon so that when you pressed on a beam, one of the wagon wheels would slip off the axle.

The Long Riders started their long distance gallop from far away, and patrols of Gaelic-speaking Saxons came out of hiding and blocked the roads the riders were using.

Meantime, the hay wagon was driven to the main gate of the town. Hundreds of farmers brought in produce for sale at the town market to the townspeople, so the wagon did not raise any suspicions. When the wagon was almost through the gate, the wheel was forced off, and the wagon prevented the gates from being closed.

Even as the city guards came over to berate the disguised Saxons, the men hidden in the hay climbed out, bows in hand. The

Welsh guards at the gate were quickly cut down, and the archers prepared to take on all defenders until the galloping Long Riders arrived."

Edward spoke. "And they were successful?"

"It wasn't quite that simple. The townspeople heard the noise of battle and rallied. The Welsh are expert archers, and soon there was a shield-wall, with archers forming up behind its protection. They began to outnumber the Saxons holding the gate."

"So what did you do?"

"We had recently rented a home not far from the gate and a group of us were hidden there. We came out behind the new Welsh battle line. We charged and hit the Welsh from behind. They broke and scattered, and we were able to reinforce the Saxons at the gate.

The Welsh commander quickly put together another, even stronger force, and started to make it hot again for the relatively few Saxons, when the thunder of thousands of hooves told us that the Long Riders had finally arrived. After that, it was all over and the town had no choice but to surrender."

Ambrose suddenly smiled. "Something tells me that you are not asking about the *Long Ride* out of idle curiosity."

Edward grinned in return. "Then you would be right, Uncle Ambrose. Polonius' spies reported last night that Benfleet is held mainly by a small number of wounded veterans and a few old men."

"And you feel that a '*Long Ride*' might be able to seize the fort?"

"Why not? We need significant reinforcements before we can go after Haesten. The Viking treasures from *Francia* and Kent are at the fort, along with many *jarls*' women and children, and their entire fleet. I know you did not want to see the Viking fleet destroyed at Appledore, since it would have stranded them on our shore, but if we destroy their fleet on the north shore of the Thames, then it might discourage any further forays south of the river."

Ambrose nodded. "And if most of the Vikings are away raiding, then we could even close the door to escape by sending the Rochester fleet to blockade the river. We either take their ships or we destroy them!"

"Then do you approve, Uncle?"

"I am not sure Polonius is up to the ride any longer, but after he has spoken to his spies and sent out a few, he should be able to pretty much guarantee a successful ride."

Edward looked up. "I thought about that. I am worried about Phillip, and I understand that Polonius barely survived the last *Long Ride.*"

"Your own father was not in much better shape at the end."

"Then why do you, Phillip and Polonius, not ride ahead with the scouts and foresters? You each speak perfect Danish, and you should be able to penetrate close to Benfleet. When the *Long Ride* reaches you, you can simply join us."

"A good idea, Nephew. It would certainly save our backsides, and Phillip's large size is hard on the biggest horses we have."

Edward smiled. "Then I will find the largest horse in Mercia and buy it just for him!"

CHAPTER 16

Benfleet Falls

Edward walked along in front of the assembled *fyrdmen*. He spoke in a voice loud enough for the men to hear him. "You all know the importance of this mission! If we manage to take Benfleet, then the Danes will be forced to withdraw from Mercia. If we seize or burn their ships, then they cannot again land on Wessex soil. The ride is daunting, and you must push yourself past exhaustion. When your horse can go no further, you will switch mounts and keep going! If we are to succeed, then we must arrive before any couriers or scouts who might bring warning. Go now, and make ready. We will ride tomorrow at dawn."

The volunteer riders of the *Long Ride* started forward, led by young Prince Edward. Close behind came Ethelred, *ealdorman* of Saxon Mercia, and close behind him came the entire London garrison, volunteers from London, and all the West Saxon *fyrdmen* Edward had called up, as well as the men Alfred had felt he could spare from his southern army.

The *drengs*, young *fyrdmen* who had not yet won their own land as a reward for battle prowess, were eager to be amongst the first. Edward was surprised to see so many *duguos* amongst the riders. These men had won land and glory already, yet here they were, ready to drive themselves to exhaustion in a mighty effort to strike at the Vikings who had invaded their island.

The Saxon scouts cut the pine tree so that its trunk fell across the old Roman road. Its tip struck the large boulder on the other side of the road, so a horse would be unable to make it easily past the barrier. Then, leaving behind two Danish-speaking men dressed in Viking garb, the men headed back along the road, bows in hand. There, they quickly found spots close to the road where they could shoot down any enemy scouts or couriers.

They waited patiently, and as the dawn threw a faint illumination across the land, they heard pounding hooves. Rousing themselves, the two disguised Saxons started swinging their axes against the fallen trunk.

Within moments, ten riders came along the road at a blistering pace. The leading rider called out when he saw the barrier ahead.

"Make way! I am a courier for *Jarl* Haesten, carrying an urgent message to Benfleet!"

The Danish-speaking Saxon turned in the faint light. "Don't tell me your problems! I have enough of my own. I'll tell you what . . . Why don't you just tell this *Odin*-cursed tree to move out of your way? You would do a lot more good if you stopped flapping your jaw, unstrapped your axe, and put it to work."

The riders were forced to stop. The leader spoke again. "There are thousands of Saxons close behind me and coming fast! We must get to Benfleet before Alfred and his Saxons!"

The disguised Saxon spoke in perfect Danish. "Then I am afraid that you are plain out of luck, unless you want to climb down and start swinging your axe!"

The man swung down from his saddle. "Bah! Tie a rope onto the tip of the tree, use your horse, and we will be out of here in less than a hundred heart-beats!"

The Saxon whistled shrilly, then smiled at the Viking courier. "I told you - it is not going to be that easy."

Suddenly, dozens of arrows struck the bunched horsemen. Horses screamed and men fell, transfixed by arrows. A quick charge from the nearby woods ended the exchange. The dismounted courier drew his sword, but the two disguised Saxons used their axes and cut him down.

The commander spoke. "Bran, collect their horses and lead them out of sight into the woods. The rest of you lot - get these bodies off the road and out of sight. Osgar, tie a rope on the tree and do what the courier suggested. Our own riders should be here soon, and they will not be amused if this road is still blocked."

Most of the Viking watchers on the hill slept beside the signal pyre. One, youngest and most junior, struggled to stay awake in the cold early morning air. He and his companions had watched for approaching riders for weeks now, and all they ever saw were cautious deer and the occasional red fox.

The sentry heard a faint sound, and yawning, he turned to see who had finally woken. He wanted nothing more than to sleep, but first he needed someone to relieve him. He had heard of sentries who slept on duty being given the dreaded *Blood Eagle*, and he wanted to live to a ripe old age, not cough out his last few breaths for the entertainment of his fellow warriors.

Neither was to be his fate, as a half-dozen Saxon arrows transfixed him before he could call out a warning to his sleeping companions. The rest joined him on his final journey within moments. The Saxon foresters slit their throats while they slept.

As the vanguard of the Saxon force swept along the old Roman road, a trio of riders spurred their mounts out of the forest and joined it. They were an odd group. A giant mounted on a giant horse, an emaciated-looking dark-skinned Byzantine, and a bastard prince matched the pace with Edward and Ethelred of Mercia.

Ambrose grinned at Edward. "How are you doing, Nephew?"

The young prince groaned. "Good of you three to finally show up! To answer your question - I am never going to be able to sit down again! I thank merciful God that I took Polonius' advice and slathered my backside with his secret concoction . . . Are we going to be able to surprise the heathens?"

"Hopefully yes. A squad of our foresters rode last night to take out a signal pyre that Polonius found out about. The rest of the men are scattered along the road. They will do their best to stop any

Vikings they see."

Hundreds of riders broke from the forest. Their exhausted mounts were pushed to their limits as the strangers approached the main gates of the Viking fort of Benfleet. Viking banners flew in the vanguard of the host, and Viking guards shaded their eyes to see which *jarls* had so unexpectedly returned to their base. Curiosity turned to anxiety when, although the banners were familiar, none of the riders could be recognized. When the galloping riders drew close enough that individual armor could be recognized, anxiety turned to panic. With the riders only seconds from reaching the fort gate, the foreign armor was recognized for what it was. While the few guards standing outside the gate tried to form a protective shield-wall, the rest tried desperately to close the massive gates. A young rider wearing expensive armor and a gold *torque* cried out in Saxon. "Charge them! For Wessex!"

The leading horsemen, spurred on by their young commander, bunched together and bulled their way through the few defenders. One sturdy defender, hefting a giant battle axe, prepared to cut the young commander in two as he rode past. To the man's utter surprise, a dagger penetrated his eye socket, and the Viking crumbled.

The tons of horseflesh shattered the rough Viking shield-wall, and within seconds the Saxons had leapt from their horses and charged the men trying to close the gates. Edward was in the vanguard, surrounded by a giant swordsman, a small man with a strange, glittering blade, and an emaciated-looking man who held a pair of daggers and clearly looked like he would much rather be somewhere else.

Viking horns blared, calling the warriors to battle, and new defenders arrived at the gates. The Saxon riders, over a thousand strong, had spread out over miles, but more and more arrived, jumped from their exhausted mounts, and joined the fray.

For awhile it was a close thing, but there were limited numbers of defenders, and the stubborn Saxons would not be pushed from the gate. Gradually their numbers swelled, and then it was the Vikings who were driven back.

The Saxons advanced far enough into the fort that they could finally form into a proper shield-wall. The line advanced step by step. As spearmen and archers formed behind the protective wall, a steady rain of missiles flew over the heads of the front rank, and the defenders' numbers rapidly diminished.

Finally there were no more defenders standing, while hundreds of slower Saxon riders arrived to add their numbers to the attacking force. Without waiting for instructions, Phillip and Ethelred led several hundred of Ethelred's Mercians up onto the ramparts. They split right and left, and the two forces easily cleared off any remaining Vikings on the walls and then ran all the way around the wall to the water gate. Shedding *fyrdmen* as they ran, the swordsmen and archers effectively cut off any escape, while Edward and his West Saxon *fyrdmen* systematically killed any remaining Viking warriors remaining on the ground.

Ambrose led a strong force to the harbor, where they raced through the water gate and hunted down any survivors who had tried to reach the ships. While Ambrose watched, two *long-ships* cut their lines and slipped into the current.

Ambrose looked down-river. The first ships of the Rochester fleet were just coming into view, and the prince smiled. The Viking sailors weren't going anywhere. In one stroke, young Edward had captured an entire fleet. Hundreds of vessels lay stretched out before Ambrose, ripe for the plucking. The prince turned to his companion.

"Polonius!"

"Aye, Master?"

"Would you be so kind as to have our captains inspect our new ships in the morning?"

"Of course, Prince. I assume that you can never have too many *sun-stones*. What else, exactly, are the captains looking for?"

"I will gratefully take any *sun-stones*. We will distribute them equally to the fleets and teach the navigators how to use them, but I really want them to focus on picking out the best ships. Then I want them to split their regular crews into skeleton crews. We are going to send as many ships to London and Rochester as we can possibly man."

"And the rest?"

Ambrose grinned. "Make a signal pyre so big that Haesten can see it in northern Mercia!"

"That, my prince, will be a singular pleasure!"

🏳

Phillip led Ethelred and his Personal Guard down the stairs from the wall, directly toward the solid building Polonius had told him contained the pirate treasure. He knew Polonius had been correct when, as they approached, an even dozen young Vikings formed up in front of them. The Viking warriors wore bright, polished armor, and had clearly not taken part in the violent street battle going on not far away.

The weapons-master drew his enormous long-sword and advanced slowly. He spoke in perfect Danish. "The battle is lost. The town is taken."

The squad commander smiled back. "And what is the fate of captured Vikings?"

"A quick death and six feet of good land."

"Your Alfred's offer is always the same.' The Dane looked up at the sky for a moment. 'I think that today is a fine day to die."

Phillip looked somber. "That is all that I can offer you, unless you want to run and take your chances."

"Do not be sorry, Saxon. Today I cross a rainbow bridge and join the gods in *Asgard . . . Skjaldborg!*"

At the sudden command, he and his companions shuffled closer together, until their shields overlapped. The Vikings calmly waited to die.

Phillip looked back at Ethelred, who had just made it around on the other wall and had joined him. "Are you ready, *Ealdorman*?"

"They will kill more than their number."

"Then we use bows and spears. I have no wish to foolishly sacrifice our *fyrdmens'* lives."

"Carry on, Weapons-master."

Phillip turned his head. "Front line . . . shield-wall! Prepare to deliver missiles . . . throw!"

The Mercians, in turn, shuffled together, while ranks of bowmen and spear throwers formed behind. On command, a barrage of spears and arrows sailed over the shield-wall. While the large Viking shields stopped most of the arrows and spears, yet some made it through, and the rest weighted down the shields, making them heavy and unwieldy.

The squad commander, still unwounded, called out to Phillip. "Step forward three paces, Saxon, and honor me by showing me why you carry a giant sword."

Phillip stepped forward, until the two were only a spear length apart. "May you have a good journey today, Viking."

"At least tell me the name of the man who is going to foolishly try and kill me today."

"I am Phillip, weapons-master to the kings of Wessex."

"The name is familiar. I have heard the name of Phillip the Weapons-master . . . He is the stuff of legends, but surely the one I have heard of must be long dead by now."

"Many Vikings have wished it so. In my time, I have stolen princesses from Vikings and served in the *Great Army*. I have called Sitric Ivarsson my friend, and killed more Danes than I can count."

The man hesitated. "Then I face one of the greatest warriors in all Britain. It will be an honor to teach you how to fight . . . Remember Dag the Dane, Saxon!"

As he spoke, the warrior advanced. His sword swept low, at Phillip's feet, but Phillip's blade was there just in time. The two blades met with a great clang, and before Dag could even react, Phillip's blade arced into Dag's shield. The power of Phillip's muscles, and the weight of his huge sword, was such that the shield split into two.

Dag tossed it aside contemptuously. "You were once good, Saxon, but you grow old."

"Today you will see *Asgard*, Viking."

With that, Phillip renewed his attack. His massive weapon struck again and again, until Dag could hardly stand.

The Viking spoke again, as he tried to catch his breath. "I underestimated you, Saxon. You have apparently not gone completely to fat in your old age."

"And you seem to have had rather too much good living and too little exercise, Viking."

As he spoke, the Dane swung his sword high. He didn't even see Phillip's sharp blade penetrate his neck. He stared uncomprehendingly at Phillip for several seconds, then fell to the ground.

Phillip stepped back into the Mercian ranks. He growled at them. "Risk no more lives. Kill them all!"

A second avalanche of spears and arrows struck the unfortunate Vikings, and before they could recover, the Mercian shield-wall closed on them. Several Mercians were wounded in the vicious shield to shield battle, but the Vikings were vastly outnumbered and quickly overcome. All died where they stood.

Phillip moved over to where Ethelred stood. "I would ask you, *Ealdorman*, to post your banner here, and a force of perhaps fifty of your most stalwart and trustworthy *fyrdmen*. If Polonius is right, then King Alfred is going to be able to finance this war with the Viking treasure behind this door. The *fyrdmen* will run amok tonight, once they have found the mead and beer. Edward has ordered that no one is to be allowed inside this warehouse."

"Should we not at least confirm that this is the treasury? It would be a shame if we found out it was elsewhere only after it was looted."

Phillip thought for a moment. "You are right, *Ealdorman*. Let me send for Polonius."

"I have a dozen stout lads here who could break the door in for us, Weapons-master."

"But there is a lock."

"It will not hold out long against a log wielded by my lads."

"*Ealdorman*, it will also not lock again. I have never seen a lock that Polonius cannot pick."

"Ah, a good point, Phillip. Then, by all means, let us send for the man of many talents."

The runner tried to catch his breath as he stood before the mysterious magician from far-off Byzantium. At last he gasped out his message. "*Ealdorman* Ethelred and Weapons-master Phillip request your presence at the treasury building, Lord! I can show you the way."

Polonius looked over at Ambrose, who smiled and nodded. "Let us go, Scholar. The men of the fleet will look after the ships until we return."

Ambrose and Polonius walked up to Phillip. Polonius spoke. "You wanted to see me, Weapons-master?"

"I have need of your unique talents, Polonius. Ethelred has quite rightly pointed out that you only think that this is the treasury building. It would actually be good to know for sure before we spend all night guarding it."

Polonius smiled. "I paid good gold for that information, Oak-tree, but if it pleases you, I will open the door and we can all confirm if the Viking treasure is stored here."

Phillip nodded. "What a good idea, Scholar. Less talk and more effort would be appreciated."

"Patience is a virtue, Oak-tree."

As Polonius teased his friend, he slipped two pieces of thin metal into the lock and wiggled them about. There was a grudging click, and Polonius smiled.

"What are you waiting for, Weapons-master? You demanded, and I obeyed."

Ambrose laughed. "Enough, you two! I will open the door and you may join me and confirm with your own eyes what I find."

With that, the prince leaned on the heavy door. With a loud squeal, it reluctantly opened. The small group entered, but could see little.

Phillip struck flint and steel. In a few moments, he had a flame, and he was able to light a resin-soaked torch that hung just inside the door.

The small group looked around, but they were surrounded by

hundreds of large wooden boxes. All had runes on them. Ambrose pointed to a large box in front of him.

"Phillip, your sword should be able to lever that top off in short order."

The massive blade easily forced the top up, exposing golden chalices and cups that could only have come from a church or monastery. Ambrose pointed randomly to five more, and they produced silver coins, golden armbands and *torque*s, and more religious vessels.

Ambrose turned to the rest of the group. "Are you all satisfied? I propose a strong guard here tonight. There may be other treasures scattered through the fort, but clearly this is the main treasury."

Ethelred nodded. "I have already assigned fifty of my most trustworthy *fyrdmen* the task, but I would be grateful if Polonius could lock the door again. There is enough gold here to tempt the Son of God himself."

CHAPTER 17

Viking Women of Benfleet

Edward walked with Ambrose along the dirty street. They had already found the slave quarters and freed hundreds of *Angelisc* women and children. There had been heartbreakingly few men languishing in chains.

The *fyrdmen* were now searching the homes and driving the Viking women and children to the square that had served as market and training ground for the Viking warriors. Many of the older girls and women who shambled past had torn clothing or were completely naked, and Ambrose knew that the *fyrdmen* had taken their revenge on the Vikings in the time-honored fashion.

Ambrose felt it was wrong to force any woman, and had, in his youth, paid a usurious amount to gold to buy the slave girl, Kuralla, from her Viking captor. He had attempted to save her from being given to hundreds of lusty warriors as a toy, but, after much alcohol, he succumbed to his own lust and forced himself upon her. While she had long-ago forgiven him, he could not, in all conscience, ever forgive himself. He knew, too, that thousands of girls and women, across the length and breadth of the island, had been raped by the pagan Vikings. The Saxon *fyrdmen* were exacting their revenge, and Ambrose knew that he could not stop them.

Ambrose saw two *fyrdmen* pull a woman out of a home. She struggled to hold on to two little boys while the warriors pawed her and started to tear off her shift. One of the little boys cried, but the other saw Ambrose and called out in Frankish to him. "Prince Ambrose! Help my mama!"

Ambrose stared. Suddenly, he recognized the two little boys. Just a few months earlier they had lived with his brother's court in Kent, and he had witnessed their baptism. If they were Haesten's two sons, then the captive who had taught her sons to speak Frankish had to be his woman.

He called out to the men who were holding her. "You men! Bring that woman and her children here!"

The men had been drinking, and they were belligerent. "Ge' your own damned doxie! This un 'ere is taken!"

Phillip took one step toward them, and they paused when his shadow fell on them. "Who the 'ell are you, big fella?"

His voice boomed. "Stand straight when your prince speaks to you, you sad excuses for a pile of shit!"

The men looked at the man's size, then at the giant sword that swung from his back. At last, his instructions sank through their stupor, and they released the woman and attempted to stand as trained.

"Sorry, sir! We 'ad a little too much ta drink."

Phillip stared at them. "Then go sleep it off. You are no good to anyone in your present condition!"

"Yes, sir!"

"Yes, sir what!?"

"Yes, sir - we will go sleep it off."

Ambrose turned to the woman, who tried to hold together with her hands the pieces of her shift.

He spoke in Frankish. "Are you *Jarl* Haesten's wife?"

"I was once his slave, but now I am the mother of his children, and his wife."

"I understood from Haesten that you were once a Frankish princess. Do you wish to be free again to return to your home?"

"Sir, to my surprise, I have found happiness in Haesten's arms. I wish only to be re-united with my husband."

"You know, Madame, that your husband lied to us, and the hostages he left with us are already hanging in trees. You and I are cousins, however, and not enemies. I will tell you what I can do. I will have you escorted to King Alfred, and he will decide what to do with you."

"Do you mean the godfather of young Marc here?"

"The same."

She smiled. "Then I will be honored to finally meet him. He

was very kind to my boys here when he arranged for their baptism."

CHAPTER 18

Ambrose rides toward Exeter and Alfred

Phillip stared back over his shoulder. Something had caught his peripheral vision, and he searched for further movement. Finally he saw what had caught his attention. A band of armored riders came from the east. Phillip caught up to Ambrose and growled a warning.

"Prince, there are riders to the east. They are armed and coming our way."

Ambrose spoke. "How many, Weapons-master?"

"At least a dozen."

"Recommendations?"

"Crest the hill and then we wait, bows in hand."

"Agreed, old friend. Make it happen."

As the riders disappeared from sight behind the hill, Phillip stopped the whole force and ordered them to form in line and string their bows. As soon as the line was formed, Ambrose, Polonius, and Phillip urged their mounts back to the hill's crest.

The fifteen riders were pushing their horses hard to close the distance. They slowed, however, when the three riders came back into sight. The lead rider, the commander by the size of his golden *torque* and the quality of his armor, advanced while his comrades slowed behind him.

"Welcome, good pilgrims. You show good sense in stopping."

Ambrose spoke. "Who are you and why are you following us?"

"Now that is a good question . . . and one I would be happy to answer. We are the guardians of Dorset's roads, and, as such, have been authorized by our *ealdorman*, Ethelwold, to collect tolls from all travelers. Since you are passing through, we require payment for the use of this road."

Ambrose sneered. "And why would I pay good silver to the

likes of you to travel a road made by the ancient Romans when I travel on the king's business?"

"I didn't say anything about silver, pilgrim. There are Vikings about, and it is expensive to keep these roads safe. We thus require gold to allow safe passage for you and your little party."

"There are several things wrong with your request, stranger."

The man smiled. "Really? And what are they?"

"Dorset ends back on the other side of the valley you just rode through. You are now trespassing on Somerset."

The big man continued to smile. "Really? Well, I see no *fyrdmen* from Somerset here, so I guess I will just have to collect on their behalf."

"The only Vikings hereabouts are trapped at Exeter by King Alfred's army."

"You see how well we protect you? It is well worth the gold coins that we charge. Do you have any more complaints before we collect your gold? I warn you, you are wasting our time, and we charge extra for that."

"I am a courier traveling to your king. Do you dare delay us?"

"Only until you are paid up, traveler. It is a few gold coins if you pay voluntarily, but my men just might take all your coins if they have to get them themselves."

"Just before you tell your brave men to do that, can you tell me your name?"

"I am Leng the Bold, pilgrim, and my patience is now officially at an end. Your toll just went up."

"Well, Leng the Bold, do you not want to know who you are attempting to rob?"

"It is not your name that I want, stranger, but your gold. You are beginning to really annoy me."

"The big man beside me is weapons-master to the king of Wessex. His name is Phillip."

"Phillip the invincible? I think you are trying to frighten me, stranger. I allow that your friend is big, but the real Phillip is a giant, and rides always at the side of the king's brother."

"Phillip, show him one of your arrows."

Phillip drew an arrow and nocked it in one smooth motion.

Ambrose continued.

"Note the abnormal size of both the bow and the arrow. It can pierce the strongest armor, and you, Leng, are the target."

Leng looked a little nervous. "There are fourteen men at my back, pilgrim, and your own comrades appear to have deserted you."

"In the ballads, Phillip has a companion who is both thin and dark, just like my second friend here. He, who you know as the wizard and the scholar, wears a special belt filled with knives that never miss their target. Polonius, show the man your belt."

Polonius smiled as he drew back his cloak, exposing his knife sheaths. Ambrose smiled again.

"And that only leaves me, brother of your king and the bearer of **Victory-Maker**. Do you know, this blade has never failed to kill any opponent I have gone against. Leng, turn your horse around while you still can. Wessex needs good warriors to fight the heathen, not rob fellow warriors."

Leng now had sweat pouring down his face. "Then pay the gold, and you can be on your way. Even the Ambrose of legend and his two companions cannot kill fifteen men."

"I think we can, but it is true that all three of us are getting a little older, so we will probably call for help."

Leng barked in laughter. "There is no one around for twenty miles, fool! Pay up and live!"

In answer, Ambrose put two fingers in his mouth and whistled shrilly. Within a second, an extended line of ten horsemen crested the hill, each holding a bow with arrow nocked and drawn.

"Leng, your next command will cause you to either live or die. Choose wisely."

Several of Lang's riders quietly turned their horses and headed back the way they had come. When the commander heard the hoof beats, he turned and watched his men abandon him. He turned back to Ambrose.

"You win this time, *Atheling*. Next time you may not be so lucky!"

Ambrose urged his horse closer to Polonius. "Well, Scholar, what do you think of our visitors?"

"I think that we should be very alarmed, Prince."

"How so?"

"Ethelwold is many things, but no fool. I cannot believe that he would allow his men to indiscriminately rob travelers."

"Then what do you think?"

"I think he has sent out patrols to ride the trails."

"To what purpose?"

"King Alfred has Ethelwold by the balls. If he makes any overt move against Wessex, then his son's life is forfeit."

"And so?"

"And so he sends out patrols. They can pretend to assist any large groups they come across. They can watch for any Viking raiders. Maybe they catch the odd courier and steal the messages that he carries. I suspect that their goal is more information than gold."

"But they backed off when we offered to give them a fight."

"Because they knew we would kill them and, in any case, they got the information they wanted. Three important allies of Alfred are nearby and vulnerable. The king might even be willing to trade us for Ethelwold's son."

"But they rode off."

"Aye, Prince, but what would you do if you saw several of Haesten's most capable officers go by?"

Ambrose thought for a moment. "If I was heavily outnumbered, I would go and get reinforcements."

"And would Ethelwold benefit from our demise or capture," questioned Polonius?

"I suppose he would, in one stroke, remove a potential rival for the crown and the king's chief strategist."

Polonius replied. "So should we worry?"

"Will we make a garrisoned *burh* tonight?"

"Not until late tomorrow, Prince, and the royal estates hereabouts have all been abandoned on the king's orders."

Ambrose sighed. "Then it is going to be armed and armored, isn't it?"

Polonius smiled. "And no blankets tonight."

The prince groaned. "We sleep in the bushes again?"

Polonius nodded. "Did it work in Calabria?"

Ambrose nodded. "I was very cold and uncomfortable, but, yes, the Byzantine soldiers came and we were able to kill them all."

"Using the foreign war arrows."

Ambrose smiled. "Yes, that did work rather well, didn't it? The authorities were busy hunting Arab pirates for weeks."

"And with the Italian assassins in Aosta?"

"The *caltrops* were a good touch there. They had removed their shoes so that they could be silent. They weren't very successful when three inch metal points speared their feet."

"And so tonight?"

Ambrose grinned. "Armed, armored, and alive it shall be, my friend!"

ᚱ

Godric, commander of the escort group, kneed his horse closer. "Prince, if they come back, they will come in large numbers."

Ambrose looked at the commander. "What are you suggesting, Godric?"

"When we stop for the evening, the three of you must ride on. You must ride through the night while we make a big fire and attract their attention."

"Godric, if they come back in strength, they will slaughter both you and your men."

"Prince, if they see that you are gone, there will be no reason for them to harm us."

"Except that you know the commander's name and are witness to who went after and possibly killed the three of us. Ethelwold simply could not afford to let you and your *fyrdmen* live."

"Then we will fight. Prince, I have sworn to protect you on your journey. I will be content if we hold them long enough that you have a chance to escape."

Ambrose stared solemnly. "Godric, you are a great warrior, and I thank you for the offer. I would like, however, to find a way for all of us to live."

Polonius interrupted. "Prince, what if we set up camp, left our horses, and then took their entire horse herd?"

"Polonius, that would assume that we can stay in hiding while they gathered around the camp, and could then locate their herd and defeat whoever is left to guard them."

"The hiding is easy, and there will be the light of a half-moon to see by. We will pick the camp location, and then we will decide where they would hide their horses. After that, we enjoy supper, cover some logs with our blankets, build up the fire and then steal away one by one to the most likely spot. If we choose wisely, we live, and obtain an entire herd of horses."

"And if we do not choose wisely?"

"We flee in the dark, or we fight to the death, unless you wish to surrender."

Godric was agitated. "Prince, there is great risk if we do not choose the right spot. Please, swallow your pride and ride for your life. You can take three of our horses as backup. We will hold them long enough that you can escape."

Ambrose smiled. "Faithful warrior, if we choose well, then we all live. I could not live with myself if I left a man to die in order to save my own life."

The little band surrounded Ambrose on his hillside. The moon was rising, casting a gentle illumination across the countryside. The tranquility was suddenly disturbed by the sound of hooves. A half-dozen riders rode slowly into sight, and then climbed down and hobbled their horses securely. The men slipped into the brush and started to worm their way toward the source of the column of smoke that climbed into the air from the travelers' camp fire. They returned in a few minutes, and sent a rider back the way they had come.

The force of over fifty riders arrived at a slow walk, and quietly dismounted. The horses were both hobbled and tied together. Two youths remained, while the rest of the warriors took up their spears, swords and shields. In complete silence, except for the occasional accidental clatter of metal on metal or displaced stones, the warriors headed for Ambrose's camp.

To Ambrose's great surprise, the men seemed dressed in Viking armor, and the symbols on the shields were definitely not Saxon. He whispered to Polonius.

"Scholar, they look to be Vikings. It is possible?"

"Vikings that made it past our coastal watchers? Vikings who come along our trail? Remember Calabria, Prince. Those Turkish arrows and the *ghutra* we left behind threw the Byzantines off our trail."

"Then you think that these are Ethelwold's men in disguise?"

"Why not? If one of our *fyrdmen* managed to escape, he would report an attack from a Viking foraging party. Ethelwold would be in the clear."

"Polonius, the Dorset men should be out of hearing now. I think we have to move soon!"

Polonius crossed himself. "May God be with us, Prince!"

The Byzantine stood up and walked calmly toward the first herd boy. As soon as he came into the boy's vision, the lad drew his axe and held it ready to strike. He spoke in a quaking voice.

"Who in God's holy name are you, stranger?"

Polonius lifted his arms so the boy could see that his hands were empty of weapons. "I am the man who is going to ask you to drop your battle axe. Tonight you may live or you may die. You must decide."

The two boys moved together, and the older one spoke. "You are but one, and not even armed!"

"I am armed with the truth. What you are doing tonight is an abomination in the eyes of God! Do you not know that you are attacking the brother of your king?"

"Stranger, I am a good Christian, and I obey the lawful commands of our *ealdorman*. What else can a sworn man do?"

"Son, to strike at the family of your king is not a lawful command. You may, however, put down your weapons and pray to God for forgiveness."

The second boy spoke for the first time. "You are the Wizard. I know of you! Have you come to steal our souls?"

Polonius looked at the two boys with pity. "I have come to save your lives. All you have to do is drop your weapons."

The second boy raised his battle axe. "Tonight I kill a wizard!" Having said that, he charged Polonius.

Only five of the dozen arrows struck home, but both boys reeled and fell back, leaking a liquid blackness in the dim light. Ignoring the fallen boys, the *fyrdmen* rushed forward. They had to release fifty horses, and do it before the Dorsetmen realized they had been tricked and returned to reclaim their horses.

In the distance could be heard great shouts of '*Odin*! *Odin*!' The *fyrdmen* chose the best mounts from the herd, and mounted up. At a shout from Phillip, they drove the entire horse herd due south.

The sun was setting as Ambrose and his escort finally saw the walls of the *tun* of Lyng in the distance. The prince stretched to ease the pain in his body, and then started his mount forward again.

"Come, my friends. Lyng is supposed to have a garrison of a hundred, plus there will be many more winter *fyrdmen* who have sought refuge here against the pagans. I doubt Dorsetmen, in Viking dress or not, would dare to approach too close. Let's ride!"

CHAPTER 19

Ambrose Reaches Exeter

Ambrose thrust aside the deer-hide door to the king's campaign tent. Alfred rose to his feet in surprise, and then hugged his elder brother. "Ambrose, this is a great surprise! I thought you were still at Benfleet."

"Benfleet fell with barely a whimper. Edward's *Long Ride* was a resounding success and your son is the hero of the army."

"Thank you for that. Ethelwold is aggressively recruiting support amongst the members of the *Witan*. He will push his case for the throne hard when I die."

"He has done more than that, brother."

"What has he done, Ambrose?"

"We were stopped on the road by a patrol of his *fyrdmen*."

"It is a time of war. That does not sound too unreasonable."

"Except that they tried to extort gold from us, brother. If you are missing any couriers, I think I know what happened to them."

"Ambrose, do you really think he would dare?"

"I have not told you the half of it, brother-of-mine."

"Then pray do, Ambrose."

"After we threatened them with drawn bows, they backed off, but Polonius warned us to prepare for an attack that night."

"Surely they would not dare!"

"They came in the night, fifty strong, and disguised as Vikings."

"And you were but twelve, thirteen?"

"Thirteen."

"Then how did you escape?"

"For that, we can thank Polonius. He had us put our cloaks and blankets over logs or brush, light a big fire, and abandon the horses and supplies. While they hit our camp, we took the horses they had left a half mile away, and rode hard for Lyng."

"I am glad that you are safe, but I am not happy that Ethelwold would dare so much. I think I will have a strong force from Somerset go sit on the border. We have, in fact, lost several couriers, but they all appeared to be accidents or the result of Viking raiders. Perhaps I can put some of my best huntsmen on it, and we can hang a few 'Viking' raiders."

"Then tell your huntsmen to look for Leng the Bold and his patrol."

Alfred pulled at his beard and then rubbed his stomach. Ambrose looked again at his brother. "Alfred, are you sick?"

"Oh, I am well enough. My stomach pains grow no worse, although I do not remember any longer when they did not exist. The quacks bleed me and make me swallow horrible concoctions, but I do not think it does any good. Only Polonius' elixir seems to help . . . but enough of me . . . what about all of you?"

"Everyone is well, brother. Your son is basking in his glory."

"Please ask Polonius to send out a royal proclamation. I want the whole world to know of Edward's success. Copies to all *ealdormen* and bishops throughout the kingdom, and include the Pope and the Frankish royal house. 'The young victor at Farnham and conqueror of Benfleet, etc, etc.' Polonius will know what to say."

Ambrose smiled. "Consider it done, brother-of-mine. Did I tell you I brought you a present?"

"Ambrose, you know how much I like presents. Why, I remember one time you brought me pieces of driftwood as gifts."

"They were planks from a sunken Viking fleet, little brother, and you told me you loved them."

Alfred hugged his brother a second time. "Aye, I guess I did, at that or, at least, what they represented. What have you got this time? Seashells or pebbles? You have never yet given me leaves."

"Much better, Alfred. It took ten captured ships to move your new riches to London."

"Ten ships?"

"Gold and silver are heavy, brother. There were not enough carts to move it all by land."

"May God be praised! Ten shiploads?"

"Fear not. It has all arrived safely at London, is securely locked up, and has a guard of Ethelred's finest veteran *duguos*. And that is only the first of your gifts."

"Brother, I am overwhelmed. You mean there is even more?"

"You mentioned the wish to expand your fleet. Well, the Danes have provided you with more than a hundred fine new warships."

"A hundred warships for free! That is a great gift, indeed. I have a question, however."

Ambrose smiled. "Speak, and I will answer, brother."

"Did not Polonius report that there were 280 ships at Benfleet?"

"There was, brother, but even with the skimpiest skeleton crews and volunteers from the land *fyrd*, I could only arrange to man so many. Even so, many of them had to be towed. Besides, we took only the newest and best. Many had seen better days and were not worth the taking."

"Then there are still ships for the Danes to return to?"

Ambrose grinned. "Not any more. We had the biggest Viking funeral pyre in history! Never have so few dead Vikings been so honored with so many ships. Each dead Dane got his own ship, and there were many left over."

"God is good! I wish I could have seen the fire!"

"It could be seen for twenty miles in all directions, brother. There are no ships and no fort left for Haesten to return to . . . Are you ready for your third present yet?"

"The suspense is killing me. Yet another present?"

"Not far behind me, and trudging your way, is Haesten's wife, both his children, and over a thousand other Viking wives, mothers and children. I took them to London, but then decided you might want to see them. I put the Frankish princess and her children on horseback, but the Viking women march in chains, pending your decision about their disposal."

"Over a thousand hostages, and all from Benfleet? Hmm. I will inspect them, and then probably send them to Winchester for now."

"To be sold as slaves?"

"Possibly . . . Not yet. Let's see if we can use them as bargaining chips first. In the meantime, they can work in the fields. We have little enough farm labor with so many men under arms.

Did you speak to Haesten's Frankish wife? Does she want to go home?"

"Yes I did, and no, she doesn't. She wants only to be re-united with her husband."

"Then let's make it so. I want her and the two children returned to Haesten, along with some generous presents.' He grinned suddenly. 'You might find some pretty trinkets in my new treasure room in London."

"Brother, you are giving away your most powerful bargaining chip."

Alfred sighed. "I know, Ambrose, but God has given us a unique opportunity to open the eyes of the pagan to the ways of the Lord. These children, and their mother, are the wedge we will use. That is more important than any petty revenge."

"Alfred, how is the siege going here?"

"Exeter is safe enough, now that we are here. The Vikings, however, chose not to slip away on their ships. They are stubbornly holding out in their own fortifications. Their behavior is most curious."

"Unless, brother, their object is to tie down as many of your *fyrdmen* as they can for as long as they can."

"If that is the case, then they are being quite successful."

"Alfred, can you end the siege here quickly?"

"You know, Polonius is right. A siege really is the lowest form of warfare. We outnumber them by ten or twenty to one, yet all we can do is dig in the mud and throw the occasional rock at them. If we approach too closely, we suffer hideous losses. Our men sleep in the mud and grow sick."

"Is there hope?"

"We have painstakingly cut off their food supplies, except for the odd ship that slips in past our defenses, and so the answer is yes. They are hungry and growing more so. Eventually they will be forced to take to their ships and abandon this area."

"Then you will be successful."

"Eventually, but in the meantime, I have tied down thousands of *fyrdmen* who would be more usefully moving into Mercia for whatever is coming next, and I have yet another army tied down besieging a second force in northern Devon. Damn it, Ambrose! I should be joining forces with my son and Ethelred, not sitting here in the mud! If it were not for you, Polonius and Phillip, then I would greatly fear for Edward and all Wessex."

"Yet Sigefrith must be taken care of, Alfred."

"You may rest assured that I will do that, brother-of-mine, whatever the cost and time, and I will not forget that Guthfrith and Eohric swore eternal peace between us. Tell Edward that as soon as this pirate Sigefrith is taken care of, then I will march to his side."

"Of course, brother."

"Ambrose, what news of Haesten?"

"Not good, Alfred. Polonius' spies report that Haesten's force has retraced its steps to Essex. That was to be expected, and, in fact, was one of the goals of the attack on Benfleet. What is more worrying are the reports of large forces from both East Anglia and Northumbria marching toward Haesten's position. Brother, I fear that your prediction is coming true."

"And what is that, big brother?"

"This is not a raid; it is an invasion."

"Merciful God! So at last the worms are coming out of the wood. Guthfrith and Eohric have finally officially declared themselves."

"We could be facing a huge army, Alfred. I was hoping that you would have been successful here and able to bring your men north. They may be sorely needed."

"Ambrose, the only way I can conclude things here quickly is if I order general assaults. Even with my superior numbers, I could not be assured of victory, and the losses would be catastrophic. I could cripple the southern army. I cannot in all conscience order that. I will, however, send north with you as many *fyrdmen* as I feel I can spare. The northern shires will just have to somehow raise the rest. I do give you permission, moreover, to dip into my treasury. Hire mercenaries if you can, and tell Polonius to be free with the bribes. Let us cause as much unrest in their home kingdoms as we possibly can."

"Speaking of treasures, how much of what you seized at

Benfleet came from churches?"

"It is hard to say, Alfred, but much of the loot consisted of chalices and other holy vessels."

"When all is said and done, I want each church in Wessex that has been raided to be able to reclaim a set of holy vessels from the treasure."

"Much cannot be identified, brother, and a clearly a lot came from Haesten's *Francian* raids."

Alfred smiled. "Then let each church claim one set of golden vessels. Of the rest, we will tithe to holy mother church. Please tell Polonius ten percent should be added to our annual payments to Rome."

"And the rest, brother?"

"Melt it down and make silver and gold coins. I fear that we are going to need to spend a lot of gold before this war is over."

CHAPTER 20

Ambrose recruits Fyrdmen

Alfred poured his brother a large horn of mead with his own hand. "Drink, Ambrose, you have earned it many fold. It is thanks to you, Polonius and Phillip, that Edward is both alive and a hero of the army. What have you decided after our talk last night?"

"Edward told me before I left London that he wishes to return temporarily to the eastern shires, which are, after all, what you assigned him to govern. They are in disarray, and there will be starvation this winter if he does not ship some food east.'

Ambrose smiled. 'I told him he could dip into your treasure to help the needy of Kent."

"Of course, brother. It is the least we can do after all the misery they have been through. What else are in the plans?"

"Well, Ethelred is worried about what Haesten is planning. He plans to call up every Mercian *fyrdman* he can get his hands on. He has already ordered the evacuations again to the fortified *burhs*."

"That won't stop the Danes from taking the larger centers if they really want them, but it will at least make it expensive for them. Ethelflæd has written and she tells me that the *burhs* are still far from complete, but they are, in any state, better than nothing.

And you, brother? What do you and Polonius want to do?"

"Polonius is worried, brother. I meant to tell you last night and forgot. His greedy Viking *jarl* has been back for more gold."

"And what did he report?"

"Pretty much what we talked about last night. Shiploads of fighting men have been arriving from the Northern Isles, from Ireland, and even from the home country. More forces from Northumbria and East Anglia are riding in. Haesten has replaced his losses and then some."

"The question is - what is he going to do with all those warriors?"

Ambrose thought for a moment. "They only come for land or loot. Such an alliance is not likely to agree to attack its own, so that basically leaves us."

Alfred grimaced. "I was afraid you were going to say that. Then the only question is, where will they strike? What does our Byzantine spy-master think?"

"Probably west. Perhaps along the Thames again. It is clear that Haesten's defeat at Farnham upset some plans. Could he have been trying to connect with Sigehelm?"

"It's certainly possible - even probable. I don't think Sigehelm planned to sit in Exeter for so long. Exeter managed to hold out against him, and then our swift arrival with the *fyrd* prevented him from moving north and ravaging the countryside. Thank the merciful Lord, after trapping Sigehelm near Exeter, I still had enough *fyrdmen* under arms to pin down and besiege the second force that landed on the northern coast."

Alfred suddenly smiled. "So what are we going to do about this Haesten, big brother?"

"With your permission, brother, I am going to call on Ethelhelm of Wiltshire and Ethelnoth of Somerset to raise every *fyrdman* they can, send word to our Welsh allies that we need as many of their fighting men as they can spare, take the men you have given me, and join Ethelred in London. The city is central enough that we can easily march either north or south, depending on the route that Haesten chooses."

"Ambrose, of course you have my permission! I have never told you this, brother-of-mine, but I truly believe that if you had not been kidnapped and taken away for so many years, the *Witan* would have chosen you as the next king."

"Alfred, I am a bastard, born of a slave."

"Ambrose, your father was a king, and your mother was a beautiful woman, who just happened to be born of a royal family that had ruled part of Britain for centuries. The truth is, I would not have been upset if they had chosen you. I wished to be king no more than our father. Given a choice, he would have joined holy mother church in some capacity, and me . . . I would have been content to be a scholar and translate books."

"But as king you have started schools, codified laws, recruited scholars from all around Europe, forced our noblemen to learn to read and write, re-organized your army and built garrisoned shelters throughout the kingdom for your people. These are not insignificant achievements, brother-of-mine!"

"There is so much more to do, Ambrose, and I am running out of time. These damned Danes never leave us alone! I have not even been able to see my wife for months . . . Speaking of families, how is my son-in-law?"

"Ethelred is ready to valiantly defend his shire, but he has enemies on all sides and cannot match Haesten's numbers. It will take the combined *fyrds* of several shires to defeat Haesten's new army. He can use all the help he can get."

"You carry my signet ring, brother, with my blessing. Raise whatever forces you think you will need - invoke my name if necessary and threaten my wrath. I will do my best to end this infestation in Devon and then join you in London."

Alfred hugged his bastard brother. "Go with God, Ambrose. You do not know what it means to me to have you and your two friends with me in the struggle against the Danes. Time and again you and your two friends have rescued Wessex. I don't know what I would do without you!"

Ambrose felt deep emotion wash over him. Rather than let the emotion show, he turned to watch the big Wessex *fyrdmen* ride by. In columns of three, more than a thousand fighting *thanes*, all Alfred could spare from his two sieges, rode north and east.

Alfred sat his horse on the little knoll, and graciously accepted the salutes of his sworn men. Ambrose eventually turned his horse back to face his brother the king.

"And may God be with you, Alfred. I hope to see you in the north soon."

༒

Ambrose watched the *fyrdmen* in the little valley below. The men were well trained, and the force deployed across the road with discipline and an economy of movement. He smiled and turned to Phillip.

"I think our old friend got word of a strange force riding through his territory and is preparing for us even as we watch. Perhaps you would like to ride ahead and wave the royal banner before someone gets hurt!"

"Aye, Prince." With that, the giant of few words spurred his horse forward. His presence on the crest was quickly noted, and a half-dozen young *drengs* rode to meet him.

Ambrose watched from above and smiled again. He knew the young *fyrdmen* were actively looking for trouble. Only a brave deed would get them the notice of their *ealdorman*, and only with accolades would they receive golden rings or even land to hold, so long as they swore to answer the *ealdorman's* summons when it was time to fight.

Phillip waved the banner for the royal house of Wessex, however, and the riders stopped in confusion. At last, one rode forward.

"Who are you, big man, that you ride alone but wave the banner of the king of Wessex?"

"It is the banner of the royal house of Wessex - not the king, but I do not ride alone. My name is Phillip, and I am weapons-master to King Alfred."

The largest young man was naturally bellicose. He wore enormous gold armbands, so Phillip knew immediately that he was either very wealthy, or he had defeated a great warrior in battle and they were spoils of war.

"Even a weapons-master of the king does not have the right to wave that flag, big man."

"Prince Ambrose, brother of the king does, and I serve him, little man! Show him respect, before I am forced to teach you humility."

"Show who respect, simpleton? The only company you have is

your horse!"

Phillip raised his hand, and suddenly a column of armored warriors rode over the crest and into sight. "You are not yet proficient in scouting, little man."

At the sight of Ambrose at the head of the column, *Ealdorman* Ethelnoth broke free from his Personal Guard and spurred forward. He called out joyfully.

"Prince Ambrose! It is a pleasure and honor to see you again. You men! Stand down! You are attempting to pick a fight with two of the greatest warriors in all Wessex!"

Ambrose dismounted when he reached Ethelnoth. He hugged the old man tight.

"Greetings to you, too, you old rascal. It is good to see you looking so well. I see that you are ready for trouble, as ever."

"Prince, when there are several thousand Danes not too far to the west, it is wise to be prepared."

"Aye, Ethelnoth, it was your preparedness some years ago that probably saved the kingdom. You hung a lot of Viking spies in order to keep your king safe."

Ethelnoth smiled. "Do you remember, some were so stupid they could not even converse in Saxon? I did what had to be done to protect my king, and I would do it again a thousand times if it was necessary. But what has brought you so far south and west? The last report I had was that you and Edward were busy looting Benfleet!"

Ambrose grinned. "Which we did, old friend. The fort fell with barely a struggle. Haesten had taken all his warriors on a raid deep into Mercia, and there were few remaining to face us.

I then came south to confer with my brother. Benfleet is a ruin and the Viking fleet was destroyed, but Haesten seems to be receiving considerable reinforcements. Last I heard, he is sitting in Essex with between five and seven thousand Viking warriors."

Ethelnoth looked thoughtful. "That is a lot of men! Do you have any idea what Haesten is planning next?"

"You know that Polonius has hundreds of spies trying to find out, but the short answer is - no."

"So how can I help?"

Ambrose smiled. "I was hoping that you would ask me that very question, my friend. Ethelred has called out his entire summer *fyrd* again to counter the threat, but, alone, he is heavily outnumbered."

"I should say so! Five to seven thousand Vikings is not a raid - it is an invasion!"

"You are right, old friend, and Alfred agrees with you completely. I have come south to find more men so we can face Haesten with some chance of success."

Ethelnoth looked somber. "And how goes the search?"

"Alfred has given me a thousand, and Ethelred has already called up every Mercian he can get his hands on. Two of our Welsh allies are sending warriors, and I am asking that you and Ethelhelm each call up your full summer *fyrd*."

"With all due respect, my prince, that is not a thousand men at your back."

Ambrose smiled. "I suspect you knew to a man how many men approached - probably since this early afternoon, but to answer your unstated question - I have sent nine hundred riders north to London. Ethelred may need them sooner rather than later."

"I hold Somerset for your brother, Prince Ambrose. The couriers will ride forth tomorrow at dawn with the war arrows. It will take some time for all to gather, however. Are you going to wait with me, here?"

"I cannot, old friend. I am on my way next to Ethelhelm, *ealdorman* of Wiltshire, to ask him to do the same."

"Then where do you want my warriors to go?"

"Bring them to London. It is central enough that we can quickly move either south or north of the Thames, depending on what Haesten does. Ethelred is gathering his forces there."

"It will be done, Prince. I and my *fyrd* will ride north as soon as humanly possible."

"Thank you, my friend. I knew I could count on you."

Ambrose, saw the *tun* of Trowbridge ahead. Polonius' spies had reported that Ethelhelm, *ealdorman* of Wiltshire was currently ensconced there with his Personal Guard. The prince had ridden a long way, and he was tired and saddle-sore.

He saw movement on the ramparts, and knew the column had been spotted; not unlikely for a force of more than a hundred riders. Unlike Somerset, however, no *fyrdmen* issued forth. Ambrose did hear horns in the distance, and the gates swung shut.

The prince approached the gates, but they remained stubbornly closed. Phillip rode ahead, holding the banner of the royal house of Wessex. He called out in stentorian tones. "Open in the name of your king, you dolts!"

The face of an old man appeared above the main gate. He was almost bald, and what hair was left was snow white. He wore a rich gown and no armor. Phillip looked up at him.

"*Ealdorman* Ethelhelm, Prince Ambrose wishes to meet with you on a matter of some urgency."

"My eyes are not as good as they once were, or my hearing. Is that Phillip the Weapons-master who is shouting in front of my gate and scaring my people?"

"It is indeed, and you have only seconds before you insult your king's brother with a closed gate."

"Dear me! I suppose I better get someone to open it, then."

Ambrose sat across the trestle table from Ethelhelm, *ealdorman* of Wiltshire. He spoke. "*Ealdorman*, there are over seven thousand enemy warriors sitting in Essex, and the best guess is that they will soon be heading west. My brother's instructions to you are quite clear. I need a full mobilization of your summer *fyrd*, as soon as possible."

"Now Prince Ambrose, I do not think your dear brother quite understands the situation in Wiltshire. Just months ago, we faced Haesten's army, five thousand strong! Many of our small *vills* were burned, women raped or kidnapped, and hundreds of brave young men died in battle. Oh, it was terrible! Where, then, was my king's army?"

"*Ealdorman*, your king's army, led by Edward himself, met this same force that you apparently lived in such terror of, not far north of here, just across the border, in Sussex. You will be happy to know we routed it utterly, forcing Haesten to abandon all his loot and prisoners, and leaving behind thousands of dead. The survivors we chased across the Thames."

"Where your young nephew trapped them and then generously decided to just let them go, Prince. I have the king's reports read to me now, since I can no longer see the words clearly, but I am not so old yet that I cannot follow the war's progress closely. Now this same army is threatening West Saxon territory again, and you expect me to send my finest young warriors to fight hundreds of miles from home."

"Ethelhelm, you have faithfully served - what? - three West Saxon kings in your lifetime?"

"Four, Prince."

"Your record of loyal service is both long and glorious, and Alfred counts on you as one of his best and most faithful leaders. A king cannot focus on a segment of a puzzle, but must see the entire picture. In his wisdom, your king has evaluated the situation, made a decision, and issued a lawful command to you. A command, I might add, you are sworn to obey until death. I suggest that you hurry to obey it!"

"Peace, Prince. Peace! I have no doubt that King Alfred would not have ordered that if only he knew the dire situation here in Somerset."

"*Ealdorman*, each of your *burhs* is manned and ready. If any people were killed on Haesten's last foray through your land, it is either because they refused to obey the instructions to move immediately to the fortified *burhs*, or their *ealdorman* did not pass on the king's commands in time. If I look into the matter and find that you were negligent in passing on the king's commands, you will be lucky to keep your head.

Your people, if a little crowded and not happy, are safe enough in the *burhs*, and the enemy is far away. I will remind you that the entire point of the *burhs* is that it gives your people defensive positions so your *fyrdmen* are freed of the burden of their defense. We can now go after Haesten with an army drawn from several shires. For the first time, we can put together forces large enough to threaten even Viking armies as large as this!"

"Prince, I understand your enthusiasm, but my responsibility is to Wiltshire. We have already suffered greatly, and I simply do not believe Alfred would ask this of me. No, I must say no. I need what *fyrdmen* I have to protect Wiltshire. There are thousands of ravaging Vikings just west of here, you know - in Devonshire."

"Being besieged by Alfred himself, with thousands of *fyrdmen* from other shires!"

Ambrose was furious. Polonius and Alfred had worked together for more than ten years to develop a system that would allow security and protection at home while freeing up thousands of warriors. At last he reached deep into his pouch.

"Ethelhelm, do you recognize this ring?"

The old man stared at it intently. "My eyes are not what they used to be. It looks to be of gold, but beyond that, I cannot identify it."

"Then I will help you, *Ealdorman*. It is King Alfred's signet ring. It has the force of law, and it was given to me by my brother himself."

The old man looked again. "Yes. Yes, it is possible."

"Then, in the name of the king, I am commanding you to call up your entire summer *fyrd*, forthwith! Is that clear enough?"

"Perhaps . . . perhaps I could write to the king and explain our situation."

"*Ealdorman*, you have long been a faithful vassal of the king, but Alfred needs your support now of all times. The king has spoken through this ring, *Ealdorman*. If you find yourself unable to obey this command, tell me now, so I can arrange to have you replaced. You and your family, unfortunately, will be banished forever from Wiltshire, and there will be a new *ealdorman* ruling in your place by tomorrow night."

"Yes, I think I see the likeness to the king's ring now. It seems to be as you say. You must, of course, give me a few weeks to prepare the messages and send out couriers."

"It is now getting late, *Ealdorman*. May I suggest you call together all the literate clerks and priests you have. They will be working through the night. I want those war arrows to be on their way before noon tomorrow."

"Yes. Yes, I suppose that is possible."

"Then send for the scriveners, *Ealdorman*. They have to get to work!"

CHAPTER 21

**"And Haesten's wife and her two sons they
brought to the king, who returned them to him,
because one of them was his godson, and the
other Alderman Ethelred's."
......The Anglo-Saxon Chronicles**

The sleek *long-ship* dropped its huge sail and drifted slowly toward
the dock. Several Danes looked up, but with little curiosity. The
largest Viking army ever to assemble in Britain was slowly forming
nearby, and hundreds of vessels had already arrived, from Ireland
and the Scottish Islands, and from the homeland itself. Word had
gone out, and thousands of Danes had responded to the call.

The *long-ship* did not head in, however, or remove its bold
dragon head from the bow. Instead, an armored officer called out to
the men on the shore.

"Would you send word to *Jarl* Haesten? It is urgent I speak with
him."

A big man, with long braided hair and a two-handed battle axe
slung on his back, looked up from his task. "Perhaps you mistake me
for a humble messenger. Come ashore and find him yourself,
stranger."

Ambrose held up the white-painted shield. "Tell him an
emissary from King Alfred wants to see him - here."

The Danes now stared at the ship and the stranger. He suddenly
had their interest.

The big man, who had spoken before, walked to the end of the
dock. "Are you truly a Saxon?"

"I am a Saxon prince, but it would be simpler if you just told
Haesten that Canuteson the Dane-Slayer is here to see him."

The big man stared some more. "Why, that would make you

Ambrose, Prince of Wessex! Be you really him?"

"In the flesh. My king, however, has sent me on a diplomatic mission to your *Jarl*. Will you send word to him?"

The big man turned and waved imperiously at two of his underlings. "Fetch the *jarl*, and be quick about it!"

Haesten, garbed in Frankish chain-mail armor, strode down the dock. "I recognize you, Canuteson. What in the name of *Odin* are you doing here?"

Ambrose smiled. "I served in the *Great Army* of the Danes. I served in the *Rus* army that conquered much of Asia. I even served in King Guthrum's army for a time. Perhaps I now want to serve in Haesten's Great Army of Conquest."

"How did you get past all my ships?"

Ambrose shrugged. "This is a Danish ship, *Jarl*. I and my crew all speak Danish, and we wore Danish garb. I just changed in your honor. Why would we not make it past your sentry ships?"

"That is not a Saxon ship!"

"I think that is what I just said, *Jarl*. Wessex has recently commissioned almost a hundred fine new vessels. Our biggest problem is not ships - it is lack of crews."

"You stole those ships at Benfleet!"

"We seized them in fair combat, Haesten. They were spoils of war."

"And you burned the rest!"

"It was a grand sight! I prefer, however, to think that we gave your dead warriors the greatest Viking funeral in history. I made sure they had the rites before I ordered the ships lit."

"Canuteson, where are our women and children? We will torture to death a hundred Saxons for every Viking woman or child that has been killed."

"They are alive and well, *Jarl*. That is one of the reasons I am here."

"Where are they, Saxon? If your answer pleases me, you may not have to suffer the *Blood Eagle*."

"Then I am safe, *Jarl*. None have been harmed, yet. In fact, they are presently helping to plant our crops in Wessex."

"Canuteson, if something happens to them . . ."

"Alfred ordered that they be well treated. He has not yet decided what to do with them, but you will be pleased to know that, so far, he has refused all offers from the Arab slavers in London."

Haesten sighed. "Would your king allow ransom?"

Ambrose spoke. "I am almost embarrassed to point out to you that you have very little to offer in trade. Do you know, it took ten ships to haul all your treasure to London?"

Haesten's face went red. "Beware, Canuteson! You play a dangerous game. Your Byzantine friend humiliated me in front of my warriors at Thorney Island, and I know that you and your magician friend were behind my defeat at Farnham.'

He grinned suddenly. 'I also have spies, Canuteson . . . I will recognize your white shield. This visit is stupid, however, even for you. Why are you really here?"

"To let you know that your families are all safe. To count boats."

"A bad answer, Saxon. I hang spies. I think that it was King Alfred who taught me that particular trick."

"I am here as an official emissary, Haesten. And you just said you would recognize the white shield."

"And can I not change my mind?"

"If you are not happy with my presence, why do you not just declare a *holmgang*? **Victory-Maker** here is just as eager as Polonius' sharp blades to taste your flesh."

"And why would I fight you if I can just kill you?"

"I am an adopted son of a Dane, and lived and fought for years as a Viking, Haesten. Your honor requires you to meet me one to one."

"And why should that concern me, Canuteson?"

"I have lost track of the number of Danes I have killed in open combat. Your death would solve a lot of problems for my brother, so I would be pleased to meet you in a duel to the death.

If that is not a satisfactory answer, then just remember the Arab slavers. It is said that they are even more cruel to their slaves than the Danes."

Haesten sighed again. "I ask you again, Saxon - what do you want, other than to bait me?"

"The truth? Alfred, in his infinite Christian mercy, has instructed me to return your little family to your bosom."

"Do not toy with me, Saxon!"

In answer, Ambrose raised his right hand, and immediately two little boys came on deck and yelled to their father. "Daddy! Daddy!"

Ambrose could see tears in the pirate's eyes. The Viking leader called out. "Are you both well?"

The elder of the two replied. "There was a terrible battle, Daddy, but Prince Ambrose rescued us from bad men, and he has brought us back to you!"

Haesten blew his nose on a corner of his cloak and spoke again. "Bless you for this, Canuteson. Can you tell me how my wife is?"

Ambrose smiled. "I can do better than that.' He raised his left hand. 'Why don't you ask her yourself?"

It took Haesten a minute to recover. At last he spoke. "Canuteson, I owe you and your brother a debt that I may never be able to repay."

"We would be friends with the Danes, Haesten. Sitric Ivarsson, king of Dublin, was my good friend and sword companion."

"Canuteson, your brother has powerful enemies, and I am sworn to a course of action. I may regret the swearing, but, whatever you think, I am a man of honor. I cannot break an oath to another Viking, least of all one made in *Odin's* name.

Wait a little while, and I will have a safe conduct put into runes . . . no! Take this ring! In all the land of the Danes, the symbol of Haesten will be recognized and you and your crew will be safe. It is my gift to you, freely given."

Ambrose leaned on the rail while his crew finished lowering the rowboat and loading Haesten's wife and children. "Thank you, Haesten. I am sorry that circumstances do not allow us to be friends. You can tell your warriors that Alfred does not make war on innocent women and children. I think, however, that the rest will not be released until Alfred is assured that you will never come back."

"Go with *Odin's* blessings, Canuteson. It is said about you that you have balls of brass. I now believe it! I think I will have my *skald* compose a new ballad about you."

CHAPTER 22

"Whilst he (Alfred) was thus busied there with the army, in the west, the marauding parties were both gathered together at Shobury in Essex, and there built a fortress. Then they both went together up by the Thames, and a great concourse joined them, both from the East-Angles and from the Northumbrians. They then advanced upward by the Thames, till they arrived near the Severn. Then they proceeded upward by the Severn."
......The Anglo-Saxon Chronicles

The rider staggered up the stairs to Ethelred's office in the old Roman fort. He stood gasping

"Ealdorman, the Danes are moving west!"

His *ealdorman,* Polonius, Phillip and Ambrose all turned, and Ethelred spoke. "How many, courier?"

"Thousands and thousands, *Ealdorman*! There were so many that the patrol just broke and ran!"

"Very well. Tell the commander at the barracks that I said you could have a hot meal and a bed. Stay there until I send for you."

"Yes, *Ealdorman.* Thank you!"

After the messenger had departed, Ethelred spoke in anger. "By the cloak of St. Peter! Another *seven-night* or two, and we would have been ready."

Ambrose looked puzzled. "Ready for what, Ethelred?"

"Right now, with the king's *fyrdmen*, my own, the garrison and my Personal Guard, we have more than enough warriors to hold the city of London, but we are likely outnumbered two to one. We do not yet have enough men to face Haesten in open battle!"

Ambrose spoke. "Then you propose we just man the walls and

let the Viking army pass?"

Ethelred spread his hands expressively. "Much as I want to crush them, I see no alternative. To have the entire Mercian *fyrd* slaughtered to a man is not likely to help our cause in any way. In a *seven-night* or two, when Ethelnoth and Ethelhelm arrive with their *fyrds*, and our Welsh allies arrive, then we can start after them."

"It will likely be a long chase, *Ealdorman*."

"I know, Prince. Meanwhile, Wiltshire, Berkshire and Mercia will likely feel the crunch of Haesten's boots before we can catch up."

"My friend, we will follow this army and we will crush it. You have the full resources of Wessex behind you!"

Ethelred sighed. "I know, Prince. I just wonder how many men will be butchered and women and girls raped before we catch this monster."

"As Polonius over there so often likes to say - wars are to be won. We will win this one . . . Did I get that quote right, Scholar?"

Polonius smiled. "Close enough, Prince Ambrose. Close enough."

ß

Ambrose swung into his saddle, and the pursuit was on. At his side rode Polonius and the ever-present Phillip, two Welsh chieftains, and the *ealdormen* of Somerset, Wiltshire and Mercia. Behind the various commanders and their officers rode thousands of Angles, Saxons, *Jutes,* and not a few Welshmen. The army of the West Saxons, along with their allies, was finally on the move. Somewhere ahead, there were dead bodies and a pall of smoke hanging over the churches and farms that had been burnt. Somewhere ahead there were well over five thousand Viking warriors, and their goal was nothing less than the conquest of the last Saxon kingdom on the island of Britain.

ß

After a week of riding, the Saxon Army was approaching

Wales, but still had not caught up to the fast-moving Danes. Countless homesteads and churches had been burned, but the major *burhs* had been by-passed. Either Haesten knew he was being chased, or he was simply too cautious to take the time to capture the well-garrisoned *burhs*. He was going somewhere in a hurry, but Ambrose was unable to predict the target.

At last, as they approached Buttington in Gloucestershire, Ethelred's scouts returned, excited. Ethelred held out his hand to stop the galloping riders. "Whoa! What have you seen that you are willing to kill your horses?"

The commander of the little troupe spoke. "Sorry, *Ealdorman*! We looped around through the countryside ahead, and we approached Buttington from the west."

"And?"

"And the Danes have fortified it, *Ealdorman*! They have stopped running."

Ambrose looked at Polonius. "Buttington?"

The Byzantine replied. "Why not? If Sigefrith managed to break free, he would be able to head right up the old Roman Road - Fosse Way, and then follow Watling Street. The *Norse* holdings are not far to the north, in case they wanted to get involved in this invasion. Haesten's sole Welsh ally is just to the west, and Northumbria could easily send down more warriors from the north."

"Polonius, they are not going to defeat us by hiding in a town in the north of Mercia!"

"Prince, our army has kept them on the move, and the *burhs* have been very effective in denying them loot and provisions. King Alfred's army has kept Sigefrith's forces from coming north. This may not be what they had in mind, at all."

"And now, Scholar?"

"They come out and fight, or we besiege them. We should have enough men to meet them in the open, and God will decide the victor. I don't see any other choices. Eventually, if they don't want to face us in the open, they will starve and will be forced to surrender."

The long glittering column of mounted and armored men moved ponderously along the old Roman road and gradually approached the *tun* of Buttington. The Danes, in the short time they had been there, had been busy. A ditch had recently been dug all the way around the *tun*, and the earth ramparts were both steep and high. Formidable as they were, they had been surmounted with a stout palisade of logs that gave the defenders good protection from missiles.

The West Saxon army flowed into a broad formation, and soon the shield-wall formed across the road and through the fields on either side. The shield-wall extended right to the forest flanking the fields. The Saxons beat their shields with swords and axes, but no challengers ventured out of the fortified *tun*.

Ambrose sat on his horse near Ethelred. They watched their warriors form up with a warm pride. It was truly an impressive sight to see the big *fyrdmen* move with such precision.

"Well, my friends, I suspect that they are not going to take the bait."

Ethelred nodded. "Are you surprised, Prince?"

"Truthfully - yes."

Ethelred looked puzzled. "They have the advantage of the walls. Using Polonius' formula of ten to one, they are quite safe inside the walls. We do not have the men to overwhelm the *tun*."

"True *Ealdorman*, but in my mind there are two times to fight."

"Which are, Prince?"

"Right now, since we have no defenses built, our men are tired from the long ride, and we have no marching fort to retreat to. We are at the most vulnerable that we ever going to be."

The *Ealdorman* nodded. "And the second time?"

Ambrose replied. "When our besieging ramparts are complete, we are rested, they are starving and cannot hold out any longer. Which would you pick?"

"When you put it that way, I will loosen my sword in its scabbard . . . unless, of course, they have a trick up their sleeve."

"Such as?"

"An army marching to join them?" replied Ethelred

"Well, Alfred is doing his best to make sure that any relieving force will not be led by Sigefrith. The only other possibilities are a Welsh force, a *Norse* army from their holdings on the west coast, or another Northumbrian land army."

"The Northumbrians have the manpower to throw one or even two large armies into the fray."

Ambrose smiled. "They also have a lot of Scots and Picts crossing their borders and raiding, brother-in-law, and even a few Welshmen who somehow managed to sneak across Mercia."

Whatever Haesten's thinking, no Vikings came out of the *tun*. Ambrose watched as Polonius and Phillip supervised the construction of siege ramparts all the way around the *tun*. The reserve units, who had carefully stayed out of sight until it was clear that the Danes were not fighting that day, exited from the forest and started on the Roman marching fort.

The Saxon army had the rudiments of their fortifications completed by sunset, so the army had a secure position they could retire to. During the night the Danes filled in much of the ditch that the Saxons had so laboriously dug that day, but the dirt was quickly removed in the early morning light. By the end of the second day, it was clear that the Danes had lost their chance for easy egress.

Polonius approached Ambrose as the prince sipped a cup of the Byzantine's strange and exotic drink that Hakim had told them were the favored food of a herd of goats somewhere in eastern Africa. "Come, my master. I would like you to take a little walk with me."

"May I bring my coffee?"

"Of course! I would hate for you to waste something so rare and precious. We have only a few beans left."

Ambrose took a sip as he walked. "I can feel new energy coursing through my veins. This is truly a great drink, Polonius . . . Where exactly are we going?"

"Not far, Prince. In fact, we are there now."

Ambrose looked around curiously. "It is a nice view of Buttington, my friend, but quite similar to the spot we just left."

"I fear I am an abject failure as a teacher, Prince."

"And I feel a failure as a student, because, even after all these years, I still don't know what you are talking about! I feel I have failed a test that I did not even know I was taking. You will have to humor me, Scholar, and give a poor dense Saxon the merest hint."

"Use your nose, Saxon prince."

Ambrose sniffed the air with deep breaths. "Ah, I think I have it! You smelled the cooking meat of your supper and decided to share the aroma with me. It is very generous of you to share it with me, but, being a poor benighted Saxon, I fail to understand the novelty of it."

"Which way is the wind blowing, benighted Saxon prince?"

"Why, from west to east."

"And are we upwind or downwind from our campfires?"

The prince wet his finger in his mouth and then held it up to the wind. "Hmm. A difficult question. I am going to go with upwind."

"So the odor of our cooking food is blowing away from our location, yet you are smelling it still? Does this not strike you as odd, Prince-of-the-Saxons?"

"Perhaps a trick of the wind . . . or the odor of cooking meat is coming from the *tun* of Buttington?"

"There is hope for you yet, Prince! And what are the implications of the Vikings suddenly roasting a lot of meat?"

Ambrose smiled. "A light begins to glimmer in my head, oh great teacher! Perhaps you are telling me, in your convoluted manner, that the Danes are hungry and also decided to cook supper."

"Why, Prince? They have no cattle of pigs left. All they have is a horse herd."

"If that is the case, rather more Vikings are going to have to learn to walk. The amount of smoke indicates that they are cooking a good number of carcasses."

"Well done, Prince! And why would they suddenly decide to cook many of their animals?"

"Hunger, my friend. It makes you do funny things."

"Or you prepare a big meal to give your hungry men strength, and perhaps prepare food for travel."

". . . which you would only do if you were planning an escape!"

"Bravo, Prince! Now we listen for revelry."

"What are you thinking, Polonius?"

"Do you remember the *Rus* berserkers, Ambrose?"

"I remember them drinking magic potions and dancing

themselves into a trance before they pledged themselves to *Odin*, stripped bare and charged."

"I hear drums and chanting, Prince."

"Polonius, you are truly a genius! You lead me to understanding even when I resist all the way!"

"And so, Prince?"

"And so, my Byzantine friend, I think that we are going to issue all the *pilums* and quivers we have in stock, and instruct the *fyrdmen* to sleep in their armor, on the ramparts.

Let's do it quietly. It would not do to let the Danes know that we are aware of their plans."

Polonius smiled. "I think that is an excellent plan, master-of-mine!"

⚑

Ambrose spoke with the *ealdormen* and chieftains, and they quietly strode off to talk with their officers. The normal fires were lit, but, right after dark, the Saxons and Welsh gradually abandoned them and quietly took up their combat positions all along the Siege ramparts.

Ambrose, lying between Phillip and Polonius, finally fell asleep. The night sentries reported nothing amiss. As the sky began to color in the east, a portion of the Danish wall collapsed into the ditch, almost filling it. Immediately, a wide column of screaming warriors charged through the gap, across the ditch and open strip of land, leapt into the Saxon ditch and started to clamber up the steep embankment. The Saxons woke almost instantly. The *fyrdmen* scrambled to the ramparts and started to harvest the Danes with spears, arrows and even rocks.

The Danes had expected to catch the Saxons and their allies by surprise, and they suffered terribly under the onslaught of missiles. The ditch and mound had been liberally sprinkled with *caltrops* and sharpened stakes, making it difficult to move quickly, but the grim Vikings just accepted their losses and kept coming. Ethelred's entire force had been held in reserve and they galloped their horses toward the area of the breakthrough.

The Viking column reached, and then overwhelmed the Saxon defense. The Saxons on both sides backed from the wall and tried to form a shield-wall, but the column of heavily armed Viking warriors separated and let *Odin's* sworn men through. Naked, the berserkers madly charged the rapidly forming Saxon line. At first the *fyrdmen* stood, but even after spears and arrows hit the crazy men, they just kept coming. At last, screaming in terror, the Saxon line broke. The *fyrdmen* ran for their lives. At their heels were thousands of grimly determined Vikings.

Ethelred and his mounted *fyrdmen* finally arrived, but it was too late. While the berserkers had finally been cut down, they had broken the Saxon shield-wall and the main column surged through. Haesten's Vikings, trapped for so long, were free again.

Ambrose and Polonius surveyed the battleground in the strong light of late morning. Polonius' warning had helped the Saxons strike hard at Haesten's forces. Well over a thousand had succumbed to the arrows, spears and swords of the Saxon *fyrd*, but the daring Vikings had fought savagely, and several hundred *fyrdmen* had been killed or wounded so badly that they had to be carried off the battlefield.

Ambrose watched idly as the last of the Viking bodies were looted, and the wounded dispatched with a quick slash to the throat. Ethelred and Ethelnoth had already ridden ahead with their mounted *fyrdmen*, and the prince knew that they intended to hunt down the Danish stragglers mercilessly. The Welshmen and Ethel helm's *fyrdmen* would follow in the morning, along with the men Alfred had entrusted to him. He sighed. He would leave several hundred of the lightly wounded to deal with the sick and seriously wounded, and ensure that the Saxons had a haven if something should go wrong.

He had already examined the Viking horse herd, but they were in pitiful condition. Without adequate fodder for several weeks, they were just skin and bone and of little value until they were allowed to graze for a few months.

⚑

At daybreak the following morning, the remainder of the Saxon army rode east after Haesten's Vikings. The rain had started at midnight, and continued sullenly into the day.

Ambrose had some scouts at his side, but it was quickly apparent that they would not be needed. The trail left by thousands of fleeing Vikings was abundantly clear, as were the tracks of thousands of riders who were in pursuit. Occasionally a body of a dead Viking could be seen lying in the mud, but Ambrose could never be sure if the man had succumbed to a battle wound taken during the escape, or if Ethelred's force had caught and killed him.

⚑

Having left the lame and the wounded behind, Ambrose was able to push his force hard, and within three days they had caught up with Ethelred's army.

Ethelred saw him coming, and trotted back to meet with the prince.

The *Ealdorman* smiled. "Greetings, cousin. How bad were our casualties?"

Ambrose became serious. "We had several hundred dead or seriously wounded. I left them with our lightly wounded and lame to take care of the sick, and bury the dead. They will hold the camp until we send them a courier with contrary instructions. How goes your hunt?"

"Frustrating, Prince. We have killed several hundred, but they are canny fighters. As soon as we appear, they make for the deepest forest they can find, or, if there are enough of them, they gather in their *skjaldborg* until we give up. We have long ago used up most of our arrows and spears, so there is little we can do when they are in formation, unless we are willing to take equal casualties."

"Ethelred, do you have any idea where they are heading?"

"No idea, Prince. We even caught a few alive and asked them."

"And?"

"They just smiled and dared us to do our worst. Even the heated irons wouldn't make them talk. They were brave men."

"You are right, *Ealdorman*. I watched the *Rus* conquer an entire river system in a matter of a few years. Hundreds of thousands of Slavs swore allegiance to thousands of Vikings. I hated the brutal savagery of the Vikings, but I greatly respected their code of honor and their bravery. They have many admirable qualities. Alfred wants to convert them to Christianity and use them as a buffer against their own kind. Perhaps it will really work."

Ethelred smiled. "Let the barbarians fight the barbarians."

"Let the Christian barbarians fight the pagan barbarians. And why not? The Eastern Romans hire thousands of barbarian riders every year, which they use against the Muslims or other barbarians.

In fact, I will have you know that I personally brokered a treaty with the emperor of Byzantium himself, that allowed him to hire the young *Rus* warriors who were looking for a little adventure."

"And did it work out?"

Ambrose replied. "Well, I had to leave in a big hurry when the Grand Chamberlain, about to be made co-emperor, decided we knew too much and decided to teach us how to swim while wearing chains, but, yes, I think it will work. The emperors always need brave soldiers, and, as you said, there are few braver than the Vikings."

Ambrose thought a bit. "What do think they are up to?"

"I suspect that they are taking the most direct route they can into Danish Mercia."

"In the hope that we will not cross the border after them."

Ambrose looked somber. "No, you are right. I think that we will stop at the border. In the meantime, however, I want to kill as many Vikings as we can catch. Death seems to be one of the few things they understand. And you know as well as I do, any Viking not killed will eventually return to haunt us."

CHAPTER 23

"As soon as they came into Essex to their fortress, and to their ships, then gathered the remnant again in East-Anglia and from the Northumbrians a great force before winter, and having committed their wives and their ships and their booty to the East-Angles, they marched on the stretch by day and night, till they arrived at a western city in Wirheal that is called Chester." ......The Anglo-Saxon Chronicles

Yet again the signal fires across Wessex were lit. Yet again a Viking army crossed from East Anglia into tired, broken, Mercia.

Ethelred sent the war arrow after the tired men he had just sent home to reap their crops. Across Wessex, *fyrdmen* were called again to service. Thousands of hostile Vikings had once again invaded.

Ambrose rode to meet Ethelred at London. The prince and his West Saxons clattered into the old Roman fort. Ethelred, hearing the commotion, went down to see who had arrived. He grinned when he saw Ambrose.

"Welcome, Prince. At least my backside has had a chance to heal."

"I wish I could say the same. I had just reached Alfred's camp in Somerset when your message arrived.

"And how is King Alfred doing with Sigefrith?"

"As well as can be expected. He finally starved him out their fort near Exeter, but the Vikings, as predicted, just took to their ships."

"Then the king's army is on its way back?"

"I wish I could say yes. The pirates left their fort, but they may have not gone far. The army has just marched to the northern Devon, to chase away the other half of the force, but Alfred will not bring the *fyrd* back to London until he is sure there is little chance of a third landing."

"You mean like in Mercia?"

"My friend, we will hunt down this army just as ruthlessly as we did the other two, and Alfred's treasury is open to ensure that your people do not starve this winter. Buy what food your people need, and the king will pay for it."

"Thank you, Prince Ambrose, for that. I will put my stewards to work buying food supplies, immediately."

"What is the word on Haesten, Ethelred?"

"They crossed into Mercia well to the north. The last report I had was that they were riding north along the Watling Road."

"Watling Road? I wonder where Haesten is off to this time?"

"We have chased him across that border two times so far and their running allowed us to inflict serious casualties at little cost to our *fyrdmen*. Maybe this time Haesten intends to stay close to the border."

Ambrose spoke. "I have brought you two thousand *fyrdmen*, Ethelred. When do we ride?"

Ethelred responded. "I have already sent for my sworn men, Prince, but they had just returned home. I have therefore called up my winter *fyrd*. I do not want the *fyrdmen* to ride all the way north just to tell me that their time is up and they are going home."

"So how long?"

"Too long, my friend. Let us go north with what we have, and my *fyrdmen* can join us on the way."

"My men are ready when you are, *Ealdorman*."

ᚦ

The *Angelisc* army rode steadily north and west. As they advanced, contingents of Ethelred's winter army joined them. Once again churches, farmsteads and *tuns* were savagely razed, but there were few corpses.

Ambrose mentioned it to Ethelred, who replied. "Prince, I sent firm instructions for a full evacuation to the fortified *burhs*. When

I have a chance, I will strengthen the system. My beloved wife has been after me to do it for several years, but I am now convinced. We can't stop the Danes from burning and looting, but they seem either unwilling or unable to take the large centers, so the livestock and people, at least, are safe."

CHAPTER 24

"Soon after that, in this year, went the army from Wirheal into North-Wales; for they could not remain there, because they were stripped both of the cattle and the corn that they had acquired by plunder."
......The Anglo-Saxon Chronicles

Polonius thrust the curtain of the command tent aside and entered. Both Ambrose and Ethelred looked up. The prince smiled. "And what did your spies report, Scholar?"

"They are having a hard time catching up to me! My favorite *jarl* sent me a message, however. Haesten has taken the old city of Chester, and they intend to hold it."

Ambrose nodded. "Good! They cannot rape and pillage if they stay in one place. We can finally catch up and besiege them."

Ethelred spoke. "I am puzzled. What is Haesten trying to do? His only chance to defeat us is to meet our armies and defeat them. Holing up in northern *tuns* only helps us!"

Ambrose turned to Polonius. "Scholar?"

"I am just as puzzled, Prince. This is his third or fourth attempt to reach northwestern Mercia. I can only assume he hoped that there would be a general rising of the East Anglians and Northumbrians to his banner . . . and I suspect that Sigefrith was actually supposed to meet him somewhere around here. Whatever his thinking, I agree - it is to our advantage - Though there is one difference between Buttingham and Chester."

"And what is that, my Byzantine friend?"

The scholar replied. "The Dee estuary. It will be very difficult to stop a fleet from sailing right up to his back door."

Ambrose smiled at his friend. "Now that's a cheery thought!

Well, at least Sigefrith's plans have been thoroughly foiled."

ᚨ

Once again the Saxons deployed in front of the city that the Danes had seized. Once more Haesten refused to come out and meet the Saxons and Welsh in open combat. An army of slaves and *churls*, protected by a shield-wall of *thanes*, ran forward and went to work. Within a few hours, the beginnings of a ditch and ramparts had formed around the old Roman walls of the city. Within a week, they had all joined and the ramparts were high enough that the Vikings were effectively sealed in.

Ambrose, Ethelred, and the rest of the force settled in for a long siege. Polonius managed to find enough iron that he had the carpenters and blacksmiths make a pair of his favorite type of catapults. Soon he and his little team were heaving rocks and flaming debris into the old Roman city. It did little practical good against the ancient stone buildings, but it entertained the *fyrdmen* and annoyed the Vikings no end.

By the end of the month, Ethelred approached the prince. "Do you not think it is time we launched an assault on the *tun*?"

"Polonius will tell you that you need ten attackers for every defender if you want any chance of success with an assault, and even those numbers guarantee nothing."

"I take that as a vote for no attack."

"Ethelred, I would like nothing better than the chance to kill these heathens. They have butchered, raped, and pillaged our lands for over a generation now. I want it to end!"

"Then you are in favor of an attack?"

"Ethelred, right now we hold a slim advantage in numbers. It is certainly not ten to one! If we make an assault and are repulsed with serious losses - which is actually very likely - the advantage will shift to them. On the other hand, if we do nothing, Alfred will eventually show up with his army, giving us a huge advantage in numbers, and in the meantime the Danes will start to get a lot hungrier. Equally important, whatever Haesten marched all this way to do - he can't do it locked inside Chester."

"You make a good case, Prince. I guess I just want to defeat these devils and go home."

Ambrose smiled. "Patience, my friend. We have frustrated Haesten's plans four times so far - and we will do it again!"

Phillip shook Ambrose and Polonius awake. "Grab your weapons! We are under attack!"

The prince put on his armor and stepped outside his tent while he strapped on **Victory-Maker**. There was great confusion. Fire arrows arced into the marching fort, and one catapult was in flames. The prince could hear Phillip bellowing for everyone to man their battle station.

Just as the men prepared for battle against an unknown force which seemed to have come from the north, Chester's city gates opened and thousands of Vikings charged out. They jumped into the Saxon ditch and clambered up the steep ramparts, but the Saxon night sentries had retreated to the marching fort when it seemed they were under attack from without. There were thus few to oppose the Viking charge.

The Danes took casualties, but the Vikings paid the price and were soon free. Without horses, they ran west.

Ambrose looked at Ethelred, Phillip and Polonius. All of the officers stared at the floor. At last the prince spoke.

"What happened last night? Does anyone know yet?"

Polonius spoke. "It now seems quite clear, Prince. A small force of Vikings, probably from Northumbria, made a diversionary attack on our fort. The guards on the ramparts responded by returning to defend the fort . . ."

". . . Leaving few to stop the Danes from escaping."

"We hurt them, but most managed to escape."

Ambrose sighed. This is not all bad."

Phillip rumbled. "How so, Prince?"

"They are without horses, they are not in any formation, and they are running for their lives. A scattered army is just many running individuals. As such, they die as individuals. The strength of the Vikings is in their *skjaldborg*, which we saw stop horsemen cold on the steppes of Asia. Our job, then, is to keep after them so they cannot re-form. Their panic must be sustained while we kill as many individuals as we can. It seems that only death will stop these stubborn men!

Then at dawn let's ride after them! They are on foot, so we should be able to catch up easily enough. We have the numbers and the horses. Let's go hunting!"

The Saxon riders caught up with and killed hundreds of Vikings. The open country made it hard for the Danes to hide from the pursuing riders. On the third day, however, the galloping horsemen reached the boundary to Gwynedd, Northumbria's Welsh ally.

Ethelred reined in his advance force and waited for Ambrose to catch up. Ambrose rode over when he saw the *ealdorman* and his troops waiting for him.

"Greetings, *Ealdorman*. Something worries you?"

"Prince, across that line lies the territory of Anarawd of Gwynedd. I would happily cross it and keep going, but I am probably embroiling Wessex in another war if I do. What do we do?"

Ambrose smiled. "It wouldn't be the first time Mercians have raided it, and Anarawd has been systematically harassing our Welsh allies, probably in an attempt to force them to keep their fighting men at home, so I would not worry that we are adding a new enemy to the list. Polonius, what do you think?"

Polonius responded. "Prince, Haesten has avoided the lands of our allies. Winter is coming soon, and it looks like Haesten and his men are going to demand the hospitality of Anarawd of Gwynedd for the winter. We do not have the supplies to wage a protracted war in actively hostile territory. I would therefore propose we withdraw to Chester or one of the other north Mercian *tuns*, settle in for the winter, and see what transpires come spring."

"What are you thinking, Scholar?"

Polonius grinned. "Let Anarawd feed the Viking army for the winter. Let us ask our Welsh allies to line the frontiers with their men who are home for the winter. We will see if Anarawd and the Danes are still friends come spring."

Ambrose laughed. "Maybe four thousand mouths to feed. That should encourage harmony between allies. Ethelred, we will be eating your food. Do you agree?"

Ethelred nodded. "I would like to send home the *fyrdmen* whose time is up in a few months anyway, but yes, I think we must have a strong force stationed nearby, and it should be reinforced in the spring. Perhaps we should also consider lending our Welsh allies some men to reinforce any border strongholds."

CHAPTER 25

"When they went again out of North-Wales with the booty they had acquired there, they marched over Northumberland and East-Anglia, so that the king's army could not reach them till they came into Essex"
......The Anglo-Saxon Chronicles

The Welsh scouts arrived just at Vespers. The ragged commander of the little force looked around helplessly, clearly not finding anyone he knew. Ambrose went over to talk with him, and spoke to him in Gaelic.

"Welcome. It is clear that you have had a hard journey. Do you have something to report?"

"Aye, Master, but I do not know who I should talk with. Sir, I can understand your Gaelic well enough, but you have a strange accent."

"I am not surprised you think so. I actually learned to speak Gaelic in Ireland."

"Ireland? That is hardly a safe place for a Saxon."

"On my mother's side of the family we are related to the ancient royal house of the Durotriges, My family ruled before the Romans came to conquer, so the Irish chose not to treat me as a hated Saxon. In fact, the Irish were very kind to me, and we fought together against the *Dubh-galls*."

"Aye? A Saxon who fought against the Irish Vikings . . . Then you can only be Prince Ambrose of Wessex. Even the Celts on this side of the water talk about your exploits there! Did you truly free dozens of Irish princesses?"

"There were dozens, but not all were Irish. Some were Welsh, and several were Angle or Saxon . . . How can I help you?"

"I have an important message, but these are not my people and I do not know who to report to."

"If you tell me the message, I promise to introduce you to the appropriate commander."

"Thank you, Prince. I am not really comfortable on this side of Offa's Dyke."

"Your king has acknowledged King Alfred as *Bretwalda*. That makes us good allies. You have nothing to fear here, my friend. What is the report?"

"Prince, thousands of Vikings are crossing Offa's Dyke even as we speak."

"Hold your words for a moment, messenger. Ethelred! Polonius!"

As the two men rushed to Ambrose's side, he turned back to the scout. "Continue, messenger. Polonius here speaks Gaelic like a native, and I will translate for the *ealdorman*."

"Aye, Prince. As I was saying, thousands of *Dubh-galls* are even now clambering over Offa's Dyke."

When Ambrose translated, Ethelred looked thoroughly alarmed. "I had better put the guards on alert, and I have to call up a lot of *fyrdmen*, immediately!"

"Hold for one minute, Ethelred. First we need to know what they are up to.' He turned back to the messenger.

'Do you know where they are going, or what they intend to do?"

"No, Prince, but I was told to be sure to tell you that they are not marching as an army."

"No? How are they marching?"

"They travel in small groups, Prince, and they are crossing the dyke at many different places, some far apart."

"Polonius?"

"They are either going to rendezvous and hoped to get there unnoticed by traveling in small groups, or they are fleeing back to Northumbria and want to avoid contact with us."

Ambrose nodded. "The former would be a cause for concern. Well, whatever they are up to, we should chivy them along with horsemen. The fear of a lance in the back might encourage them along and keep them from re-forming. Ethelred, how many horsemen can we scrounge up at short notice?"

One or two thousand - if you give me a few days. You have a thousand of Alfred's mounted *fyrdmen* within a few hours ride, many of whom have trained with Polonius' *pig- stickers*."

"Polonius?"

"They can ride with the dawn, Prince. They are bored from a long winter and are restless."

"Even when Ethelred's *fyrdmen* catch up, we will still be outnumbered."

Polonius spoke. "Most of Haesten's Vikings will be on foot, and the very act of splitting up their forces works to our advantage."

Ethelred looked puzzled. "How so, Polonius?"

"They only outnumber us if they rendezvous somewhere and again form a single army. As long as they stay in small groups, we will outnumber them."

"And if they re-form?"

Polonius smiled. "Our men will be mounted, and the Vikings are not. Our men will attack or evade, depending on the circumstances."

⊱

The war arrow was again sent to every *fyrd* commander in northern Mercia. Each *burh* sent out scouts, and thousands of *fyrdmen* rode to their own rendezvous. Slowly, Ethelred's mounted army re-assembled.

The Danes were quick, however. Unencumbered with much in the way of loot or prisoners, they jogged north and eastward, steadily heading for Northumbrian territory and safety.

Hundreds of Vikings were spotted by the Saxon horsemen, and died. Several thousand more, however, avoided the many patrols, and safely crossed the border into Viking lands. Haesten's army was badly mauled, but not broken.

CHAPTER 26

Winchester

Ambrose, Polonius and Phillip rode into the bustling *burh* of Winchester on a glorious June day. Behind them rode the last remnants of the Saxon *fyrdmen* who had been sent the previous fall by Alfred to join Ambrose in northern Mercia.

As soon as the remaining *fyrdmen* were settled in, Ambrose headed for Alfred's Great Hall. There, his brother met him at the main door.

Alfred smiled. "Come, brother, give a king a hug!"

As they embraced, Alfred spoke quietly in his ear. "It is good to have you back, brother!"

Ambrose looked happy. "It is good to be back.' He ruefully rubbed his backside. 'I only hope that I will not be riding anywhere for at least a few days!"

"Come, rest your bottom on a cushioned chair, and let us compare notes."

Ambrose sat down, and Alfred's servants brought horns of mead.

Alfred smiled. "I thought that you might be a little dry after your epic ride. Drink, brother!"

At last Ambrose finished the horn and got down to business. "What has transpired in my absence, Alfred?"

"Both the Northumbrians and East Anglians have finally abandoned Devonshire."

"Thank the Lord! I cannot believe they were so tenacious."

"Nor I. I can only assume that it was part of a massive conspiracy that went wrong. One of the fleets, however, put in to Sussex and the Danes reverted to their old ways."

"Oh? What happened?"

The king grinned. "Our faithful *thanes* gathered every man who could hold a stick, met them in open battle and trounced them! Then they managed to seize several of the pirate vessels before they could escape."

"Your fleet continues to expand! That is excellent news. And have we heard of Haesten?"

Alfred looked instantly more somber. "In spite of the best efforts of you and Ethelred, the majority of his army made it safely to Northumbria, and from there to East Anglia. His army has now settled on the island of Mersea, in Essex."

"Damn! His luck continues to hold!"

Alfred smiled. "You are too hard on yourself, brother! You harried him all the time he was in Wessex. He took almost no *tuns*, and he did not win a single battle against us, in spite of the fact that he led the largest Viking army we have ever faced."

"He slipped through my fingers - twice, after we thought we had him securely trapped."

"And in the process lost so many warriors that his army was crippled and had to run. He kept recruiting more, and you kept killing them. Polonius' friend, *Sun Tzu*, said something about the best strategy being to attack the enemy's strategy. Four separate armies invaded us, one several times, and to the best of my knowledge, not one managed to meet their objectives. I consider that a momentous victory, big brother! Oh, and another piece of news that will entertain you."

"What is that?"

"As you know, Polonius wrote me a complete report about how you decided to avoid invading Gwynedd and let Haesten and his army descend on Anarawd's kingdom for the winter. Well, Anarawd has written me. He was so unhappy with Haesten's continued pillaging of his territory last winter that he has renounced his treaty with Northumbria and begs to be allowed to join us as allies."

Ambrose laughed. "Polonius called it, and this time you didn't even have to let Ethelred's young wolves loose amongst them."

"No. Anarawd of Gwynedd learned the hard way what the Vikings are really like. When Haesten's men met the Welsh warriors you arranged to have stationed along the borders, they turned back and ravaged the lands of their faithful ally!"

Ambrose replied. "There is a twinkle in your eye. What exactly did you tell Anarawd?"

Alfred smiled. "He is going to lend us six hundred good archers for the duration of our struggle, and I will eventually have the honor of being his godfather. Once he has met these conditions, I will allow him to call me *Bretwalda*."

CHAPTER 27

"Then, in the same year, before winter, the Danes, who abode in Mersey, towed their ships up on the Thames, and thence up the Lea."
......The Anglo-Saxon Chronicles

The lean ships slid silently from the fog and neared the shore. Without a word being spoken, the sailors lowered the ship square sails and took up their oars. One by one the ships turned north, left the Thames and started up the Lea River.

Alfred's main fleet was split between London and Rochester, and so no Saxon ships came out to meet the Viking vessels. The Danes traveled upriver, until the fleet commander saw what he wanted. It was only a small settlement, on the Mercian side of the river, but its site was eminently defensible.

The Viking fleet headed for the shore, and more than two thousand warriors swarmed ashore. The Saxon villagers, when they saw the dreaded shape of *long-ships* appear on the river, screamed, prayed, and ran for the woods. To a Saxon, there were few worse things than to be captured by Vikings!

The Vikings were efficient, and all too aware that London, with its strong garrison, was only some twenty miles away. Using what few prisoners they caught, and their own sweat, they worked feverishly to fortify the site. Within two days, the *tun* had become a fort. A ditch, solid ramparts, and a palisade on top now greeted any new arrival. The Danes sent out foraging parties in all directions. They knew that the Saxon *fyrd*, though a slow and ponderous beast, would eventually respond to their presence, and it was vital to have sufficient food stored before the *Angelisc fyrdmen* arrived to besiege them."

🏳

The courier was gasping for breath, and his mount was in worse shape. He finally just handed the message to the guard at the city fortress, and collapsed. The burly man who now held the message was clear on his task. He ran to wake the Byzantine scholar who King Alfred had appointed as spy-master.

He pounded on the door leading to Polonius' quarters, and a beautiful older woman answered, wrapped only in a woolen robe. The man stammered. "Sorry, Lady Kuralla! It is urgent - for Lord Polonius! His standing orders are to bring anything to him immediately!"

"Thank you, sentry. You are quite right. I will wake him right away."

Polonius smiled at his wife as she returned to their bed chamber. "Have you come back to our bed because you are feeling wild and exotic desires that only I can fulfill?"

She smiled. "I have just been dragged from my bed, my love. My greatest desire for the moment is for my chamber pot."

"Then perhaps I should just slumber until you are ready to molest me again."

"If only, my beloved husband! Unfortunately, duty calls. This message just arrived."

Polonius reached out, took the folded and wax-sealed letter, and broke the seal. As he read, he became more excited. "May God have mercy on us!"

Kuralla looked up, startled. "What is it, love-of-mine?"

"Whatever it is, it does not make me happy. There is a newly built Viking fort on the Lea River, barely twenty miles from here! I had better get dressed and see the king!"

🏳

Alfred stared at his little group of advisors. Phillip, Polonius, Ambrose and Ethelred stared back. At last the king spoke.

"What can it mean? A Viking fort within a hard day's ride from London is a cause for serious concern!"

Ambrose spoke. "I am not sure it matters, brother."

"How can it not matter?"

"Whether it is a base for invasion or just an obscure outpost, our response is the same."

"It is?"

Ambrose smiled. "Of course. We move against it, isolate it, and besiege it, whether it is in East Anglian territory or ours. If Eohric doesn't like it - too bad! We have already had to hang his six hostages because of his treachery."

Alfred nodded his head. "Simple. Direct. Let's call up the men and do it!"

Polonius spoke. "Hold, good king. There is another report that came bundled with this one."

"Well, Spy-master? By the beard of St. Peter, don't keep me in suspense."

"The governor of London, in Ethelred's absence, raised a force of militia and sent them northward."

"And why does this concern you, Polonius?"

"Two words. 'Commanders. Numbers.' To put it bluntly, the joint commanders are not known for their intellectual prowess."

Alfred nodded. "Joint is the first problem. Too many commanders just sow confusion . . . You said numbers?"

"Even if they pick up some *fyrdmen* on the way, it is not likely that they have sufficient men to properly besiege, let alone attack a Viking fort. We do not know the exact Viking numbers yet, but the London force probably barely outnumbers the Danes."

"Polonius, if they did not have adequate numbers, why did the fool send the men?"

"I can only speculate, Sire."

"Please feel free to do so, my friend!"

Polonius held up a parchment that he was reading. "Possibly greed. According to my source in London, there were rumors of treasures being stored in the fort, and soon after these rumors swept through London, hundreds of volunteers showed up."

"The bloody fools! Do they think the Vikings will just meekly hand them their treasure?"

"Many warriors came back from Benfleet rich men, Sire, and

that didn't include the ten boat-loads of treasures we seized on your behalf."

Alfred nodded. "So they thought it would be their chance. Well, what is done is done. Let us pray that the London force achieves success. Meantime, what are we to do?"

Ambrose spoke. "Based on the calculation of Polonius' old friend, *Sun Tzu*, we will have to assume that the force will not be successful in taking the fort. I would therefore suggest that we start gathering an adequate force, just in case we have to take action."

Alfred looked around the room at his advisors. "Then we are agreed? So be it! Polonius, would you arrange for the war arrows to be sent out to increase our numbers? Ethelred, send out your Mercian messengers yet again, and let's you and I take our Personal Guards and ride for London in the morning. Phillip, would you please alert the men of both Personal Guards and the garrison? I want to move a force north as soon as possible."

🏳

They came upon the first of them a half-day short of their target. Bloodied and battered, many without their weapons, the retreating *Angelisc* warriors trudged, limped or crawled southward. Most headed instinctively toward the forest when the Saxon horsemen came into view. Alfred sent some riders to stop one big man, still in armor and with his weapons prominent. The man was brought to Alfred.

Phillip spoke to the man. "Kneel in front of your king!"

The warrior slid slowly to one knee. "Greetings, King Alfred."

"And greetings to you, warrior. What in God's name has happened to cause this flood of broken men?"

"I fear God had little to do with it, Sire. We were sure you or *Ealdorman* Ethelred were on your way, so our leaders commanded us to try and overwhelm the Viking fort with a concerted rush."

"With how many men?"

"We had a little over two thousand, Sire."

"And the Vikings?"

"We estimated about the same, Sire."

"Warrior, it takes ten men for every one in a fort to attack successfully. Why would you so rashly attack a strong force behind stout walls when you might not even outnumber them?"

"Sire, I am ashamed to answer. Many of the *fyrdmen* at Benfleet made their fortune when they searched the Viking houses. We hoped to do the same, and it is God's truth that our commanders did not want to share the glory and our good fortune with you."

Alfred frowned at the man. "That is at least an honest answer, Warrior. What happened?"

"We went forward behind large mobile shields, and threw loads of dirt into the ditch until it was full. Then we charged. We were scrambling up the steep outer wall when they hit us with rocks, spears and arrows. Hundreds fell, but we kept going. It seemed more dangerous to retreat than to continue. We made it to the palisades, and there the Viking warriors met us with naked steel. Hundreds of us pressed forward, and then died on their blades. Finally, the survivors broke and turned to run. That is when the gates opened and the horsemen came after us! We were cut off from our horses, and we ran blindly. King, I can still hear the screams as my comrades were cut down by grinning Viking horsemen.

We ran for the forests, where the horsemen could not go. As soon as the sun set, we started back along the road to London. The Vikings rode ahead, however, and have hunted us for the last two days. I was afraid when I saw your column that it was them having yet another go at us."

Alfred spoke. "Return to London with the blessings of God, Warrior. You have been a fool, but at least you are alive."

"May you have better luck, King. I hope you kill every single one of them. They just laughed as hundreds of my companions bled to death. They didn't even have the grace to slit the throats of the badly wounded. They are truly the devil's spawn!"

Alfred's scouts stood in front of their king, who spoke. "Well, what did you learn?"

"The fort is formidable, Sire, and might contain two thousand warriors."

"What gives you that number?"

"We counted the ships, Sire, and then divided. It is just an estimate."

"Good enough! Go get some food, and then report to Lord Polonius. I want you to sketch out the shape and location of the fort on the maps he will show you."

The men pulled themselves straighter. "Yes, Sire!"

ﯓ

Ambrose, Polonius, and Phillip faced Alfred across his campaign table. The king spoke.

"Well, my friends, we know now where the Vikings are, and we know more-or-less how many. The question is, what do we do about it?"

Ambrose looked thoughtful. "It would take considerable time, but we can send out the war arrows until we gather enough *fyrdmen* that we could besiege the Vikings. Ethelred is still in London trying to sort out the problems there, but he could bring us two thousand *fyrdmen* before the next full moon. The problem is, when we push too hard, the Vikings will just climb aboard their damned ships and sail off down-river, to land and try somewhere else. Meantime, we will have a problem starving them out, since they will just send their ships into East Anglia for supplies, or for that matter, have food hauled overland."

Polonius spoke. "Sire, we are not going to gather twenty thousand warriors without stripping every *burh* in the empire of their complete garrisons, and that leaves everyone terribly vulnerable."

Alfred nodded. "True, Scholar. So what do we do?"

"With Ethelred's arrival, we will have more than enough *fyrdmen* to besiege them, but across the river is East Anglian territory."

"What are you saying, Polonius?"

"In order to complete the noose around the Viking fort, we must invade Eohric's territory, or we can wait to see what Haesten is up to."

Alfred spoke. "Polonius, I have no problem attacking Eohric and East Anglia. He swore an oath that he has hardly respected. He sent a fleet to land at Devonshire, and we have killed hundreds of his warriors who were fighting under Haesten's command."

"True, King, but Eohric sent only a small fleet to Devonshire, and neither he nor Guthfrith have openly called up their entire army and marched against you, although it seems clear that was what Haesten was expecting. Last autumn was the third time Haesten has fought his way to Northern Mercia, taken or built a fort, and waited for allies to show up. Each time, they didn't, and Haesten was eventually forced to retreat."

Alfred looked thoughtful. "What are you proposing, Scholar?"

"I think that Eohric and Guthfrith have been testing the waters by sending Haesten deep into West Saxon territory, but both seem afraid to step in with both feet. They are afraid of you, Sire, and Haesten's debacles just reinforce their fear."

"Then what do we do, my Byzantine friend?"

"We take the army north to watch, and perhaps allow the people to gather their crops. We make no hasty moves against such a strong fort, and, for now, we do not cross the river into Eohric's territory."

Ambrose spoke. "Then we cannot bottle them up."

Polonius replied. "With his fleet secure by his fort, Haesten rules the river. If he wants to stop us from crossing, he can do so."

"Polonius, that would mean that we have a strong Viking army poised just twenty miles from London itself. That makes me very nervous," said Ambrose.

"It is illusion, Prince. I think we all agree that assaulting the fort would cost too many lives. We could besiege them, but to do so we must cross the river and risk stirring up all East Anglia. More important than that, Haesten can destroy any ship we might use to cross to the far side. If we leave them alone and they march out of their fort, we are less than a day away, and we would considerably outnumber them."

Alfred came to a decision. "Very well! We will move the rest of the *fyrd* up to this position and build our own fortification, and then we will see what they are up to."

Polonius spoke. "Sire, all the people north of the Thames have retreated to the defensive *burhs*, as you ordered, but they are now afraid to return to their fields to harvest their crops. London depends on those fields to supply much of their food."

Alfred smiled. "And no doubt the Vikings intended the food to supply them, as well. Polonius, write the orders. The *fyrd*, along with all the reinforcements we can pick up on the way, will move immediately to just south of the Viking fort.

Send messengers to the *burhs*! I want every *churl* and slave within two days' travel to come and harvest the fields, from London all the way to the fort itself. We will dare the Danes to come out and meet us in open combat. If they do come out, we will crush them with our superior numbers, and if they don't, then they can enjoy watching us harvesting the crops they are probably relying on for the winter.

CHAPTER 28

The Saxons Harvest their Crops

The West Saxon *fyrd* moved into position. To the thunder of Viking swords on shields, the Saxon column thickened as it approached the Danish fort. Just outside of bowshot, the column completed its transition, and the shield-wall was ready for the foe. Shield touching shield, the line stood ready, but the Danes manning the walls only threw insults.

At an unseen signal, the slaves and *churls* ran forward. Safe behind the shield-wall, they went to work digging a ditch and piling the soil on the inner side of the excavation. Within two hours, the construction of the Roman marching fort was well underway. Within four, the many hands had completed the task, and Alfred's *fyrdmen* had a secure fortification.

Without even a pause, the peasants then dug out sickles and scythes. The backbreaking August ritual began in full view of the Danes. A handful of stalks was grasped by a hand, and the sickle swept in low for the cut. Hundreds of farm wagons rolled forward to receive the bountiful crops and haul them southwards.

There was a mutter of anger from the walls. It was clear that the Vikings had intended the rich fields to provide them with sustenance through the winter. The Saxon *fyrdmen* went on the alert, but no Danes issued forth from the fort, and the Saxons took to jeering the frustrated Vikings.

Wheat, barley, oats and the last hay of the season were all systematically cut and hauled away. The crops could mean the difference between life and death for the many slaves and *churls* who normally worked the fields, but were now crammed into the garrison *burhs* for their own safety.

⚑

Polonius faced his king across the planning table. "Sire, the *churls* and slaves are hard at work, and no Danes have yet dared to try and stop us."

"It makes my heart glad, Scholar, but, short of an all-out assault, I want to put more pressure on these heathens."

Polonius suddenly smiled. "Perhaps there is a way, Sire!"

Alfred looked at his spy-master. "What have you got in mind, Polonius?"

"Sire, we did it at Wallingford, Sashes, Southwark and Cricklade. Your *Francian* cousins have started to emulate you. It has singlehandedly stopped the Thames from being a Viking roadway."

Alfred's face broke into a smile. "Of course! If we can't take their fort, then we build two of our own! We build twin river forts and close the lower reaches of the Lea. We turn their biggest asset into a liability! Their ships will never see the open seas again, and we cut off their main supply route.

Polonius, would you start on the plans for the two river forts? Once the last of the food is hauled away and the people are safely back in the *burhs*, we will make the forts our next priority."

"King, one of the forts must be on Eohric's territory. Is that acceptable?"

"Why not? If we can get the forts operational before Haesten is aware of them, he will not be able to get his fleet down-river far enough to stop us. Once we control the lower reaches of the river, we can ferry men back and forth as needed."

⚑

Alfred hugged the Byzantine. "Scholar, are you sure you would not like more men as an escort?"

Polonius smiled as he swung into his saddle. "Fear not, Great King. You have Haesten and his men pretty well boxed in hereabouts, and I do not intend to cross the river into East Anglian territory. I should be back in a day or two. I will just scout out the spot you proposed, and then ride right back. As soon as I return, I will start on the plans for the twin forts."

Alfred smiled in return. "Go with God, Polonius."

"Thank you, Sire." With that, the Byzantine kicked his horse into motion, and he and his escort of a dozen *thanes* thundered south along the river path.

↬

Ambrose and Phillip were talking with Alfred in his planning tent when a breathless *thane* interrupted. "Prince Ambrose! Lord Polonius has been taken!"

"*Thane*, what are you talking about," questioned Ambrose?

"Lord Polonius was riding down-river with his escort, when a party of Vikings killed the *thanes* and took him prisoner!"

Alfred looked upset. "Merciful God! I sent him down-river to check out a site for our twin river forts that I remember seeing on the way up. It looked like it had possibilities."

Ambrose spoke. "*Thane*, do we know how large the raiding party was?"

"The scouts said it looked like not more than fifty, Prince."

"Do we know where they went?"

"The tracks show that they crossed the river, retrieved horses, and then rode eastward."

Ambrose whirled about until he faced Phillip. "Weapons-master, we need fifty Danish speaking *thanes*, dressed in Viking garb! We need fifty of the best archers we have, also dressed in Danish clothing. Let's take a spare mount for each man and food supplies for five days. We will be riding fast. We need transport for the horses and men to cross the river. Oh, and I want a jarl's or *hersir's* banner, preferably from Northumbria."

Phillip replied. "Prince, the best archers we have are the Welshmen. They practice for hours every day, and their bows are far more powerful than most."

"Then let's ask for fifty of their best. Although I want them in Danish clothes, it is not necessary that they speak Danish."

"Prince, when do you want all this by?"

"I want to be ready to ride before the sun is high tomorrow. The horses can be ferried across during the night, and we can follow at dawn."

"It will happen as you command, Prince!"

Alfred grasped Ambrose's shoulders and spoke to him. "If there is anything else you need, brother, you have but to ask."

"You might send a force of several hundred armored *thanes* along our trail in a day or two, Alfred."

"Why not just take them now?"

"I need to travel fast and we will use guile rather than brute force.' Ambrose grimaced. 'If that doesn't work, then we will use the big club that you are sending after me. They can also cover our line-of-retreat. It is just possible I will stir up a hornet's nest."

"If you survive the first encounter, Ambrose."

"Starting tomorrow, my name will again be Canuteson."

Alfred sighed. "May God watch over you, brother! I will pay any ransom they ask to get that skinny Byzantine back! I owe him my kingdom."

"By guile or by force, brother, I will bring Polonius back!"

With an eye to the north and the possibility of being surprised by a Viking *long-ship* slipping down-river to the Thames, the barge crewmen slid the clumsy vessel out of the shallows and into deeper water. A team of horses on the eastern bank and a long rope gave the barge the necessary momentum, and within a minute the tubby vessel was nosing into the eastern bank. Within seconds, a horse team on the western bank had it on its way back to pick up the last passengers.

As the sun was rising, the pursuit party mounted their horses and took the leads of their spare mounts. At Ambrose's signal, they started off on the clear trail left in the soft ground.

One of the Mercian scouts trotted back along the trail and vigorously waved his hands over his head in a silent signal for the band to halt. Ambrose and Phillip rode forward to meet him, and Ambrose spoke quietly when he drew near.

"What is the matter?"

"It looks like the Vikings are camped in a glade about half of a Roman mile ahead."

"Did you see Polonius?"

"I saw a thin man who appeared to have his hands tied, but I could not make out enough details to be sure if it was Lord Polonius."

"Good enough. Ride ahead, but do not get spotted. Your task is to ensure that we are not surprised by any other Vikings."

"Understood, Prince!"

Phillip spoke to the man he had helped raise from a young boy. "What are your orders, Prince?"

"I will go ahead with thirty of the *thanes* who are most fluent in Danish."

"Then they will outnumber you if things go wrong."

"I don't want them to be too nervous when we approach. They will be less anxious if they considerably outnumber us. I will fly the Northumbrian banner, and I am counting on you and the other seventy men to worm your way in as closely as possible. If things go wrong, then I will be relying on the archers to even the odds."

"In that case, Prince, you will have to let us start forward now, and only follow at, say, a two thousand count."

Ambrose smiled. "You are right, as always, old friend! Leave a couple of men to watch your horses, and I will start my count now."

Phillip smiled. "May God be with us today, my Prince!"

"Go with God, old friend!"

The Danes they had been following were dismounted and sitting around a campfire cooking food when Ambrose and his little troop rode into view. The Vikings were about fifty in number, and they rose to their feet in alarm when the column of disguised Saxons approached. They only sheathed their weapons when they saw the banner of Rollo the Black, an important *hersir* of Northumbria."

Ambrose held his hands high to show they were empty and spoke in fluent Danish. "Greetings, strangers. May we join you?"

The big man who seemed to be in command, replied. "And greetings to you stranger. Climb down and rest at our fire. I do not recognize either you or your men, although I well know the banner of Rollo of Northumbria."

"I am known by most as Canuteson."

"And I am Hagar . . . I am fairly sure that we have not met, Canuteson."

"I am surprised, Hagar. I have been swinging a sword for a long time. I fought with the *Great Army*, served with King Guthrum for a time, and saved the life of Sitric Ivarsson not once, but several times."

"Then it is strange our paths have not crossed."

"No man knows how the *Norns* spin our threads, Hagar. May we ride a ways with you?"

"Why not? I always welcome good companions, and more swords would certainly be welcome if the Saxons dare cross the river to follow me."

Ambrose looked alarmed. "And is that likely, Hagar?"

"Who knows, Canuteson? I do have something they will want back badly."

"Well, Hagar, I assume you mean the captive that I see over there. He is a pretty scrawny specimen. He actually looks a lot like King Alfred's tame Greek - what is his name - Phillip? Polonius?"

"I am surprised, Canuteson. How do you know this man?"

"You forget. I fought both with the *Great Army* and King Guthrum. This man was present at several negotiations."

"You have a good memory, Canuteson, and be careful what you say. That Greek understands every word that we speak. We caught him yesterday just across the Lea River - in Mercia," said Hagar.

"Surely so important a man would not be traveling alone."

"He was foolish enough to think that a dozen warriors was adequate to protect him."

"Clearly he thought wrong. Where are his companions?"

"They fought well enough, but with odds of fifty to twelve, it did not take long to cut them all down. This one may not look like much, but do you know, when we took him, he threw six throwing daggers, and killed four of my men. We were about to slit his throat, when one of my warriors recognized him."

Ambrose nodded. "Polonius the Greek. He is a fine catch. What do you intend to do with him?"

"I thought my king would like to meet him. Perhaps he could entertain us by showing us how he flies as a *Blood Eagle*."

Ambrose stared at Polonius for a long time. "This man is also known as the Wizard. My master has often expressed the wish to have this man in his grasp. We know that this Polonius was behind several of the Pictish raids into Northumbria. I would give you five gold coins for him."

"It is a generous offer, but I want to make a present of him to my king."

"I think I would be willing to go to ten," said Ambrose.

Hagar frowned. "He is King Alfred's right-hand man. The favor I gain from delivering him to my king is worth much more than a mere ten gold coins."

Ambrose shrugged. "I wish you would reconsider my offer, and I am even willing to double it again. The real truth is, Hagar, that I am this man's master, and I would really like to have him back."

Confused and suddenly suspicious, Hagar put his hand on the shaft of his battle axe. "Master? He is no *thrall* to anyone that I know of. He is a free man and serves a Saxon king."

"Funny, I have been telling him the same thing for years, but he still insists on calling me 'master' and 'friend'. Why don't you just ask him who his master is?"

Hagar looked puzzled, but turned toward his prisoner. "Polonius, who is your master?"

The thin Byzantine looked up. "The man you are talking with is he who I am sworn to serve."

Hagar turned back to Ambrose. "Canuteson, I think you had better explain to me just what the two of you are talking about? This man serves King Alfred."

"True, Hagar, but then, so do I. Many people have recently taken to calling me Canuteson the Dane-Slayer."

Hagar looked in puzzlement at Ambrose. "The Dane-Slayer? There are legends of such a man, a Saxon prince of Wessex, but they were invented by our *scops* to entertain us on cold winter nights."

"Hagar, take the twenty gold coins, and ride away. Return this man to his rightful master, become rich, and live."

"I cannot do that, Canuteson, and you abuse my hospitality by asking yet again."

"Hagar, I only ask because I want to save your life. The Saxon prince you are referring to is called Ambrose by the Saxons, and he carries a magic sword called **Victory-Maker** that looks just like the one at my waist."

Hagar looked at Ambrose in shock. "Then . . . then you are this Ambrose . . . a prince of the house of Wessex?"

The Viking commander smiled suddenly. "My king would pay much more gold for you. We outnumber your men by almost two to one. Why should I not just capture you and take both of you to my king?"

Ambrose weighed his words carefully. "Because you have freely offered me your hospitality. Because I really am the adopted son of a free Dane. Because I would rather make you rich then kill you."

Hagar snorted. "I think you have listened to too many of your own legends, Canuteson, or Ambrose, or whatever you choose to call yourself today. You and your men have no chance against my warriors."

"Hagar, what does the legend about me say?"

"That there are three great heroes who trick Danes."

"Polonius and I make two. Who is the missing man of the trio?"

"I remember now . . . A giant of a man, the greatest warrior in all Wessex, who carries a sword that normal men can not even lift - but he is just a legend."

"Hagar, Hagar. Do you think that I would just ride into your camp blindly?"

Hagar made a show of looking in all directions, then smiled. "Canuteson, I see no one else. I think that you did exactly that."

"Do you remember the ballad when the giant uses a bow that no one else can even draw?"

"I think so, Canuteson. What is your point?"

"Phillip is aiming one of his giant arrows at your heart even as we speak."

Hagar again looked around, this time nervously, and then laughed. "I don't think so, prince-of-the-Saxons!"

Ambrose raised his hand horizontal but over his head. He called out in Slavic. "Phillip, in the tree, just over his head!"

A second after the name echoed through the glade where the Vikings had stopped, an arrow thudded into the tree two hand widths above Hagar's head.

Both Hagar and Ambrose stared at the arrow, while all the Vikings drew their weapons. "Hagar, the first was a warning. The next shot will kill. Take the gold and turn over Polonius, or you will see *Asgard* before sunset this very day."

"I admit, it was a brilliant shot, Canuteson.' As he spoke, he swung up his shield.

'But why should I fear any one man, whatever his prowess with a bow?"

"I never said that Phillip was alone, Hagar. Take the gold. No one has to die today."

"Canuteson, you are trying to bluff me with a lone archer hidden in the woods. Do I look like a simple child?"

As Hagar spoke, he made a circle motion with the weapon in his right hand. The Vikings immediately shuffled toward each other, formed a ring, and stood with their weapons ready and shields up. The Saxons backed in the other direction, and also shuffled into a defensive ring.

Ambrose put two fingers in his mouth and whistled shrilly. Suddenly, as if the god Cadmus had sowed more dragons' teeth, armed warriors rose from the ground.

Ambrose spoke to Hagar. "Note the longbow each warrior holds. These men are Welsh, and are particularly adapt with them. Their bows are so powerful that they can put a bodkin point through the best armor at this range. I will give you three choices, Hagar."

"I am listening, Canuteson."

"First, you can take the gold I have already offered you, leave Polonius, and depart peacefully. Second, our two forces can attack each other, but I suspect the archers will make short work of your warriors. Third, you can meet me, face to face."

"For what purpose, Canuteson?"

"One of us dies, and no one else is involved. If I win, your men free Polonius and leave."

"And if I win?"

"I will be dead, and my men will lower their bows and let you ride away with Polonius."

"Canuteson, you should know that I am famous for my prowess with the battle axe. I have never been bested."

"And I am called Dane-Slayer. It seems that we are well matched. What is your preference?"

"As you say, Canuteson, who knows what fate the *Norns* have spun for us? No real Viking would allow himself to be bullied into releasing a prisoner he does not want to release, and I do not wish to be responsible for the useless deaths of some or all of my companions."

"That considerably narrows your choices, Hagar."

"You give me your word that you will respect the agreement as stated?"

"You have my word, Hagar.' He called out to Phillip in Danish. 'Phillip, did you hear the agreement?"

"Aye, Prince."

"And you will honor it?"

"I will honor it, Prince."

Hagar hefted his axe and smiled. "Then there is nothing left to say. Draw your sword and learn how a true Dane fights!"

Ambrose unhooked his shield from his saddle and drew **Victory-Maker**. He spoke. "This does not have to be, Hagar."

In answer, Hagar's axe thudded into Ambrose's shield, making him step back a pace to regain his balance. Almost before Ambrose recovered, the heavy axe head came at him again. This blow was so powerful that it pushed him to his knees. This time, however, **Victory-Maker** flickered out and struck Hagar's armor.

The Dane paused as he felt the sharp blade strike. "Well done, Canuteson! Few can recover so quickly from a blow from *Man-Killer*."

Ambrose smiled. "Your power surprised me, Hagar. You move that heavy axe like it weighs no more than my light sword."

"Canuteson, your shield is badly splintered. Surrender now and I will let you live."

"I have worn the iron collar thrice, Hagar, and I have vowed never to wear it again."

"You, a prince, were once enslaved?"

"It is how I came to be adopted. My Danish master thought of me as his lost son, and granted me freedom and his name."

Hagar swung at Ambrose with a horizontal motion that made Ambrose move quickly back. "You said 'thrice'."

"The second time, I was captured by Moorish pirates off Greece, and was taken to Crete in chains."

"But here you are."

"The three of us, along with some new friends, organized a slave rebellion and managed to escape, along with a lot of our master's treasures. Without Polonius, I never would have made it. I owe the man my life, many times over."

"And a third time?"

"Slavers in the mountains north of Italy took us."

"And you escaped again?"

"Only with the help of a naked woman, but we were freed and killed many of our captors."

Hagar swung again, and Ambrose stepped back to preserve his battered shield. The Viking grunted with the effort, and then spoke.

"I understand you wish to free your friend, Canuteson. I would do no less. I am only sorry that I cannot allow it."

"I, too, Hagar. I have no wish to kill a brave and honorable man." As Ambrose spoke, he stepped forward and used his slim sword like a thrusting spear. His second strike hit a vulnerable part of Hagar's armor, and pierced it deeply enough that it drew considerable blood.

Hagar looked down in surprise at the blood running down his torso, and Ambrose stepped back, unwilling to take advantage of the man's surprise. "That is first blood, Hagar. You can withdraw gracefully, with no loss of honor."

The Viking stared at Ambrose. "Well done, Canuteson, but you are wrong. My honor would not allow it."

As Hagar spoke, he threw away his shield and grasped his axe with both hands. The heavy head arced over and over in Ambrose's direction, splintering and then shattering the prince's shield. Ambrose threw his shield aside, and then started a series of swings that made Hagar step back.

Hagar's axe was massive, and contact with it against Ambrose's sword would likely shatter the blade. Ambrose therefore moved in and quickly out, before Hagar could connect with one of his mighty blows.

As Hagar's axe head went by Ambrose's head with inches to spare, Ambrose struck. Before the Viking could recover his balance, **Victory-Maker** pierced Hagar's right wrist. Suddenly unable to control his heavy axe, the weapon fell out of hands. Hagar just looked at Ambrose.

Ambrose spoke. "Well fought, Hagar. Are you ready to yield yet?"

The man smiled. "You are good, Canuteson. No man has ever bested me as you just did."

"My offer is still good. Take the gold and go home, Hagar."

The Viking warrior awkwardly drew his *sax* with his left hand, and smiled again. "That is no way to reach *Asgard*, Canuteson. Prepare to die!"

Even as he spoke, he raised his blade above his head and charged. Ambrose was forced to make an instant decision, and he held his sword straight out. Hagar made no effort to evade the point, and it penetrated right through the chain mail, deep into the Viking's chest. Hagar's face showed the sudden pain he felt, but it was over in seconds, and the dead man collapsed onto the already blood-soaked ground.

Ambrose turned to the gawking Vikings, still standing in formation, and spoke directly to them. "Your leader was a brave man, and he died a warrior's death that you might live. Take your horses and ride away. I promised Hagar that we would not kill you."

Several warriors sidled toward Polonius. Ambrose spotted it immediately, and spoke again. "But if any man steps any closer to Lord Polonius, the archers will show you their prowess with their bows and our agreement will be rescinded, with unhappy results for you. Polonius, walk this way - now! Vikings, ride away while you still can."

↩

The outriders doubled back to Ambrose's side when they detected motion somewhere ahead. "Prince, riders come!"

Ambrose didn't hesitate. "Archers, hide your horses and string your bows! *Thanes*, form into a line over there . . . by the trees where the archers are hiding!"

Several scouts came at a gallop, followed by a mass of armored horsemen. In front was a tall man, wearing a helmet surmounted with a golden crown.

Ambrose called out in Saxon. "Alfred! Have you come to rescue your brother?"

The *thanes* slowed when they heard the words and saw Ambrose waving happily at them. Their king galloped ahead of the slowing *thanes* and leapt off his horse to greet a thin Greek and a big brother.

"Thank God that you are both safe and well! Come and give your king a hug!"

↩

The stalemate continued. Alfred did not have enough *fyrdmen*, at Polonius' ten to one ratio, to assault the fort, but he had enough to win in a fair fight on open ground.

On the day the wagons hauled away the last of the grains and hay, Alfred's army formed up in front of the Viking fort, and then turned south. To the accompaniment of jeers and cheers, the *fyrd* rode south, following the river downstream.

When the army reached the point Alfred had noticed on his way north, the *fyrdmen* broke ranks, and, while one quarter stood guard, the rest went to work. Polonius' engineers had hammered in stakes, so the dimensions were known. A full dozen ships arrived from the London fleet, and immediately started to ferry men and supplies to the east bank. Within hours, twin forts had arisen on both sides of the river. A Viking long ship was seen nosing its way south, but a half-dozen Saxon vessels took off after it and caused it to turn and flee back up-river.

On the second day, Ambrose was amused to see columns of Viking riders on the opposite bank, in East Anglian territory. It was already too late, however. Although they could be greatly improved, the twin forts were already secure against attack. Once Polonius' catapults were built and several of Haesten's older captured ships were filled with stones and scuttled in the channel, the river would be effectively closed to any unfriendly vessels.

CHAPTER 29

Ambrose meets with Haesten

The leaves were dropping fast, and the brilliant reds and oranges were now a dull brown, or gone. It was the time of animal butchering when the Mercian scouts returned to Alfred's river fort. The tall leader, his hook of a nose looking like a hawk's beak, stood before his sovereign and spoke.

"Sire, they are gone!"

"Who is gone, Treddian?"

"The Danes, King!"

"What do you mean - gone?"

"We climbed a tree on the hillside to see if we could see what the devils were up to."

"And?"

"Sire, we saw nobody, so we climbed back down and started to sneak up on their fort. The ships were tied up like normal, but there were no Danes anywhere!"

"So what did you do?"

"We snuck right up to the fort walls, and there was still nobody about! Little Werian scampered up the wall. He's a spry lad, he is!"

Alfred was becoming exasperated, but he controlled his temper. "And, Treddian?"

"Nobody inside, Sire. The fort is deserted. When we saw that, we ran to where we had left the horses, and galloped all the way back here to report!"

"Well done, Treddian. You and your men deserve a rest. I will send a force in strength to see where the Danes are going."

Ambrose reined in his tired horse. Behind him was almost a thousand mounted *fyrdmen*, and before him was the plain trail of thousands of Vikings heading northward. When he signaled a stop, Polonius rode close.

"What do you think, Prince?"

"I think we are off on another wild goose chase. I am guessing they are heading for Watling Street again, but it is possible they are heading for Danish Northumbria."

"So what do we do, Master?"

Ambrose replied. "What else can we do? We follow, and harass."

Polonius looked unhappy. "I feel like a fly chasing a spider. If we catch up to the spider and it turns, we could easily find that we have bitten off more than we can chew!"

"True, Scholar. That fact, and your oft stated fact that you intensely dislike big rusty blades, especially in the hands of barbarians, should motivate you to send word to Alfred to follow with all haste."

"If you will let us pause here for more than a few moments, great Prince, then I will have a chance to write your letter."

Ambrose turned to Phillip. "Old friend, would you give the order for the men to stand down. We could be here for an hour or more."

With that, Ambrose turned back with a smile to the Byzantine. "You see, Scholar, your wish is my command."

Polonius climbed down and removed his leather case from his saddlebag. "Let me reiterate, Master. You humbly suggest Alfred follows with maximum speed, bringing all the forces at his disposal."

"Not my words, my wordy friend, but quite satisfactory."

"And the ships?"

"I don't think we can take ships far along Watling Street, Scholar."

Polonius sighed. "Are we going to leave them for the Vikings to return to after we abandon our river forts?"

Ambrose replied. "Are we abandoning the forts?"

"We either have a large garrison holding the twin forts, or we have a strong army riding after fleeing pirates. We do not currently have enough men under arms to do both."

Ambrose smiled. "Polonius, you are quite right - as usual. I knew there was a reason I saved your skinny butt so many times and dragged you all the way from *Kiev* to this blessed isle."

"And the answer is, oh generous master?"

"My brother the king shall decide."

"But we are his advisors. What do we advise?"

"Okay. One. Send most of the force after Haesten and his army. Two. Leave a small garrison at the twin forts but send to London for more *fyrdmen* to hold them before the East Anglians arrive in force and take them over.

Three. Send the dozen Saxon ships up-river to watch over the Viking vessels until the best of them can be crewed and sailed to London. Four. Have another Viking funeral with the remaining ships. Pile on any dead Vikings and let the ships burn to their water lines . . . Have I missed anything, good scholar?"

"No. Quite well done, my master."

"That's what you were going to write, anyway, isn't it?"

"Of course, Master."

Ambrose laughed. "And you call me master, while you shamelessly manipulate a barbarian Saxon king and his dumb older brother."

"Some days you barely make it a challenge, oh prince-of-the-West-Saxons."

Ambrose's force caught up with the Danes two days to the north. The Vikings threw their famed *skjaldborg* across the road, and the Saxon pursuers were forced to halt. Without the *fyrdmen* Alfred commanded, there were not enough to meet the Viking host in any near enough numbers to offer a reasonable chance for success. Ambrose waited impatiently for his brother to arrive.

Scouts sent to the tops of the tallest trees reported that the head of the Viking snake was continuing north and west, while the Saxons were forced to follow the slow Viking rearguard or sit in the late autumn rains and wait for their reinforcements. The Danes were careful to fire each and every *vill* they found, leaving only smoldering ruins for the already cold and hungry West Saxons. At the end of the second week, Alfred caught up, along with his best horsemen.

"Greetings, brother," said Alfred.

Ambrose responded. "Greetings, King-of-mine. As happy as I am to see you, I long almost as much for the sight of the supply wagons."

Alfred looked crestfallen. "Oh. They are on their way, brother, but we rode ahead."

Ambrose looked somber. "We have had little food for a week now. The Danes have made sure that we cannot find so much as a crust of bread or a scrawny chicken."

Alfred nodded. "Then I am pleased to report that I have some presents for you, brother-of-mine. It seems only fitting, after all the treasures you have brought me over the years. Faithful Polonius sent an urgent request for supplies. The wagons are slow, so I did bring over a hundred pack horses, each laden with meat and supplies. I hope that is satisfactory?"

Ambrose grinned. "Bless that man! You owe him your kingdom. I owe him my life, many times over, and now I am obliged to him for my supper!"

ⵡ

With Alfred's *fyrdmen* in the ranks, the Saxons were a match for the Danes, and they harassed the Viking rearguard constantly. The Vikings were forced to keep moving, but their rearguard managed to hold off the probing *Angelisc* riders, though with considerable casualties.

The weather grew colder, and Ambrose was sure that the winter snows were not far away. He wondered where the elusive Danes were off to this time.

ⵡ

The scout commander stood straight before his king. He stank of horse and sweat, but he grinned. When Alfred nodded encouragingly, the big man spoke.

"We got 'em, King! They have seized the *tun* of Bridgnorth and fortified it. They have the harvest from the nearby fields, but it is only enough for a few hundred townspeople. It will not feed the entire Viking army for a whole winter!"

Alfred smiled warmly. "Well done, warrior! Get yourself something to eat and then report back after dark to Lord Polonius."

༄

The king looked at his advisors sitting around his planning table, then spoke. "Well, my friends, now we know where the Vikings were going. The question is - what do we do about it?"

Ambrose looked at his brother. "With your permission, I would like to speak to Haesten."

Alfred looked surprised. "You are welcome to speak to anyone in the kingdom, big brother, but may I ask why Haesten?"

Polonius smiled. "I think Canuteson wants to ask him his plans for the future."

Alfred looked surprised. "Ambrose, do you really think he will tell you?"

"It is at least possible,' Ambrose smiled. 'if we talk Viking to Viking."

Alfred nodded. "Then go for it, brother-of-mine. You have done dumber things in your life, and, most amazingly, you generally manage to succeed!"

༄

Polonius approached the Viking fort slowly, his white shield prominent. A lanky Viking called out to him. "Hold it right there, Saxon!"

"I am no Saxon,' he replied. 'Some say I am a wizard, capable of stealing Viking souls.'

Polonius was amused to see the man wince, and a momentary

expression of fear flitted across the warrior's face.

'. . . but the simple truth is, I am a Byzantine scholar who serves King Alfred of Wessex."

"Now I know who you are, Byzantine. You are also called the Spy-master, and you carry magical knives that never miss. Why are you here?"

"I would have hoped that my shield would speak for itself. I carry a message to *Jarl* Haesten from Prince Ambrose, who you might know as Canuteson the Dane-Slayer."

Haesten himself looked down from the ramparts at Polonius. "And what is the message, Spy-master?"

"My master would like to meet with you. He guarantees your safety with his own life, and suggests you could both meet on the small island close to your fort."

Haesten smiled. "Tell your master the answer is yes - but with one condition."

"And that is?"

"Your master brings the food and drink. I fear he would not enjoy such delicacies as we are currently serving."

Polonius laughed. "It is agreed, *Jarl*! Would you prefer ham or roasted pheasant?"

"I care not. I only ask that it not be horsemeat!"

"Done, *Jarl*. Would tomorrow at high noon be satisfactory?"

"If Canuteson brings the food, I will be there anytime he wants."

"The servants will cross to the island in the morning, to set up a tent and prepare food. They will leave, however, before the prince rows himself to the island."

"That is acceptable, but hardly necessary. If Canuteson has guaranteed my safety, then I have no fears. Canuteson is known as a man of his word."

ɮ

Haesten sat across from Ambrose. He took in a mouthful of ale and savored it in his mouth. Smacking his lips, he spoke to the prince.

"Ah, that, by itself, has made this visit worthwhile. When you don't have enough grain to feed the horses, or even the men, you cannot waste any of it on making good ale, more's the pity!"

Ambrose sipped from his own horn. "*Jarl*, I am puzzled why we are even here. If you had settled in East Anglia, or even Essex, we would not be enemies facing each other across your fortress ditch. This is the fifth time you have marched into Mercia, but each journey has cost you dearly in the lives of your loyal followers."

"We have taken much loot, Canuteson."

"I suppose there are some pots and copper coins about, but most of the real treasure is stored in the *burhs* you were unable to take. And, in exchange, you have given us more than ten ship loads of gold and silver and two entire fleets. I doubt you have broken even, Haesten."

"Aye, it is true that *Loki* has been having a lot of fun at my expense, Canuteson."

"*Jarl*, my brother has to make a decision, and soon. Knowing what you are planning might help us make that decision."

"And what decision does he have to make?"

"When Ethelred arrives with his winter *fyrd*, we will probably have enough men on hand to assault the fort and wipe you out."

Haesten sat back in his chair and stared at the tent ceiling. "That may be possible, Prince, but it will cost you dearly, and if you are no longer able to field a strong force, then I know several Viking kings who would invade your little kingdom in a heartbeat."

"Haesten, let there be truth between us. Excluding the disaster at Farnham, this is the fourth time you have invaded Mercia. The Viking kings are not coming. These invasions have gained you nothing, but cost you much. You told me once that you fought my brother because you had sworn a sacred oath to do so. It is obvious to me that you swore to hold a base here until Guthfrith of Northumbria and Eohric of East Anglia joined you with their armies. Only Northumbria has called up its army, and that was for the purpose of fighting an unexpected invasion of Scots and Picts over their northern borders. Eohric has yet to send out a general call-up, and I doubt that he is planning to do so.

Perhaps you also expected the *Norse* and your Welsh ally. After your little visit to his lands, Anarawd has forsworn his treaty with Northumbria and begged to become an ally of Wessex. I have an understanding with Sitric of Dublin, and pray God he does not get himself involved in all this.

In fact then, in spite of all the sweat and blood spilled by your followers, you have been abandoned. An oath, Haesten, is a mutual agreement that an honorable man cannot break. You once told me that."

"What did it cost to send the Scots and Picts south?"

"A small part of your gold. It was not expensive - they hate Vikings with a passion and love to raid."

"Canuteson, what do you really want?"

"I want you to go home, Haesten, and to leave my people alone."

"What do you want today?"

"I want to know if we should pay the price in blood and massacre you and all your warriors, or if we should enjoy a peaceful winter and watch you leave - forever."

"Canuteson, whatever you think of me, I keep my word - at least to a man of honor. I have done what I swore to do, and more."

"Then consider yourself released from your vow, *Jarl*, and go home! You have been betrayed, you have no hope of defeating Wessex, and I think you now realize it."

Haesten sighed. "I had a very good chance, Canuteson, but Eohric and Guthfrith are old women. They feared your brother, and you, so when they should have led every fighting man they had across your borders to crush any opposition, they procrastinated and sent small contingents, which were never enough to decisively defeat you."

"I think that perhaps their full armies would still not have been enough, Haesten."

"Ah, Canuteson, the plan was bigger than that! I am still sworn to secrecy, but I will tell you this. Alfred should look within his own ranks. Oaths were not kept to us. We came very close to paralyzing your entire army."

Ambrose smiled. "Unfortunately for you, *Jarl*, Alfred ordered the sons of the two traitors we are aware of to serve in his Personal

Guard. Their fathers were both told that the sons would be returned in small pieces if there was even a hint of betrayal, and the sons were given special bodyguards who were personally loyal to Alfred."

Haesten stared at Ambrose, and then broke into laughter. "Your brother Alfred is not such a fool after all! That is worthy of your wily Polonius!

But I am curious. Wouldn't it have been simpler to just send assassins or order the men to court, where you could perform the *Blood Eagle* on them? Allies of mine or not, that is what such traitors deserve!"

"Haesten, do not think it was not discussed. Instead, their shire *fyrds* fought gallantly and helped defeat you. I was but a young man when Northumbria fell, but I remember it well. Aella and Osbert, having chased away their common Viking enemy, fought a bitter civil war for the throne. The Danish invaders came back and this time were able to conquer the weakened kings. Alfred is very aware that a civil war at this time would probably have lost us the war."

"We were counting on it, Canuteson. It was the last throw-of-the-*bones* that would have given us victory."

"Then you have answered your own question, Haesten."

"Aye, I must admit that it was a shrewd move on your brother's part. You may also tell your brother that his fortified *burhs* are very effective. And the summer and winter *fyrds* - that is brilliant.

I will sign no treaties with your king, Canuteson. As you know, they are worthless in my eyes, anyway. I have already broken my word too often to a man I have come to respect. We will forage as much as we can, and come spring we will head north into Northumbria. Whether we go through you or around you will be up to your brother."

"Haesten, we will kill any Vikings we find on our side of the ditch."

Haesten smiled. "I expect nothing less . . . if you can catch them! And your brother will pay one thousand ounces of gold, or five thousand of silver."

Ambrose shook his head but smiled in return. "The days of *Danegeld* are done, Haesten, but I will make you an offer."

"And what is that, Canuteson?"

"If there is no sign of your warriors for one full year, Alfred will send the captive women and children he holds across the border into East Anglia."

"That is a great incentive to my warriors. What happens if Vikings do invade again?"

"Mark my words carefully, *Jarl*. Then the Arab slavers with their gelding knives will have their way with the boys, and the girls and women will be sold into slavery. We are counting on you to convince two kings that the invasions are over and done. *Jarl*, go home!"

Haesten sighed. "The real truth is, Canuteson, I have no home. We know we have been betrayed, and we have discussed our future. Some of my men will settle in Essex or East Anglia, and a few prefer Northumbria, but I am not ready to settle down."

"Then what will you do?"

"There are still some provinces in *Francia* that I have not finished looting. I think I will go back and throw the *bones* with *Loki* again."

Ambrose stood. "Haesten, I hope you will not be insulted if I leave the rest of the meat and drink on this island. It is a lot to carry back in my small boat."

The pirate chief stood. "Canuteson, you treated my wife and children with kindness, when you did not have to. I would consider you a friend if I had not sworn a sacred oath to defeat you and your brother both."

"I think that Eohric and Guthfrith have absolved you of that oath, *Jarl*. I would take your hand in friendship."

Ambrose and Haesten exchanged firm hand shakes, and then hugged each other.

Ambrose looked at the burley pirate chief. "Go in peace, Haesten. The Dane within me calls you friend. The Saxon in me will kill you if I can catch you outside of your fort."

"That is how real men play the game, Prince. If we meet in battle, I will do my best to kill you. Until then, I would call you friend!"

Ambrose rowed his little boat down-river, well within arrow

range of the thousands of Danes assembled on the shore. Not one thought to raise his bow, however. Canuteson, the legend, rowed calmly past them all.

℞

Alfred waited impatiently in his planning hut, along with Phillip, Polonius, and Asser. When Ambrose thrust the deer-hide curtain aside, letting in a blast of cold and damp, each looked up at the prince as if he were newly born.

The king spoke first. "Well, brother? Is it to be peace or war, and why are we even in this Godforsaken part of Mercia?"

"Peace, brother! One question at a time!"

Alfred spoke. "Very well - did he tell you why we are here?"

"Yes. He was part of an alliance with Guthfrith of Northumbria and Eohric of East Anglia. There may have been other actors, but those two were the principal conspirators."

"Then why did Haesten keep marching back to this area?"

Ambrose responded. "He had sworn to hold a fort in this area until the others could reinforce him."

"If they promised that, they betrayed Haesten and all his brave men."

Ambrose nodded. "We agreed on that, brother. He finally feels absolved of that oath."

"Then do we fight?"

"His pride will not let him sign a peace treaty. I would suggest we patrol all winter, Alfred. We kill any foragers they send out. Come the spring, he has promised to break camp and head north into Northumbria, where his army has voted to break up."

"Then we should harry them as far as the border, but not force a flat-out fight."

"A fight will cost us needless lives, brother. We have already won. They will defend themselves, but will not go out of their way to attack us. They really want their families back."

"You told him one full year?"

"And that Haesten was responsible for stopping Guthfrith and Eohric from crossing the border."

Alfred laughed and then got up to hug Ambrose. "May God bless you, brother! What would I do without you?"

APPENDIX I

Glossary

Ambat: Female Viking *thrall* or slave.

Angelisc: The name the Angles, Saxons and *Jutes* had started calling themselves.

Angleland: The land of the Angles, Saxons and *Jutes*. England.

Asgard: Where Viking warriors go if they fall bravely in battle.

Bones: Dice.

Athelings: were 'princes of the blood'. The Saxon kings were chosen from the group by a Council, or *Witan*. The usual tradition was for the *Witan* to choose the eldest son, but this was not always adhered to.

Athelstan, King: When King Guthrum was baptized by King Alfred at Wedmore, he took the Christian name of *Athelstan*.

Black Arrow: One of King Alfred's small and fast courier boats.

Blood Eagle: When a person's ribs are broken and the lungs are pulled out through the back. The lungs will pulsate outside of the body until the man dies.

Bretwalda: A ruler of Britain so powerful that all of the other kings recognize him as overlord.

Burh: A fortified settlement with a permanent garrison. When Alfred was through building these forts, no Saxon was more than twenty miles from the protection of one.

Caltrops: A sharp metal object made up of two or more sharp nails or spines arranged in such a manner that one of them always points upward.

Churl: A peasant. His property was guaranteed, but he had to farm and provide military service.

Danegeld: Is a payment to the Danes so that they would leave the land in peace. It was reportedly first paid in 865 by the *Ealdormen* of Kent.

Dreng: Young warriors who serve as the king's companions. If they serve well, they may be given land and elevated to the status of *duguo*.

Dromon: was a three-decked war galley of the Eastern Roman Empire's navy.

Duguo: The proven warriors who have been allotted land by the king. They are expected to answer the king's summons at the head of their own household troops.

Ealdorman: A nobleman next in power to the royal princes. The Saxon kingdom of Wessex was divided into shires, and an *ealdorman* was in charge of each Shire. It was the *ealdorman* who called out the *Fyrd*, or local militia.

Dubh-galls: Dark foreigners, or Danes.

Francia: is, in this case, roughly, the area of France, or, more accurately, Francia Occidentalis.

Frisian: Were sea-faring traders who were located on the mainland coast just south of Viking territory. One of their main cities was Wyk Te Duurstede.

Fyrd: Militias made up of *thanes* and *churls*. For every five *hides* of land, one *fyrdman*, mounted and armed, was obliged to answer the call-to-arms.

Great Army: The name given to the large Viking army that invaded England in 865 AD. Its leaders included Ivar the Boneless, Ubbi, and Halfdan.

Ghutra: a traditional Arab headdress fashioned from a square.

Hersir: A minor Viking nobleman.

A **Hide** is a unit of measure. It generally denoted enough land to support a single family. In Alfred's day, every so many hides (generally 5) held meant that you had the obligation to send one armed and mounted warrior to join the *fyrd* when so instructed.

Held his Stomach: Bishop Asser reported that Alfred 'suffered from a nervous affliction' that affected him throughout his life.

Holmgang: A duel that followed very specific rules.

Jarls: They were important Viking land-owners, who acted as both priests and judges.

Jutes: The Jutes were, with the Angles and the Saxons, the three major Germanic tribes to have conquered Roman Britain. The empire of Wessex was made up of people from all three of the original tribes.

Khazars: A powerful nomad tribe that was quite supportive of trade, and controlled the territory where the Dnieper River enters the Black Sea.

Kiev: was a town just north of the open steppes on the Dnieper River. It was apparently seized by Dir and Askold sometime soon after 860 A.D.; after the death of three brothers who had ruled there.

Loki: Is the Viking god of mischief.

Long-ship was a Viking sea-going vessel somewhat smaller than a dragon ship. It was up to a hundred feet in length, and carried up to 200 crewmen.

Long Ride or Long Gallop: A technique Ambrose and Polonius used to seize Carnarvon. With multiple mounts, the riders start a fast ride toward the target from far away. By changing horses and posting scouts in advance to ambush any couriers, they attempt to outride any news of their approach, thus achieving complete surprise.

Lundenwic: A Saxon settlement of craftsmen and traders just upstream of the depopulated London.

Man-Killer: The name of Hagar's battle axe.

Miklagard: 'Great City', the name the Vikings gave to the city of Constantinople.

Nights: The Anglo-Saxons counted time by nights instead of days.

Norns: The Norns spin the threads of fate at the foot of Yggdrasil, the tree of the world.

Norse: Norwegian

Odin: Was considered by the Vikings to be the chief god and ruler of the universe.

Pig-Stickers: Polonius had been trying to teach the mounted Saxons the lance skills of the heavy cavalry of the Russian Steppes. He had helped the *Varangians* of *Kiev* and of the Dnieper River Valley fight off a massive invasion of these fierce warriors. Though the Vikings had emerged victorious, Polonius had learned to respect the steppe-warriors' skills. He had seen at first hand the shock value of their ferocious charge.

Pilum: A Roman spear with a long soft neck of iron that bends easily and a small hardened head.

Practice archery: Edmund, king of East Anglia, was used as an archery target by Danish Vikings when they took over his kingdom.

Rus: A tribe of Vikings that lived in what is now Sweden. Their traders traveled all the way to the Black and Caspian Seas by boat, and were thought to have taken over Novgorod and *Kiev* around the time of this story.

Scop: A Saxon bard or poet.

Sax: A Saxon or Viking dagger.

Seven-night: For the Anglo-Saxons, each day began at sunset. Thus, a week before was a 'seven-night ago.'

Skald: professional Viking storyteller.

Skjaldborg: Viking shield-wall formation of overlapping shields.

Sun-stone: The mineral Cordierite, which can show the direction of the sun on cloudy days.

Sun Tzu: Refers to the book - The Art of War, by Sun Tzu. This text was written some time between the fifth and the third century B.C.

Svinfylka: or 'boar's snout'. It was an arrow-shaped mass of warriors who would press forward and try to break an enemy shield-wall.

Thane: An Anglo-Saxon warrior who is granted land in exchange for yearly service in the king's army or *fyrd*.

Thor: The son of *Odin* and the god of thunder.

Thrall: Male Viking slave.

Torque: A band of metal worn around the neck.

Tuns: Towns.

Valkyries: were the divine maidens who took fallen Viking warriors to *Asgard*.

Varangian: I use it to mean the various Viking tribes that traveled the Russian rivers. The *Rus* was but one of the *Varangian* tribes, though it was they who provided leaders for Novgorod, *Kiev*, and several other towns.

Victory-Maker was the name of the priceless foreign-made sword Canute had given his young *thrall* when Ambrose was still a captive in Denmark. It was originally taken as loot from Arabs on the North African coast.

Vill: Village.

Wergeld: Money paid as compensation for injury inflicted on another.

Witan: is the council made up of Saxon noblemen and Church elders. They had the final choice over the selection of each king.

APPENDIX II

The History of Wessex, of Russia, and of Ambrose and his Son and Friends in the Ninth and Tenth Century AD.

Historical facts are in plain text.
Fictional stories in this series and comments are in italics.
Parts specific to this story are in bold.

793: First recorded attack by (Norwegian) Vikings on England.

832-865 AD.: Danish Vikings attack East Anglia, Wessex, and Kent.

838: Cornwall surrenders to Wessex.

845: The king's mistress gives birth to AMBROSE.

849: Alfred the Great is born.

850: Vikings winter in Kent for the first time.

853: Alfred is sent to Rome where he is made a Consul by the Pope.

855: Ethelwulf, king of Wessex, takes his son Alfred to Rome again.

856: Ivar the Boneless and Olaf the White take Dublin.

858: Ethelwulf dies. Ethelbald becomes king.

(Trader of Kiev)
860: *Ethelbert becomes king. Vikings sack Winchester before being driven out of Wessex.* Ambrose and Phillip are enslaved in a raid on the coast of Wessex.

861: *Pope Nicholas sends envoys to Constantinople to investigate Photius' ascension as patriarch.*

862: Rurik, a leader of Varangian Rus Vikings, is invited to rule at Novgorod.
Ambrose, Polonius and Phillip arrive in Sweden after escaping from Denmark. Pursued by their former captors, they hurriedly agree to go south with Rurik and his Rus tribesmen.

863: Dir and Askold, Rus jarls, take over the Slavic town of Kiev. Nb. There seems to be considerable debate about both this date and whether Dir and Askold actually really existed. After setting up a trading post in Novgorod, the friends join Dir and Askold's force going south to Kiev.

864: The Pechenegs, a savage steppes tribe, attacks

Kiev. Only with Polonius' expert help, and the fanatical fighting bravery of the Vikings, do they survive. An attack on the Pechenegs at their most vulnerable point not only ends the siege, but forces the Pechenegs to pay to cross the Dnieper River.

(Emissary to Byzantium)

865: Kent is invaded by a Viking force and Danegeld is paid for the first time to stop the destruction. The Great Army (Danish Vikings) arrives in East Anglia from France.

Dir and Askold lead a combined Slav and Varangian force against Constantinople because of a perceived injustice. With both the Byzantine fleet and army away, they manage to do considerable damage, although they never seriously threaten the city. On the way home, a savage storm sinks many of the Viking and Slav ships. Meantime, Kuralla is kidnaped in Kiev. That there was an attack by Varangians, and a storm, within a few years of this date seems inconvertible. Since the Russian Primary Chronicles set the date somewhere between 863 to 867, I arbitrarily assigned it to 865.

866: Reign of Ethelred in Wessex. The Great Army seizes York. Ambrose and Polonius are sent by Dir and Askold as official envoys to Constantinople. They return north to find word from Kuralla waiting for them. The friends rush north, free Kuralla, turn around, and travel again to Constantinople.

After attempts by Basil to involve them in a plot against the emperor, Ambrose, Kuralla, Polonius and Phillip sail for Wessex. Basil, aware they know altogether too much, sends agents after them.

(Southern Journey)

Basil is told by the Byzantine emperor, Michael III, to divorce his wife so he may marry Michael's mistress.

Bardas plans a sea campaign to retake Crete.
Michael has Basil kill Bardas.
Michael adopts Basil and makes him junior emperor.
Ambrose and his friends are captured and enslaved by Muslim pirates operating out of Crete. Polonius' skills allow them to break out of their prison, and they escape to the dubious safety of a Byzantine Fleet. When they realize one of Basil's agents recognizes them and intends to kill them, they flee to Egypt, where they join a caravan heading west.
The Byzantine admiral harries them across North Africa, but Ambrose and his friends do manage to strike back and damage the Byzantine ships. Ambrose then finds a Muslim slaver to transport them to Calabria. Attacked and hunted, the friends finally cross the border from Calabria to Benevento. Ambrose feels that they are finally

safe.

(Journey Home)

The friends start north. Ambrose and his friends pay a visit to Admiral Demetrious in Naples. They escape and make it back across the frontier just ahead of vengeful Byzantine soldiers.

Ambrose makes it to Rome, where he meets Pope Nicholas. He and his friends then head north for the mountain pass to France. They arrive after the pass is closed for the winter, and must spend the winter in Aosta.

867: Aelle, king of Northumbria, is killed trying to retake York.

Basil 'the Macedonian' kills his own sponsor, Michael III, emperor of Byzantium. (September) Ambrose and his friends survive an attack by assassins, and in the spring they head north into the mountains where they are captured and enslaved. After Kuralla rescues them, they reach France and relative safety. They reach Paris and meet the king. Then they head for Calais and a ship to England. The Vikings, however, are raiding along the coast. Finally, after many adventures, they reach Calais and Phillip finds a captain willing to risk the dangerous crossing.

867: Finally, Ambrose and his friends arrive in England, where Ambrose is welcomed back to the court.

Ambrose meets a beautiful girl and falls in love.

(Warrior of the King)
868: The Great Army occupies Mercia. King
   Ethelred and his brother, Alfred, ride north to
   support Burgred of Mercia. The Vikings are
   besieged at Nottingham, but Burgred decides to
   pay Danegeld. The West Saxons go home.

   Alfred marries a Mercian noblewoman -
   Ealhswith.
   Ambrose and his companions return north and
   join the Great Army as spies. After finding out
   the Vikings are going north, they flee. Ambrose
   is wounded and nursed by his loved one. The
   Great Army pursues, and catches up. Strangely,
   the attack is called off.
   Ahmad ibn Tulun, a Turk, is appointed by the
   Caliph to rule Egypt.
   Pope Nicholas the Great dies.

(Gretchen; Future Princess)
   Gretchen and her father head south for Wessex
   and her marriage. She is kidnaped and taken to
   Wales.
   In Wales, Vikings attack the group, and
   Gretchen is taken to the Viking stronghold of
   Wexford in Ireland. Ambrose visits Wexford,
   but is unable to free Gretchen.

869: The Great Army returns to York in the north
   for a year.

Ambrose attacks the Viking ship carrying his beloved north. They are finally re-united.

870: Danes kill King Edmund of East Anglia, then invade Wessex under the Danish leader Halfdan.

871: Alfred becomes king. After fighting nine battles, Alfred pays Danegeld to buy peace for five years.

873: Ivar the Boneless, 'king of Dublin and York', dies in Ireland. His brother, Halfdan Ragnarsson, becomes king in his place.

874: Edward, son of King Alfred and future king, is born.

(Alfred the Great; Viking Invasion)
875: Alfred takes out a small fleet and routs seven Viking ships. (Nb. For dramatic purposes, I arbitrarily moved this event to the following year, where I tied it in with Guthrum's invasion.)

876: Danes under Guthrum break their word, slip past Alfred and seize Wareham.

877: Guthrum agrees to a truce, but slips away to Exeter, which the Danes fortify.
After a Viking fleet is dashed on the rocks in a storm, the Danes agree to withdraw.
Halfdan Ragnarsson is killed in Ireland fighting

Norwegian Vikings.

878: Guthrum, a Danish chief, rides south across the
Wessex border in winter.
Alfred at first hides in the forest of Selwood.
A second Viking army, led by Ubbi Ragnarsson
and invading from Wales, is defeated in Devon.
As spring approaches, Alfred builds a military
camp on the island of Athelney.

Battle of Edington: Alfred's forces meet the
Vikings here in May. The Danes break and run
to Chippenham.
The Saxons blockade the Danes within their
fortress of Chippenham for 14 days.
At last Guthrum surrenders and agrees to be
baptized.

879: Guthrum takes his retreating army to East Anglia,
where the men eventually settle down.

882: Alfred fights a battle against four Danish ships.

883: Halfdan dies. Guthred is recognized as king of
Jorvik.

884: Ethelflaed, daughter of Alfred, marries Ethelred
of Mercia.

(Alfred the Great: King's Revenge)
885: A Danish army crosses to England and besieges
Rochester. Alfred relieves the city before it falls.

885: Later that summer Alfred fights a naval battle at the mouth of the Stour River. He takes all 16 enemy warships.
Guthrum breaks his treaty. He gathers every Viking vessel and attacks Alfred's laden fleet. He wins.
Alfred calls up his entire force and marches on London. He takes it and garrisons the city.

886: Alfred signs another treaty with Guthrum, where he gets London and control over part of Mercia.

889: Edgar, son of Ambrose and Gretchen, is born.

891: Danes in France suffer two serious defeats.

(Alfred the Great; Young Edward)
892: Five thousand Danes land in Kent and seize an unfinished fort at Appledore. A second fleet follows, led by Haesten, and lands at Milton Royal. Alfred arrives with his army, drives Haesten away, and then moves against the Danes at Appledore.

893: Haesten's fleet sails away, to Benfleet, and is eventually joined by the second, larger fleet. The Danes then raid deep into Hampshire and Berkshire. Edward, son of Alfred, inflicts a major defeat, and then chases the Danes across the Thames. After being forced to surrender, the Danes give hostages and

depart. The Danes of Northumbria and East Anglia send two fleets to Dorset as a diversion. Alfred rushes to the west, while Edward marches on Benfleet. Edward wins a great victory.

The Danes gather all their forces and march along the Thames again. They are besieged, break out, gather fresh forces, and try again. Besieged at Chester, the Danes break out yet again and flee to Wales.

Late summer, 893: Edward, Ethelred, volunteers from the London garrison, along with reinforcements from the West Country, gather and march on Benfleet. The Viking army is away raiding, and the Saxons take the town.

All Danes now gather at Shoebury in Essex. They march west to the Severn River. They build a camp at Buttington, in Montgomeryshire. Though besieged, the Danes break out and make it back to Essex.

Early autumn 893: The Danes in Essex march without pausing along the old Roman Watling Road, into Cheshire, where they seize the tun of Chester. Besieged, the Vikings break out yet again, though they suffer heavy losses. They flee to Wales.

Spring 894: **The Danes split up and flee back to Essex via different roads.**

Winter 894: **The Danes sail up the Lea River and build a fort.**
London men attack, but are repulsed. Alfred arrives and guards the peasants who harvest the local crops. Alfred then moves his army to the mouth of the river, where he builds twin forts to blockade the Viking fleet. The Danes abandon their ships and ride north and west, to Bridgnorth in Shropshire.
Athelstan, future king and son of King Edward, is born.

895: **In the spring the Vikings sneak back to Essex or move to Northumbria or East Anglia.**
Guthfrith, king of Northumbria, dies on August 24.

896: *Sitric Ivarsson dies.*

(Edward the King)
899: King Alfred dies. Ethelwold seizes two royal estates and kidnaps a nun. Faced with an army under Edward, he flees northward. The Danes of Jorvik (Northumbria) accept him as king.

902: Ethelwold arrives in Essex with a Northumbrian fleet, and the Danes there submit to him. The Norse are expelled from Dublin. Ingimund attacks Wales. Driven out, he settles on the Wirral Peninsula with the permission of Ethelflaed, since Ethelred is sick. (While the exact date is in doubt, the most likely year of this event was in 902.)

Elfweard, second son of King Edward, is born.

(Introduction to 'Ethelflaed, 'Lady of the Mercians')

903: Ethelwold convinces Eohric of East Anglia to join him, and together they raid Mercia and Wessex as far as Cricklade and Braydon before retreating. In retaliation, Edward gathers his fyrdmen and ravages the Viking lands as far north as the northern fens. He then orders a retreat, but the Kentish fyrdmen are slow to obey and the Danes catch up with them on December 13. Ethelwold and Eohric are killed on the Danish side, while Sigehelm, the Ealdorman of Kent, falls on the other side. Both sides suffer serious losses. This is known as the Battle of the Holme.

(Ethelflaed, 'Lady of the Mercians')   (902 to 919)

905: The Norse under Ingimund demand land and the old fortress of Chester. When their demand is rejected, they revolt and besiege Chester. Ethelflaed provides extra fyrdmen and the garrison is able to hold the Norse off.

Edgar is Kidnaped by Ingimund and Ambrose goes after his family in Hitchingford.

906: King Edward concludes a truce with East Anglia and Northumbria, and probably pays Danegeld.

907: Ethelflaed refortifies Chester.

909: Ethelflaed & Edward raid Danish East Anglia and bring back the body of St. Oswald.

910: The Saxons and Mercians defeat and kill joint Jorvik kings Eowils and Halfdan II at the Battle of Tetenhall. Ethelflaed builds the fortress at Bramsbury.

911: Ethelred dies.
Ethelflaed is chosen by the Witan as 'Lady of the Mercians'.
Edward annexes London and Oxfordshire.

912: Ethelflaed builds two more burhs along the Welsh border - along the Severn River.
1. Bridgnorth - main crossing point to Wales.
2. Scargeat- location is unknown. Probably upriver north and west from Bridgnorth.
Edward takes his army to Essex, builds a fortress at Witham, and receives submission from Essex. Some of Edward's supporters moves to the burh of Hertford and work on it.

913: Danish forces at Leicester look west and see two new burhs: Tamworth and Stafford.
Danes march south to the village of Banbury, joining forces with Danes from Northampton for

a coordinated attack. The Angles meet them in battle and defeat the Vikings.

914: Ethelflaed fortifies the largest town south of Danish Northampton - Buckingham.
She builds a fort on either side of the River Ouse. Danish armies of Northampton and Bedford submit to Ethelflaed's army at Buckingham. Jarl Thurcetel submits.
A Viking army arrives from Brittany, led by Ohter and Hroald. They land in the Severn estuary. They go inland, but the men of Hereford & Gloucester meet them and put them to flight. The Vikings finally leave in the autumn.
A Danish Viking, Ragnald, seizes power in Northumbria after Tetenhall, and defeats the Scots in the First Battle of Corbridge in 914.

915: This allows Edward to establish a fort at Bedford, directly across the Ouse from the former Danish camp.
Ethelflaed now had a nearly straight line of forts from Chester to Hertford.
There are two gaps. Ethelflaed closes the Mersey gap with several more burhs.
914 - Eddesbury. Warwick.
915 - Runcorn.

916: Edward builds a fort at Maldon.
Ethelflaed sends her army into Wales. An abbot had been killed. The army destroys a town and captures a Welsh king's wife.

917: Ethelflaed signs a treaty with two Scottish kings, both called Constantine, insuring their alliance against Jorvik.

Ragnald is unwilling to face Ethelflaed. He fights the Scots and Picts again at the Second battle of Corbridge. He wins again but the numbers of his army is cut in half.

Edward fights the Danes in the east - Towcester, Bedford, Wigingamere, Tempsford. He kills King Guthrum II at Tempsford and all resistance in East Anglia collapses.

Ethelflaed's troops march into the Danish center at Derby and take it.

All Danish leaders now submit to Edward and accept him as their protector.

They are granted their estates and allowed to live according to their Danish customs.

918: Edward builds a burh at Stamford. The Danes there submit without a fight.

To the west, Ethelflaed marches into Leicester, where Danes surrender without bloodshed, probably led by Danes seeking support against the Norse threat from the west.

The last two Danish enclaves, Nottingham and Lincoln, fall to the West Saxons by the end of summer, but Ethelflaed dies on June 12, 918.

(Elfwynn, Traitor Queen)

The Mercian Witan gives the title of queen to the twenty year old daughter of Ethelflaed - Elfwynn. Ambrose and Polonius kidnap her during the winter. They return to rescue the boys of the Royal School in the spring of 919.

919: Edward calls Elfwynn to his court and officially annexes Mercia.
Edward moves his army to Gloucester and Betlic flees. Ambrose and Polonius chase him northward. They fight on the way, and Elfwynn finally kills Betlic.
Norse adventurer Ragnald storms York and establishes a line of Norse kings.
During his reign he gives nominal allegiance to Edward, who recognizes his new kingdom.

921: Edmund, son of King Edward, is born.

(Athelstan, First King of England)
924: There is a Mercian revolt in Chester. King Edward is killed at Fardon-on-Dee. Mercia supports Athelstan as king. Wessex supports Elfweard, his half-brother. Elfweard suddenly dies a few months after his father.

925: Athelstan is finally crowned as king. He is crowned at Kingston-upon-Thames, by Ayhelm, Archbishop of Canterbury. This is the first time a Saxon king is crowned with a crown instead of a helmet.

926: Athelstan arranges for his sister Edith to marry Sihtric of York. They agree not to invade each other's territory and not to support the other's enemies.

927: Sihtric dies. Cousin Guthfrith leads a fleet from Dublin to try and take the throne. Athelstan captures York and receives the submission of the Danes. (It is not known if he fought Guthfrith). The Northumbrians are outraged at this usurpation.

July, 927: at Eamont, King Constantine of Scotland (Alba), King Hywel Ddn of Deheubarth, Ealdred of Bamburgh and King Owain of Strathclyde accept Athelstan's overlordship, which leads to seven years of peace. Athelstan is now the first king of all the Anglo-Saxon people.

933: Prince Edwin drowns, possibly after a rebellion where someone called Alfred attempts to blind Athelstan.

934: Athelstan invades Scotland, though the reasons are unclear. Sometime thereafter, Constantine of Scotland marries his daughter to the Norse king of Dublin.

937: The Norse king of Dublin, Olaf Guthfrithson, joins with the Scots and Strathclyde Britons under Owain to invade England in the fall. Ambrose meets with the Scottish king. The opposing armies meet at the Battle of Brunanburh. Athelstan wins an overwhelming victory, though he also takes heavy losses.

Ambrose and Polonius die protecting the king.

939: (October) Athelstan dies.

(Edmund, King of England)

939: Edmund is proclaimed king. Crowned in
November.

939-940: King Olaf III Guthfrithson conquers
Northumbria and invades the Midlands.
Conquers as far south as Watling Street.
Olaf marches south from York to Northampton.
When that siege fails, he goes on to Tamworth,
which he takes by storm. King Edmund besieges
King Olaf and Archbishop Wulfstan at Leicester,
but they escape by night. Battle is averted when
Archbishops Oda and Wulfstan reconcile the two
kings and a truce is concluded. Watling Street
becomes the new boundary.

941: Olaf Guthfrithson raids Bernicia and dies shortly
thereafter. Olaf Sihtricson succeeds him on the
Northumbrian throne. He has his cousin Ragnall
as co-ruler.

942: Edmund defeats Idwal of Gwynedd.
Edmund reconquers the Midlands.

943: Edmund becomes godfather of King Olaf
Sihtricson of York.

944: Edmund reconquers Northumbria.

Edmund drives out of Northumbria both Olaf Sihtricson and Ragnall Guthfrithson.
Congalach Cnogba, High King of Ireland, sacks Dublin.

945: Edmund conquers Strathclyde, but cedes the territory to King Malcolm I of Scotland in exchange for a treaty of mutual support. Blacaire of Dublin driven out by Olaf.

946: Edmund is killed in a brawl by an exiled thief named Leofa. Eadred, Edmund's brother, succeeds to the throne.

APPENDIX III

The Kings of Wessex

EGBERT
802-839

▼

ETHELWULF
839 - 858

▼

ETHELBALD   ETHELBERT   ETHELRED   (*Ambrose*)   ALFRED
858 - 860   860 - 866   866 - 871   871 - 899

         ▼   ▼

     (Ethelwold)   EDWARD I
(Alfred chosen over him)   899 - 924

                                           ▼

                                       ELFWEARD
                                       924 - 924

                                           ▼

                                      A THELSTAN
                                       925 - 939

                                           ▼

                                        EDMUND
                                       939 - 946

Appendix IV

APPENDIX V

About the Author

After counseling teenagers and adults for more than forty years, Bruce Corbett retired to concentrate on his writing and photography. To date, he has written a collection of Science Fiction short stories and two Science Fiction novels. The project closest to his heart, however, is his series of well-researched historical novels based on a family of fictional heroes, set in the time of Alfred the Great, his children and grandchildren. **Alfred the Great; Young Edward**, is the third in the King Alfred Sagas and the ninth in total for the overall series.

These novels are arguably the most comprehensive series of novels ever written based on the time of the Anglo-Saxon Chronicles. A complete description of the various novels, including samples, links and supplementary information, may be found on Bruce Corbett's web site:

www.brucecorbett.com

Bruce Corbett lives in Pincourt, Quebec, Canada. He is an avid landscape and wildlife photographer, and is generally found reading anything historic.

APPENDIX VI

Other Books Released by the Author

In chronological order

HISTORICAL
I. The Ambrose Sagas
1. Ambrose, Prince of Wessex; Trader of Kiev
2. Ambrose, Prince of Wessex; Emissary to Byzantium
3. Ambrose, Prince of Wessex; Southern Journey
4. Ambrose, Prince of Wessex; Journey Home
5. Ambrose, Prince of Wessex; Warrior of the King
6. Ambrose, Prince of Wessex; Gretchen, Future Princess

II. The King Alfred Sagas
1. Alfred the Great; Viking Invasion
2. Alfred the Great; King's Revenge
3. *Alfred the Great; Young Edward*

III. The King Edward Sagas
1. Alfred the Great; Edward the King
2. Queen Ethelflaed; 'Lady of the Mercians' **2023 release**
3. Elfwynn, Traitor Queen of Mercia **2023 release**

1V. The Anglo-Saxon Kings of all England
1. Athelstan, First King of England **2023 release**
2. Edmund, King of England. **2023 release**
3. King Eadred of England (Under construction)

SCIENCE FICTION
Bruce Corbett's Speculative Short Stories
The Goldmines of Alpha Centauri (coming soon)
The Vuorran Pogrom (coming soon)

The above novels are available worldwide as e-books from your favorite online book sellers, and the paperbacks are available from Amazon and Drafts2Digital.